"What do we do now?" Selina asked.

Her whisper, broken by tears, tugged at his heart. He hated seeing a woman cry, no matter how angry he was.

What did they do now?

He folded the letter from her—supposedly from her—that he'd been reading, stacked it on top of the rest and tied the string around them. What he wanted to do was burn them along with his marriage certificate.

The way he saw it, they had no other choice. Vows had been spoken. The Bible made it clear about the wrongness of breaking vows. Like it or not, he and Selina were legally married. There was only one answer to that question. "I guess we head home."

Her gaze flew up to his and the color drained from her face.

Michael understood exactly how she felt. But they had no other choice. He hoisted his body off the log and offered Selina a helping hand up. "We made our vows before God and we need to honor those vows. Let's go home."

Books by Debra Ullrick

Love Inspired Historical

The Unexpected Bride
The Unlikely Wife

DEBRA ULLRICK

is an award-winning author who is happily married to her husband of thirty-six years. For more than twenty-five years, she and her husband and their only daughter lived and worked on cattle ranches in the Colorado Mountains. The last ranch Debra lived on was also where a famous movie star and her screenwriter husband chose to purchase property. She now lives in the flatlands where she's dealing with cultural whiplash. Debra loves animals, classic cars, mud-bog racing and monster trucks. When she's not writing, she's reading, drawing Western art, feeding wild birds, watching Jane Austen movies, *COPS,* or *Castle.*

Debra loves hearing from her readers. You can contact her through her website, www.debraullrick.com.

DEBRA ULLRICK

The Unlikely Wife

Love Inspired

™ LOVE INSPIRED BOOKS

Recycling programs
for this product may
not exist in your area.

ISBN-13: 978-0-373-82902-6

THE UNLIKELY WIFE

www.LoveInspiredBooks.com

Printed in U.S.A.

Dear Reader,

Welcome to Love Inspired!

2012 is a very special year for us. It marks the fifteenth anniversary of Love Inspired Books. Hard to believe that fifteen years ago, we first began publishing our warm and wonderful inspirational romances.

Back in 1997, we offered readers three books a month. Since then we've expanded quite a bit! In addition to the heartwarming contemporary romances of Love Inspired, we have the exciting romantic suspenses of Love Inspired Suspense, and the adventurous historical romances of Love Inspired Historical. Whatever your reading preference, we've got fourteen books a month for you to choose from now!

Throughout the year we'll be celebrating in several different ways. Look for books by bestselling authors who've been writing for us since the beginning, stories by brand-new authors you won't want to miss, special miniseries in all three lines, reissues of top authors, and much, much more.

This is our way of thanking you for reading Love Inspired books. We know our uplifting stories of hope, faith and love touch your hearts as much as they touch ours.

Join us in celebrating fifteen amazing years of inspirational romance!

Blessings,

Melissa Endlich and Tina James

Senior Editors of Love Inspired Books

This book is dedicated to
my dear sister Marlene Baylor.

Every time I've needed a friend,
or a listening ear, or encouragement,
or needed lifting up, you've been there for me.
Thank you so much! You'll never know how much
that means to me. How much YOU mean to me.
I luv ya high as the sky, Marlene.

God bless you.

* * *

For the Lord does not see as man sees;
for man looks at the outward appearance,
but the Lord looks at the heart.
—1 *Samuel* 16–7

Chapter One

Paradise Haven, Idaho Territory
1885

This has to be a nightmare.

Standing in front of Michael Bowen at Paradise Haven's train station was the woman who claimed to be his wife. His eyes traveled up and down the length of her. Instead of a dress, she wore a red scarf draped around her neck, a black cowboy hat with a stampede string, black cowboy boots and brown loose-fitting trousers. In her hands she held a Long Tom black powder rifle.

A rifle? The woman was holding a rifle. No matter how hard he tried he couldn't pull his gaze away from the weapon that was nearly as long as she was tall.

Michael bore down on his teeth until he thought his jaw would snap. Even with her heart-shaped face, stunning smile and beautiful brown eyes, the person standing before him looked more like a female outlaw on a wanted poster than the genteel lady he had been corresponding with for the past five months. The woman he had fallen deeply and passionately in love with. The woman he had legally married sight unseen.

This woman was nothing like what he'd expected. Nothing. There had to be some mistake. There just had to be.

Suddenly, she lunged toward him and threw her arms around his neck. He stiffened and struggled to draw in even the smallest amount of air because she squeezed him so tightly. *Dear God, have mercy on me.*

"Oh, Michael! It's so nice to finally meet ya." Selina Farleigh Bowen pulled back and stared into her new husband's face. She knew Michael would be handsome—no one who wrote letters that sweet could not be. But even if he were uglier than a Kentucky toad, she'd still love him.

She took a second to study his face. Jaw, nice and square. Nose, straight. Eyes, breathtaking and smiling, the color of a sapphire necklace her ma once had when days were better. Lips, bow shaped. The man was so handsome. And he was all hers. "I just can't believe I'm finally here."

Michael stared down at her with wide eyes.

Her husband wasn't smiling, and he looked like he'd just swallowed a giant cricket. Her joy evaporated.

She took a step back and dipped her head sideways, wondering if she'd done something wrong or if he was disappointed in her looks. Maybe she shouldn't have grabbed him and hugged him like she had. After all, that was a mighty bold thing to do, but she couldn't help herself. She'd waited five long months for this day.

Still, maybe her boldness had upset him. She reckoned she'd better apologize. "I'm sorry, Michael. I oughta not tossed my arms about you like that. Forgive me iffen that was outta line."

He continued to stare, saying nothing.

"Bear got your tongue or somethin'?"

"You—you can't be Selina."

Whoa. She wasn't expecting that. "What do ya mean I can't be Selina? Of course I'm Selina."

He tugged his gray cowboy hat off his head and ran the back of his hand over his sweaty forehead, then settled the hat back into place. "You can't be. The Selina who wrote me was…" His eyelids lowered to the wood planks under his feet, but Selina still caught sight of the hurt in his eyes.

Quicksand plopped into her belly. "Michael." She waited until he looked at her. His expression was blank. "You said the Selina who wrote you was… Was what, Michael?"

"She was…"

She was what?

The longer he stood there not saying anything the more skittish her insides got. "Tell me, Michael. She was… I mean, I was what?"

"Well, will you look at her? That's repulsive." Disgust oozed from a woman's voice as she passed by them.

Selina swung her attention to two young women standing about five yards away with their fancy dresses and matching hats with long feathers sticking out of them.

"Are you sure it's a she? Looks more like a man to me."

Selina caught sight of their faces.

They looked her up and down with a snarl on their

faces. *Jumpin' crickets*. Did those women have their corsets in a twist or what?

"I can't believe she would be seen in public like that."

Selina had dealt with their type all her life. People who thought they were better than her just because they had money and could afford fancy clothes.

Selina narrowed her eyes, pursed her lips and gave them her meanest stare while patting her rifle.

Their eyes widened. They linked arms and scurried off like a herd of scared mice stuck in a shack filled with cats. Worked every time.

Selina turned back to Michael.

His eyes followed the women until they disappeared around the train depot building. She wondered what was going through his mind. "Michael, would you mind iffen we found someplace over yonder so we can talk? I need you to tell me what was in them letters."

"What do you mean you need me to tell you what was in the letters? You wrote them." A frown pulled at his face. "What's going on here, Selina?" His voice was harsh and loud enough that people stopped what they were doing to stare at them.

"Whoa." She held up her hand to ward off the roughness of his words. "Just back up your horses, cowboy, and I'll explain everything. But not here. Come on." She tugged on his shirt sleeve. He balked like a stubborn mule, and she had to practically drag him all the way to the edge of the trees out of the earshot of others.

She sat down on a log and hoped Michael would do the same, but he just stood there, towering over her.

"Won't you please sit a spell? I'll have a crick in my neck iffen I have to keep lookin' up at you like this."

He lowered his backside onto the log but as far to the other end as possible.

He removed his hat and worked the brim of it into a curl.

Such a waste of a mighty fine hat.

Why, Pa would skin her and her brothers alive if one of them ever treated a hat like that. But she wasn't here to talk about that. "Michael, I don't know what the problem is, but I want you to know that I told Aimee to tell you that I had no book learnin' and that I couldn't read nor write because I had to help my pa raise the youngins after my ma took sick and died."

"What do you mean you can't read or write?" His shocked face made her want to find a rock to crawl under. She dropped her head in shame. "And who's Aimee?" he asked.

"You don't know?"

"No. Why should I?"

"Aimee's my friend who wrote them letters for me."

"I'm confused."

"I can see that. I'm a mite confused myself because Aimee was supposed to tell you that she was writin' for me. Must have slipped her mind." At least Selina hoped that was why Aimee hadn't told him.

"Well, she didn't."

"What did she tell you then?"

"The letters said that your father was dying and that was why you answered my advertisement. When I mentioned that I didn't want someone to marry me because they needed a place, you…Aimee…suggested we correspond a time in order to get to know each other. Then after a couple of months if neither one of us cared for the other, we would find someone else. But the more I wrote, the more I fell in love with..."

"Finish what you were fixin' to say, Michael. You fell in love with who? Me or Aimee?"

"I—I don't know. The woman in the letters?" He placed his elbows on his knees and his head in his hands. "Only now I don't know who that person is."

"Me, neither." She hated having to admit that. "There's only one way to find out. You got them letters with you?"

"Yes."

"Would you mind fetchin' them?"

He stood. "They're in the wagon. I'll be right back."

Selina had a sick feeling as he walked away. If her doubts were right, Aimee hadn't told Michael everything Selina had asked her to. And if Aimee hadn't, then her best friend had done not only Selina wrong, but also Michael.

But surely Aimee wouldn't have done such a wicked thing. Her friend loved her and had always treated her kindly. Unlike those other rich folks she'd worked for who had treated her worse than an unwanted critter. Her friend had even rescued Selina when Aimee's brothers had tried to drown Selina in the river. If Aimee hadn't shown up when she had, she wasn't at all certain she would be here today.

Still, she couldn't help but wonder if Aimee had tricked them. If so, did that mean Selina had up and hitched herself to a man who loved someone else? Namely her beautiful friend Aimee?

Michael took his time walking to the wagon. He needed to get his thoughts together. He had a hard time believing the woman sitting on the log was his bride. The word *bride* stuck in his throat like a chicken bone.

For years, Michael had prayed for God to send him someone like Rainee, his first real crush, but Selina was nothing like Rainee. His sister-in-law was a woman he admired and respected. She was the epitome of femininity, a Southern belle who was educated and smart, beautiful inside and out, genteel yet strong, feisty but sweet, able to hold her own when need be and a real survivor. Everything he wanted in a wife.

Tired of living alone at the age of twenty-seven, with women still scarce in the Idaho Territory, he had decided to take out an advertisement. After all, it had worked for Rainee and Haydon.

If only it would have worked for him.

If only he would have taken the time to get on that train and head out to Kentucky to meet Selina before actually marrying her by proxy. But he couldn't be spared.

The coming of the railroad had made getting feed and supplies much easier. Because of that, he and his family had purchased more property and livestock.

Even with the extra hired help, Michael was needed to tend the cattle and hogs, the apple, plum and pear orchards, the hay, wheat, oat and barley fields. His absence would have put too much burden on his family, and he had refused to let that happen.

He thought his heart had been in the right place at the time, but now he was stuck with the consequences of that decision and had no one to blame but himself. With a heavy sigh, he retrieved the letters from behind the seat of the wagon and headed back to Selina.

Her cowboy hat now rested against her back. Sunshine glistened down on her head, exposing rivers of copper and blond streaks flowing throughout her molasses-colored hair.

Her skin was flawless.

Her teeth were even and white and her striking, rich, coffee-colored eyes held a million questions. Questions he didn't know the answers to.

No denying the woman was beautiful, but none of that mattered. She wasn't what he had wanted or prayed for. Of that he was certain.

He lowered himself at the opposite end of the log from Selina. Without looking at her, he tugged at the string around the parcel and opened the first letter he'd received from her. He practically had it memorized. Neat penmanship and feminine curves looked back at him, mocking him with their precise, dainty script. Script filled with lies and deception.

"This is the first letter I got from you. 'Dear Mr. Bowen. My name is Selina Farleigh. I'm twenty-five years old, five-foot-three inches tall with brown hair and brown eyes. I am responding to your advertisement because my father has taken ill. You see, the man my father works for provides our lodging. Once my father passes on, I will have to leave as I will no longer have a home.'"

"That's not true," Selina interrupted him.

He glanced at her.

"It's true about my pa taking ill but not that other stuff. No wonder you said you didn't want someone to marry you because they needed a home. Well, I didn't need a home, and Aimee knew that. My pa owned a place in the hills. Wasn't much, but my brothers own it now. I could've stayed there with my brother and his wife."

"Why did you answer my advertisement?"

"I let Aimee talk me into it. My pa's dying wish was to see me hitched to a good man. Pa said he could die in peace knowin' I was happily married and far away from Bart."

"Who's Bart?"

"A fella back home who wanted me to marry him." She scrunched her face. "No way would I have married Bart even iffen he was the last man on earth. Somethin' about him gave me the willies. Pa didn't much care for him none either. Said he drank too much moonshine. So when Pa found out about the ad and how Aimee was encouragin' me to write to you and all, he agreed. Said he wanted me to have a better life."

She looked away. "'Course, when he found out you were a pig farmer, he said it wouldn't be much of a better life but at least I'd be far away from the likes of Bart and would always have food to eat. That made Pa feel a whole heap better. Plus, he knew I never wanted to marry a rich man."

Michael's attention snagged on that last comment. Why didn't she want to marry someone rich? What was she going to say when she found out she already had? Did he even care?

"Then again, Aimee was supposed to tell you all a that."

Well, she hadn't. And Michael couldn't help but wonder who the real villainess was here and if all of this was some elaborate scheme to snag a husband. He had no way of knowing the truth. What he did know was, he felt the deception through every inch of his body and the largest portion of that deception settled into his heart.

From the way she was looking at him, he knew she was waiting for his response, but instead of responding, he raised the letter and continued to read.

"'Your advertisement states that you cannot travel as the work on your ranch needs your attention. I am willing to travel, but my father will not let me leave without first being married.'" Michael glanced over at her. "Is that true? Your father would not allow you to leave until you were married first?"

"Yes, sir. And neither would my brothers."

He nodded, then continued to read. From the corner of his eye, he could see Selina pulling the bead up and down on her stampede string.

The more he read, the faster she raised and lowered the bead. And if he wasn't mistaken, a shiny wet spot covered her cheek.

As he read one letter after another and Selina refuted one thing after another, anger replaced any love he felt toward the person who penned them.

"I've heard enough. Please stop."

She'd heard enough? He'd heard plenty. Plenty enough to know he'd been lied to and tricked.

His gaze fell to the stack of letters in his lap that at one time had brought him more love and joy than he'd ever known before. He had loved the sense of humor in them, the wit, the charm, the way the person saw beauty in the smallest things, the feistiness and confidence the person in them possessed. Only that woman no longer existed.

Or did she?

He didn't know anymore.

Didn't know what to believe or who to believe.

This whole thing was making him crazy.

Who could do such a wicked thing? And why? What could their motive be? He folded the letter he'd been reading, stacked it on top of the rest and tied the string around them. What he really wanted to do was burn them and his marriage certificate.

"I'm so sorry, Michael." Selina's voice cracked. "Everything I told her to say, she twisted or made it bigger than it was. She even wrote things I never did say." She shook her head, looking lost, alone, terrified even.

He couldn't help but wonder if it was all an act. He hated thinking like that, but he didn't know the truth or how to find it.

"Can't believe Aimee did that. I don't understand *why* she did this to me. To us." Her gaze dropped, along with her voice. "I—I don't rightly know what to say except…" Her chest rose and fell. "What do we do now?"

Her whisper, broken by tears, tugged at his heart. He hated seeing a woman cry, no matter how angry he was.

What did they do now?

Vows had been spoken, and the Bible made it clear about the wrongness of breaking vows. Like it or not, he and Selina were legally married. There was only one answer to that question. "I guess we head home."

Her gaze flew up to his and the color in her face fled.

Michael understood exactly how she felt. But they had no other choice. He hoisted his body off the log and offered Selina a helping hand up. "We made our vows before God and we need to honor those vows. Let's go home."

Selina picked up her rifle and slung the sling around her neck.

They shuffled their way back toward the train depot.

"Where's your luggage?" he asked without looking at her, his mind and body numb. Dead, even.

"I only have the one bag." She headed toward a patched-up gunnysack, picked it up and faced him.

He stared at the bag, shocked by her obvious poverty. "Here, let me take that for you." His focus trailed to her face.

She raised her head and jutted her chin before shifting her bag away from his reach. "Thank you kindly, but I can carry it myself."

He didn't mean to hurt her pride. He nodded, then pointed to his wagon, the only one left at the station now.

She slipped her hat back on, strode to the back of the buckboard, laid her rifle and sack down, then leaped onto the tail of the wagon, leaving her legs dangling.

That wasn't what he had in mind when he pictured taking his bride home. And what if his family was around when he got back to the ranch? What would they think if they saw her sitting back there and not up front with him?

Indecision tugged him in several directions as he debated what to do. Embarrassed by her appearance, he preferred she stay back there. But then again, if she did, his family would wonder what was wrong and he certainly didn't want to tell them he'd made the biggest mistake of his life. They already thought he was crazy because of some of the poor choices he'd made in the past.

Like the goats he'd bought on a whim.

The little brats had destroyed his mother's garden, chewed up some of the laundry and had even wreaked havoc at some of their neighbors' places. It had taken him a long time to make amends and to get rid of them. No one wanted the goats. He finally had to give them away. His family still gave him a hard time for that one. They'd have a field day with this one.

"Selina." He scuffed at the dirt with his boot. "Would you mind sitting up front with me?"

She frowned. "Why?"

"Because... Whether we like it or not, we *are* man and wife, and I think it would be best if we acted like it."

She tilted her head and studied him. "I see what you're sayin', and I won't shame ya by not sittin' next to you." Before he had a chance to help her, she hopped down and seated herself up front, leaving the sweet scent of field flowers in her wake.

He stared, shaking his head. He wasn't sure he would ever get used to a woman who acted and dressed like a man. And yet, what choice did he have? For better or worse, she was now his wife. And he had a bad feeling it was going to be for the worse.

Chapter Two

Selina scooted as close to the side of the wagon seat as possible. Touching Michael was something she didn't want to do. Her heart ached something fierce knowing Michael didn't love her and that she'd pretty much come all this way for nothing.

If only she'd known all of this back home, she would've never gotten hitched then. She'd seen the ugliness of what a marriage without love could do to folks, to the whole family, and it wasn't a pretty sight.

Long ago she had made a promise to herself to never get married unless the man truly loved her and she loved him. When she'd said yes to Michael's proposal, she believed she was honoring that promise.

Why did she ever let Aimee talk her into answering that stupid ad? If she hadn't, then neither she nor Michael would be in this mess.

Poor Michael. What he must be going through. "Michael."

"Yes?"

"I'm really sorry for what my friend did. I had no

idea she wrote those things and lied to you. Iffen I'd known, I would never have come."

"What's done is done, Selina. We'll just make the best of it."

He sure seemed to be taking it a lot easier than she was. Either that or he was mighty good at hiding it.

Silence followed them the rest of the way home. That was fine with Selina. Gave her time to take in the scenery.

Layers of green rolling hills stretched before her, ending at the base of a mountain covered with trees. Well, if a body could call these here mountains. They weren't nearly as big as the ones back home. In Kentucky, these mountains would be called nothing more than hills.

One thing for certain, this place was nothing like where she'd come from. But then again, nowhere on God's green earth ever would be to her. Born and raised in the Appalachian Mountains, she loved Kentucky and all its beauty. Before she left, she had fastened every little detail of them and her home into her memory so she'd never forget what they looked like.

The sun bore down on her back, heating her body something awful. She sure could use a drink. She licked her lips.

Michael twisted in the seat and reached for something behind him. He handed a canteen to her.

"How'd you know I was thirsty?"

His only response was a hike of his shoulder.

Wasn't long before they rounded a bend in the trees.

"Whoa, girls." Michael pulled the horses to a halt in front of a house five times bigger than the shack she grew up in.

Selina turned to Michael. "Why we stoppin' here?" She gawked at the large two-story house with rocking chairs, small tables and a big wooden swing on the porch that went clear around the place.

"I live here."

"This is yours?"

"Yes. It is."

"Well, I'll be hanged. You told me you were a pig farmer. Or did Aimee lie about that, too?"

"No. She didn't. I am a pig farmer. But I said that I also raise cattle."

"Oh, no," she groaned. "I can't believe I up and married myself a rich man."

Michael turned his head her direction. "You sound like that's a bad thing."

"It is. Iffen I'd a known you was rich, I'd never have answered that ad."

"What do you have against rich people?"

"Lots of things. Folks who have money think they're better than poor folk. Treatin' us like we're lower than dirt. Like we have no feelin's at all."

"Hey, now just you wait a minute. You can't go judging all rich people by the ones where you come from. My family and I do not turn up our noses at poor folks or treat them like dirt, either. Nor are we mean. I resent you clumping us into some category when you don't even know us."

"You might resent it, but the truth is you're just like them rich folks back home. Back at the train station I saw you turn your nose down at me and how I look. My whole life people been judgin' me by the way I dress. All I can say is, I'm mighty glad the good Lord looks at the heart and not the outside like some folks do."

His cheeks turned the color of a rusty-pink sunset.

"Aimee was rich, too. And look what she did to us." Selina spoke under her breath, still in shock at what her friend had done. She didn't want to think about that right now though. It hurt too much.

She hopped down from the wagon and grabbed her bag. Good thing she'd found a flour sack and put it to rights the best way she could, or she wouldn't have had anything to put her few belongings in.

Her eyes trailed to the huge house again and she wondered how many people lived here.

Michael was waiting for her at the end of the steps, looking uncomfortable.

Well, he wasn't the only one who felt that way. *C'mon, Selina. You can do this.* She met him and followed him up the stairs.

Michael opened the door and waited for her to go in first. One thing about the man, he was a gentleman. She stepped inside and stopped. Never in all of her born days had she seen anything so fancy.

The place was filled with more furniture than she'd ever laid eyes on. Her focus slid to the rich brown kitchen table and the six matching chairs with fancy carved legs and arms. Fresh flowers flowed from a large vase in the center of the table, which was covered with a lacy tablecloth.

And the cook stove, why, it was mighty fine. Unlike the old potbelly stove back home. That thing was harder than the dickens to keep burning and the door barely hung on.

Selina stepped farther inside, taking in the whole room. Two cream-colored rockers with gold squiggly lines running through the fancy curved tops and arms sat on one side of the fireplace, facing a matching sofa with blue, gold and cream-colored pillows on it. Betwixt them was a long table. A large oval blue-and-cream rug had been placed underneath the table. Sure was pretty.

Heavy drapes held back by a braided rope covered six tall living room windows.

On the mantel of the large stone fireplace sat a clock, with three different-sized brass candlestick holders on each side of it.

Selina strode toward the fireplace and crouched down, peering past the metal screen.

Why, the thing went plumb through to the other side into a bedroom with a cherry-colored dresser topped with a long mirror, another dresser that was taller and a four-poster bed, and all of them were done in the same fancy carved wood as the rest of the place. On top of the bed was a white quilt with light and dark blue circles and dark blue pillow covers. Pale blue drapes swagged the windows.

She loved blue. A tear slipped from her eye. She thumbed it away and wouldn't allow any more to escape. Knowing Aimee had told Michael that Selina loved blue made her wonder if the blue bed quilt and house curtains were done on purpose. Well, even if they had been, who were they done for? Her or Aimee?

Selina turned to see Michael standing in the doorway with his hat in his hands, watching her. Never before had she felt so out of place or uncomfortable. And she didn't like it. Not one little bit. She pressed her shoulders back, determined to not let it show. "Your home is beautiful, Michael. Whoever took the time of it did a right fine job."

When he said nothing, she played with the bead on her hat string. No longer able to stand the silence, she said, "Well, I reckon you must be hungry. Let me get my rifle and I'll hunt us up some grub."

His head bobbed forward like a rooster. "Grub? Are you serious?"

She raised her chin, not liking how he made her feel with his tone. "Yes, sir, I am serious. You wanna eat, don't ya?"

"Well, yes, but you don't have to hunt for any *grub,*" he said the word *grub* as if he hadn't ever heard it before. "I'm assuming grub refers to food."

Sure enough, he hadn't.

"I have a cellar and a pantry full of meat and anything else you might need. Here. I'll show you." Michael walked over to a small room off the kitchen, opened the door and stepped to the side.

Selina came up beside him at the doorway entry and peered inside. Her eyeballs nearly popped out of their sockets. The room was filled with canned goods, a large bag of flour and sugar, eggs, coffee, cornmeal and just about anything a body would need to fix a meal. Except she didn't see any meat.

"That door at the end of the pantry leads into the cellar," he said from behind her. A little too close behind her as far as she was concerned. She squirmed forward, but his broad-shouldered body took up most of the small space. Thing was, it didn't seem that small before he stepped into it.

Wood, soap and peppermint scents drifted from him. He sure smelled nice.

Swallowing to stop the thoughts, she moved farther into the room, putting even more space between them.

"You'll find whatever meat you need down there along with fresh vegetables and canned fruit."

Selina opened the door and squatted, trying to see in the dark hole but couldn't. It was coal black. When she stood, Michael picked up a lantern and matches from one of the shelves and lit it.

"Here. Take this."

She took it from him and made her way slowly down the steep, narrow stairs, expecting one of them to give way any time, but they never did. They were nothing like the rickety steps back home. These were nice and sturdy.

At the bottom of the steps, she held the lantern up. *Jumpin' crickets!* she thought, unable to believe her eyes. One whole side of the room was filled with hanging meat. All sorts of canned goods lined two of the walls. Barrels of taters, carrots, dehydrated apples, turnips and onions lined the other wall. More food than a body could eat in a year.

Michael stepped into the cavelike room, filling it with his presence. She struggled to keep her wits about her as she continued to take in what was before her. "How many will I be feedin'?"

"Just you and me."

Selina whirled. "All a this food is just for the two of us?"

"Yes. I wanted to make sure there was plenty when you got here. We butchered a few head of cows and some pigs and divided the meat. Mother, Rainee, Hannah and Leah canned all the fruits and vegetables and the fish and chicken, you see."

"There sure is a lot of it. Must've taken them a long

time to put up so much. Well, from now on, I can do ours so they won't have to."

"You know how to can?"

"Sure do. I told you so in my letters." Her heart dropped to the dirt floor of the cellar with that slip of the tongue. Now why'd she have to go and bring up them letters for? All that did was remind her that she wasn't the woman her husband was expecting, that she wasn't loved and that this wasn't a real marriage and probably never would be.

"Well, I need to go and finish my chores." He turned and headed toward the steps.

She followed him, hoping to do something to reclaim her pride. "I'll help you."

He stopped on the stair and looked down at her. The man sure had pretty blue eyes.

"Help me? You don't have to help me. Chores are man's work."

"Not where I come from they're not. Besides, I aim to do my part to earn my keep and to help out around here."

He raised his hat and forked his fingers through his hair, then put his hat back on. "Selina, you don't have to *earn* your keep. You're my wife."

A wife you don't want.

"And no wife of mine is going to do chores."

Did she just hear what she thought she'd heard?

She planted her hands on her hips. "And no man is ever gonna tell me what to do."

Not even her husband—no, make that especially not her husband. She'd never let him bully or boss her around or tell her what she could and couldn't do like her cousin Mary's husband had done. Mary had always been a cheerful and happy sort until she'd gotten hitched. Her husband stripped the life out of her with his controlling, bullying ways. He'd broken Mary's spirit until she was walking and acting like some dead person. Even worse, Mary had let him.

Well, not this gal.

Michael came back down the stairs and looked her right in the eyes. "I'll say it again. Chores are man's work and no wife of mine is going to do men's chores."

Just who did this sidewinder think he was, bossing her around like that? She stepped even closer, coming toe-to-toe with him. "And I'll say it again. No man is ever gonna tell me what I can or can't do." Selina refused to be beholden to anybody. She'd seen the ugliness of that, too.

He closed the distance between them until they were almost nose-to-nose. "You're not doing chores and that's final." With one more hard look he whirled and stomped up the stairs.

Well, she could stomp just as hard as he could and she did, too, until she met up with him. Then, she bolted past him and was out the door and in the buckboard before he even made it to the wagon.

He climbed aboard and glanced at her. "You're incorrigible. You know that?" He snatched up the reins and slapped his horses on the behind. The wagon lurched forward.

She didn't know what that word meant, but she had a feeling it wasn't good.

Michael rounded the trees by the main ranch. *Oh, no.* He should have known his family would do something like this. Neighbors, family and friends filled the ranch yard, along with benches, tables loaded with food and two large signs.

One read: Congratulations Mr. & Mrs. Michael Bowen.

The other: Welcome to our family and community, Selina.

The first thought that struck him was his wife's attire; the second was he hoped she wouldn't open her mouth. He wanted to turn the horses around and head back home before anyone caught sight of them.

"Here they come," his sister-in-law Rainee hollered. Rainee waddled toward them as fast as her pregnant belly would allow. Before he could think of a good way to get them out of there, she stepped up to Selina's side of the wagon and offered her a big welcoming smile. "Selina. Welcome to the family."

With no grace whatsoever, Selina hopped down. "Thank you kindly, ma'am."

Immediately Michael detected suspicion in Selina's voice. One look at her face confirmed it. He figured it stemmed from her earlier comments about rich folks. Well, she'd just have to put her prejudice aside and learn that not all folks who had wealth treated poor folks badly. Sure, he had turned his nose up at her when he first saw her, but she needed to understand it was the shock of seeing her dressed like a man and not a woman. Like a tomboy. An outlaw even.

The sad fact was, rich and poor alike would find her attire inappropriate. He knew many a poor woman and they didn't dress like her, so wealth had nothing to do with people judging her. Her lack of propriety did.

Before he had a chance to introduce her, Rainee said, "I am Rainelle Victoria Bowen." She curtsied.

"But, please, call me, Rainee." Rainee looped arms with Selina and led her to the crowd of people.

This whole thing was a nightmare come true.

Seeing no way out of it, Michael hopped down from the wagon and followed them. When he caught sight of the surprised look on the men's faces and the horror on some of the women's as their gazes traveled over her, anger surged through him. He didn't like her appearance, either, but how dare they openly show disrespect for the woman who was, after all, his wife.

He strode to Selina's side and placed his hand at the base of her back.

Selina looked up at him, at his arm and then back at his face, a question lingering in her untrusting wide brown eyes.

His gaze remained fixed on her, taking in her face, her high cheekbones and perfectly shaped lips. The woman was beautiful. Why did she hide it under that hat? Perhaps she didn't know she was beautiful.

Leah and Abby rushed up to meet her.

"Selina, these are my sisters, Leah and Abigail."

"Pleased to meet you." Leah gave her a quick hug.

"It's Abby, not Abigail. That sounds so stuffy. Just like you, Michael." Abby wrinkled her nose at him and then turned her focus onto Selina. "I love your outfit." His sixteen-year-old sister smiled, beaming as her gaze raked over Selina's clothing.

Dear Lord, don't let Abby start wanting to wear pants, too.

His sister-in-law Hannah looked up from wiping baby Rebecca's mouth. She handed the baby to her oldest son, Thomas, who took her willingly. He'd make a fine father some day. Just like his father, Jesse.

"Selina!" Hannah rushed over and gave her a hug. "Welcome to the family. We're so happy to have you here."

"Selina, this is my sister-in-law, Hannah."

"Pleasure to meet ya, ma'am," Selina said.

"Mama, where's my drink? I'm thirsty." William, Michael's five-year-old nephew and Hannah and Jesse's middle child, tugged on his mother's skirt.

Hannah rolled her eyes. "Sorry—I need to get my son something to drink. We'll talk later. You must come and see me. I live over there." She pointed to her and Jesse's house, then swung William into her arms and like a whirlwind she was gone.

Michael's mother scurried up to them. "Selina, I'm Katherine. Michael's mother."

"Pleased to meet you, ma'am."

"Welcome to the family, Selina. You must come by the house tomorrow so we can get better acquainted."

"That's right neighborly of you." Skepticism shrouded Selina's face once again.

"Hi, son." His mother barely glanced at him. "You don't mind if I borrow your wife, do you? There's someone I'd like her to meet."

"Hi to you, too, Mother." He smiled. "No, I don't mind at all."

"Good. Because even if you did, I was going to steal her anyway." Mother reached up and kissed his cheek before she looped arms with Selina and scampered her over to the same group of ladies he'd seen scowling. He watched, waiting and ready in case Selina needed his intervention.

"She isn't what you expected, is she?"

Michael turned toward his brother Jesse. With those

seven words, Michael knew his acting hadn't worked. Making sure no one was within hearing distance he said, "No, she sure isn't. I'm so angry and confused, Jess, I don't know what to do. I married the wrong woman."

Jesse frowned. "What do you mean 'the wrong woman'?"

With a shake of his head, Michael beat back the awful truth. "Selina didn't write the letters—her friend Aimee did."

"I don't understand."

There was no reason to hide the truth. Jesse had been with him through this whole thing from the beginning. In short detail, Michael explained everything to his brother. How the woman he fell in love with didn't really exist. Or if she did, she existed in two different people. One of whom he married. The other of whom he might have actually loved.

Jesse's concern was written all over his face. "Now that's a tough one. But remember, you did pray about it."

"I didn't pray for this, Jess. You know what I prayed for. Why would God do this to me?"

"God didn't do anything *to* you. He did it *for* you. He has a plan, Michael. We talked about this, remember?"

"A plan? What? To humiliate me? And how could you say God did it for me? What could God possibly have in mind? I mean, look at her, Jess. She's..." He couldn't even finish.

Jesse slid his gaze toward Selina. "She's um...different, but she seems friendly enough and she's very beautiful."

"She's different all right. She might be beautiful, too,

but she's nothing like what I had my heart set on marrying."

"Look, I know you wanted someone like Rainee. But there's only one Rainee and she's married to our brother."

"I know that. It's just… Well, every time I prayed for a wife, I asked God to send me someone just like her."

"Maybe He did."

Michael's brows spiked. "I don't think so. I don't mean to sound cruel, but look at the way she's dressed. And the way she talks." He rubbed the back of his neck. "I think the woman who wrote the letters comes closer to what I was wanting in a wife than Selina ever could."

"You don't know that. From what you told me, the person in the letters is a mixture of Selina and Aimee and a lot of things were exaggerated. So you have no idea what Aimee is really like except that she's the kind of woman—"

Michael finished Jesse's sentence. "Who would send her friend out West knowing she had lied, that she had deceived not only her, but also the man she had married. Leaving Selina to deal with the consequences." That thought alone secured his compassion toward Selina.

Nobody deserved to be treated that way. Especially by a friend she trusted. Indignation roiled through his gut. If Aimee were here right now he'd tell her exactly what he thought of her.

"Why did I have to come up with that ridiculous plan to say my vows of marriage in front of Reverend James and sign the marriage certificate and send it to her so she could do the same in front of her minister? If I hadn't, then neither one of us would be in this miserable situation." He caught his brother's gaze. "What am I going to do, Jess? I'm in love with a dream woman who doesn't exist. And even worse… I don't love my wife. She's a complete stranger to me."

All of a sudden, his stomach churned and he thought he might be sick as unbidden flashbacks of another loveless marriage came rushing in on him.

Unbeknownst to anyone, as a young boy Michael had witnessed time and again his brother Haydon's first wife Melanie's rage toward Haydon.

From afar Michael heard Melanie's cruel and spiteful remarks about what a poor excuse of a man she thought Haydon was. How she resented him for bringing her to this desolate place. How she hated him and wished she had never married him. How she had never loved him and had only married him for his money and his position in society.

To this day the memory of the pain on Haydon's face still haunted Michael. His brother's unhappiness had crushed Michael's young heart. His brother changed after Melanie. He was no longer his confident self until years after Melanie's death when God had sent Rainee into Haydon's life. Because of her, Michael now had his brother back, and Haydon was happier than Michael had ever seen him.

Michael wanted the special kind of love Haydon had found with Rainee. With all his heart, Michael believed he had—until a few hours ago. But it was fully clear to him now that his marriage to Selina was nothing but a farce and that his worst nightmare of being stuck in a loveless marriage had now come true. How had he let this happen?

Jesse squeezed his shoulder, yanking Michael from the cave of darkness his thoughts had taken him to.

"I know this is hard, Michael."

You have no idea how hard this thing is. No one does.

"But I have faith in you that you'll do what's right. Keep in mind that when Rainee first came, Haydon didn't want anything to do with her, either. He didn't believe God was in that whole situation, yet look how it turned out. They have two beautiful children and one on the way. Listen, I've got to run. Hannah is waving me down. If you need to talk, you know I'm here."

"Thanks, Jess." Michael pulled his brother into a quick hug then watched him head toward Hannah.

"Hey, buddy." Michael stiffened. The town heckler, Jake Lure, stepped alongside him and slapped him on the back. "Well, I guess we know who wears the pants in your family." Jake cackled and twitched his thick blond eyebrows in a mocking gesture.

Michael clenched his fists at his sides.

Jake looked around and then leaned closer to Michael. "You know, I think I've seen that beautiful face somewhere before. On one of the wanted posters at the jail." He cackled again.

Even though the man was a few inches taller than Michael's six-foot, broad-shouldered frame, Michael found himself wanting to punch Jake. But, he refused to stoop to this man's lower-than-dirt level.

Yet, hadn't he already done that by judging Selina's outward appearance, too? He had even justified his actions by reminding himself that she was not what he was expecting and it was the shock of seeing her dressed in trousers that had made him act so unbecomingly.

Thinking about how despicable his ungodly thoughts had been, he repented immediately. In that second, he decided no man or woman was ever going to get away with talking about his wife like that again.

"I'll thank you not to insult my wife ever again. Now, if you'll excuse me, I need to find my bride." Michael turned to leave.

"Just look for the lady in trousers." Jake's hooting laughter grated on Michael's nerves, but he refused to give into the temptation to pummel the guy.

Instead, he pushed his shoulders back and headed toward Selina. "I will." He tossed the words over his shoulder.

All the way to Selina, Michael fumed. Just who did Jake think he was, anyway? How dare he or anyone disrespect his wife like that? He may not like the way she dressed, either, but maybe that was all she could afford or had or grew up with. So who was he or anyone else to judge her?

He walked up next to Selina, standing amid a group of women who were laughing at something his wife had said. These were the very same people who when they had first laid eyes on her had shown disgust.

He slipped his arm around her shoulder. "Excuse me, ladies. You won't mind if I steal my wife away, will you?"

"We do, but we'll let you," said Sadie Elder, who came out West four years before to marry Tom Elder, a widower with nine boys. She took Selina's hands in hers. "You're just what we needed around here, Selina. It's a real pleasure meeting you. When you get settled, you must come by for a visit. Michael can show you where we live." Sadie looked at Michael seeking his permission.

He nodded.

"Oh, yes, you must come by my house for a visit, too," Mrs. Hawkins chimed in, and the other married ladies put in their requests, too.

Selina had obviously made a good impression on them. They not only seemed to accept her, outfit and all, but liked her well enough to invite her to their homes. That was a good sign. Wasn't it?

"It's right neighborly of y'all to invite me to y'alls homes. Iffen any of you need help, you let me know, and I'll be there quicker than a frog snatchin' a fly."

They all laughed.

"Oh, Selina. You say the funniest things," Sadie said through a chuckle.

Selina looked surprised by Sadie's comment, then she wagged her finger at Sadie and said, "Don't you go hurtin' yourself liftin' that cannin' kettle. I'll come by in a couple days and do it for you." Selina glanced up at Michael and smiled. Her teeth were as white as freshly fallen snow and not a crooked one to be found. The woman really was beautiful. Judging from the way she was willing to help everyone, she must be beautiful on the inside, too. Only time would tell.

"And when that baby is ready to be birthed, I can help you. Iffen you want me to, that is. Like I told you, I helped birth many a baby."

"Thank you so much, Selina. I feel better just knowing you're here. I'll see you soon then." Sadie turned and waddled toward her husband.

Sadie, who was twenty years younger than her husband, was carrying Tom's tenth child. Michael wondered if it would be another boy. For Sadie's sake, he hoped it was a girl.

The loud ringing of the dinner bell jarred his attention.

"Everyone, it's time to eat," his mother hollered.

Each woman took a turn shaking Selina's hand before they left in search of their husbands. Not one of them seemed to mind how heartily she returned their handshakes.

When the crowd quieted down, his mother turned her attention to him and Selina. "Michael and Selina, you get your plates first."

Michael glanced down at his wife. "You ready?"

"Yes, sir. Ain't had nothin' to eat since last night. I'm so hungry I could eat a herd of lizards—skin and all."

Lizards? The thought of eating lizards turned his stomach inside out. He hoped she was kidding. "Why haven't you had anything to eat since last night?" He placed his hand on her back and led her toward the long food table.

"I ran outta money. Couldn't afford none."

Michael instantly felt horrible. "I'm sorry, Selina. I thought I sent you plenty of money to take care of everything."

"Oh, you did. You did. But I couldn't sit by and watch that poor widow woman strugglin' to feed her three youngins."

"What poor widow woman?"

"Mrs. Morrow. Her husband died and she was comin' out West to marry up with a Mr. Clemens. From the way she tells it, he has four youngins himself. His wife died two years ago and he couldn't keep up with them and his chores, so he placed an ad and she answered it. Mr. Clemens sent her enough money for the trip, but some polecat stole it from her. Can you believe some snake would do such an evil thing? And to a widow woman with three youngins no less. Why, iffen I'd caught him, I would have put a load of buckshot into his sorry hide to make sure he never did it again. I'm just so glad you sent me plenty enough that I was able to help poor Mrs. Morrow."

She stopped and looked at him. Concern dotted her eyes. "Don't worry. I'll find some way to repay you. But I ain't sorry I did it. Ain't no way I was gonna sit by and listen to them youngins beg their mama for somethin' to eat when I had plenty."

What an unselfish thing she had done. To go without food so that another woman, a complete stranger and her children, could eat.

Maybe getting to know her wouldn't be such a bad thing after all.

Chapter Three

Back at the house, Selina picked up her bag to ready herself for bed. She had a good time meeting all her new neighbors. Some of them were friendly, too. But all that visiting had tuckered her out. All she wanted to do was find some place to curl up and go to sleep. She wasn't sure where that place was, though. The barn would suit her just fine, but she knew if someone saw her there, Michael would be shamed and she didn't want that for him.

She hoped to one day share her bed with Michael just like her mama and pa had. But that wasn't likely to happen with the way things were. Still, she wouldn't give up hope. Later on, during her evening prayers, she'd tell God's ears that if there was any way for Michael to love her one day, she sure would appreciate it.

Michael. This being her wedding night and all, just thinking about him sent shivers through her. She sighed. No sense pondering on him and making herself feel even worse than she already did. She needed to place her mind somewhere other than him. And she'd start with looking for a blanket or something to cover up with.

She searched a trunk and found one. While Michael was out at the privy, she put on her patched-up nightgown, tossed herself onto the living room sofa and pulled the blanket over her chest. Surprised at how soft the sofa was, she wiggled her way down into it.

The door clicked open.

Michael stepped one foot in and stopped to stare at her.

Selina yanked the cover up under her neck. "I hope you don't mind me helpin' myself to a blanket."

He shut the door behind him. "Selina, this is your home now, too, and I want you to make yourself comfortable here. And you don't have to sleep on the sofa, my bedroom is—"

"I ain't gonna share your bed," she blurted. *Until I know for sure you're in love with me and not Aimee,* but she didn't voice the last part. Thinking about what she'd said, white-hot flames licked their way up her neck and into her cheeks.

With a sigh he took another step in. "What I was going to say was, my bedroom is over there." He pointed to the door off of the living room. "If you'd like to sleep in there, I can move my stuff into one of the upstairs bedrooms. Or, if you would like more privacy, you can take one of them. Whatever you decide is fine with me."

What? No argument? No fight about his husbandly rights? She didn't know whether to be relieved or insulted. Considering their situation, she was definitely relieved. "I'll take one of the upstairs bedrooms. Ain't no sense in you movin' all your belongings."

He looked down at her flour sack, then back up at her. "Tomorrow, I'll see if Leah can take you into town to purchase you some women's shoes and material to make yourself some women's clothing."

It didn't get past her none that he stressed the word *women's* louder and longer than the rest of his words.

"I'm sure Mother and Leah would be more than happy to help you make a few dresses and bonnets and nightgowns and whatever else you may need."

She sprung into a sitting position. The blanket fell from around her shoulders.

Michael's eyes widened. He swung his attention away, looking everywhere but at her.

She snatched the cover up and tucked it back under her neck. "Just you back up your horses, cowboy. I don't need dresses, and there ain't a thing wrong with my clothes. Why, they've still got plenty of wear left in them. Besides, I don't cotton to wearin' dresses. They're just too confinin' and troublesome. You can't even hunt in them."

Michael's attention flew back to her. He crossed his arms over his chest and spread his legs. His stare went clean through her, but she wouldn't let him see that he unsettled her.

"That might be so. But no wife of mine is going to wear men's clothing."

"Listen here, Michael. I've been wearin' them most of my life and I ain't stoppin' now. Men's trousers are more practical."

"They might be more practical, but in case it's slipped your notice, the women around here do not wear pants. They wear dresses."

"I ain't other women. I'm me. And I won't be puttin' on airs for you or anyone else."

His eyes slammed shut for only a moment before bouncing open. "You're a stubborn little thing, aren't you?"

"Ain't tryin' to be stubborn." She wrapped the blanket around her and stood. "But I won't be bullied into being somethin' I ain't, neither." Michael wanted her to be something she wasn't and never would be. A lady. Tomboy was more her style. She'd been one all her life and loved it. Maybe she was stubborn. But some things were worth being stubborn about—and wearing trousers was one of them.

Before Michael could give her the wherefores about propriety and proper attire, his mouth spread into a wide yawn he couldn't stop. After the trying day he'd had, a soft bed and sleep sounded good. So, for right now, he'd let the subject drop, but he would definitely pick it up again in the morning. "It's been a long day, and I'm ready to go to bed. I'll show you to your room first."

He motioned for her to precede him up the stairs, which she did after picking up her sack. At the top of the landing, he stopped and faced her. "There are three rooms. Take your pick."

She peeked inside the first bedroom, then the second and then the third. "Iffen you don't mind, I'll take this one here."

"That's fine." He managed to keep his head from shaking in frustration. "Whatever you want." Somehow he had a feeling she would take the sparsest bedroom. The smallest room with the iron-framed bed, light blue quilt and matching curtains. Only a single dresser, a night stand with a lantern, a wash bowl and basin, three paintings on the wall, and one small closet occupied the room. The other two, which were larger and decorated as nicely as the rest of the house, didn't seem to fit her. One thing for certain, she was a simple woman who liked simple things.

"Well, good night, Selina. I'll see you in the morning."

"Night, Michael," she spoke softly in that melodic voice of hers, the one that in no way, shape or form matched her masculine attire or attitude.

Trying not to think about any of it, he headed to his bedroom, undressed and slid between the new cotton sheets. He rolled onto his side and stared at the blank pillow next to him. Tonight was the night he was supposed to be sharing with the woman of his dreams. Yet he'd felt nothing but relief when Selina said she wasn't going to share his bed.

But he couldn't bear the idea of spending his wedding night alone, without the woman he had dreamed about for five long months. A phantom woman who now only existed in his heart and his imagination. Grief barreled through him as the death of his dream came crashing in on him. Though he was exhausted, he dragged his weary body out of bed, threw on his pants and headed out onto the porch, where he leaned against one of the posts and stared up at the stars and the quarter moon.

Mosquitoes and gnats buzzed around his head. He waved them away as he watched the fading and returning lights of the stars dancing in the darkness above him.

Wind blew through the leaves of the trees and across his face, whispering a mournful sound that reflected the sad state he now found himself in.

He had no idea how to deal with his swirl of feelings.

Minutes ticked by while Michael berated himself for placing that ad in the first place. For not going out to meet her. For falling in love with a fantasy. If he hadn't done that, then none of this would have happened. "Lord, I know I did this to myself, but what am I going to do about Selina? She's a woman who is the complete opposite of everything I ever dreamed of. Imagined. Prayed for. She's a woman—" He stopped and sighed.

Selina *was* a woman. That much was obvious when the blanket had fallen from her shoulders. Through her thin nightgown, he could see the outline of her womanly curves, curves that would be the envy of most women. Yet the way she dressed did nothing to show her femininity.

He sighed heavily and scratched his neck.

"Lord, You know I've been talking to You for eleven years, asking You for a woman like Rainee. Why would You send me someone like Selina? Why? Please, help me to understand."

He listened for that still, small voice, but the only sounds he heard were coyotes howling in the distance, frogs calling out into the darkness and an owl hooting somewhere off in the trees.

Selina stepped up to the door in time to hear Michael ask why God had sent him someone like her. Her heart broke knowing she was causing Michael so much pain and heartbreak. But there was nothing she could do about it. Still, it hurt something fierce that he didn't want her. Her dreams of them becoming truly hitched disappeared like smoke in the wind.

Careful not to make a sound, she backed away from the screen door and hightailed it back upstairs and into her bed. Not one normally given to crying, she buried her head into her pillow, soaking it with her tears. Something akin to bear claws tore at her heart, shredding it to pieces.

Being in love with a man who didn't love her back hurt something fierce. Living with him every day was going to be the hardest thing she'd ever come up against. "Lord, give me the grace I need to survive. And I'd be right beholden to You, iffen You'd ease this awful pain in my heart and in Michael's, too."

After a few hours of fitful sleep, Selina lit the lantern next to her bed and slid into her garments. She grabbed the lantern in one hand and her boots and stockings in the other and crept down the steps and into the kitchen.

Careful not to make any noise, she made her way down the cellar ladder and cut off a slab of bacon and fetched a couple of eggs before she commenced to fixing breakfast. Coffee, bacon, eggs and fresh flapjack scents made her stomach growl.

Selina stood in front of the dish cabinet. Back home, she had a handmade breadboard counter to hold her dishes. It sort of reminded her of this piece of furniture, but her breadboard counter had a flour bin and several drawers and it didn't have glass doors like this fancy piece did. Plus, hers was covered with oil cloth and this one had a shiny finish to it. Made her afraid to touch it, it was so fancy. But she didn't have any choice. Not if she wanted to serve Michael his breakfast.

She opened the door, pulled out a couple of plates and froze at the sight of the dainty blue flowers and leaves. They were blue, not yellow, not pink and not any other color but blue.

Her favorite color.

Sure seemed like someone went to an awful lot of trouble to get dishes with blue in them. But, she sighed, they weren't meant for her. She set the table and then sat down with a hot cup of coffee. Bowing her head and closing her eyes, she clasped her hands together and said her morning prayers.

"Good morning, Selina."

Selina yanked her head upward to find Michael standing in front of her with a look of a man who didn't know what to do.

Bags sagged under his bloodshot eyes. His hair was all muffed up, and his clothes looked as if he'd slept in them.

"Did you sleep well?" *Jumpin' crickets, Selina. That was a stupid question. Anyone could see he ain't slept but a wink.*

His gaze slid over her face. "About as well as you, apparently."

Selina wished she had stopped in front of the looking glass before she came down. She had no idea what she looked like. Slowly raking a finger through her hair, she stood and put her back to him. Having him study her like that made her skittish. "Can I get you some coffee?" she asked, even though she had already grabbed him a cup and started to fill it.

"Yes, thank you. That would be nice."

"You just sit yourself down and I'll fetch ya some vittles."

Selina placed a plate with four pieces of bacon on it, six biscuits and a small mound of scrambled eggs onto the center of the table.

He looked up at her. "Aren't you going to have any?"

Selina glanced at the food and frowned. "Yes, sir." Confused by his question, she lowered herself onto the chair.

Before she could ask more, Michael reached over and clasped her hand in his.

Her attention flew right to him. Warmth spread up her arms and into her body as she yanked her hand away. "Wha—whatcha doin'?"

"Getting ready to pray." His eyes softened.

"Oh." She nodded, feeling dumber than a fence post for asking. She slid her hand back across to his.

His eyes drifted shut.

She knew she ought to close her eyes and concentrate on his prayer but her mind took a turn in another direction. While he prayed, she studied his face, wondering if those full lips were as soft as they looked.

Strength flowed through his rough hand even though he held hers with the softest of touch. Having her hand in his felt right nice, a little too nice considering their circumstances.

Her eyes trailed up his arms. Arms with muscles that were so big they pulled at the seams of his shirt sleeves. What would it be like to have him slip them around her and pull her close? Would she ever be close enough to his heart to hear it beating?

Her attention slid up to his eyes. Heat barreled up her neck and her cheeks felt hotter than the red coals in the cook stove over yonder. Just when had Michael stopped praying and caught her stealing her fill of him?

She looked at their hands, jerked hers from his and all but shoved the plate of food in front of him. "You— you'd best start eatin' before—before it gets cold."

Eating was the last thing Michael thought about doing right now. When he'd reached for Selina's hand, the instant he'd made the connection, warmth spread up his arm and slipped into his heart. He had no idea what that was all about nor did he want to know. Confused over what had just happened, he struggled to pull himself together so he could pray.

When he opened his eyes and saw Selina studying his arms and chest, saw the longing on her face, something stirred inside him. That foreign feeling made him vastly uncomfortable.

He rammed his fingers through his hair, but they snagged on some tangles. What had he been thinking coming to the breakfast table without combing his hair first? Even when he lived alone, he groomed himself before sitting down to eat. This whole situation had him so upset and confused he was no longer thinking or acting rationally.

To get his mind off the situation, he looked at the paltry plate of food she had placed on the table. Selina said she hadn't eaten yet. If they shared what little food was there, that amount wouldn't hold him long at all. He normally required twice as much as that just to make it until lunchtime.

He didn't understand why, when he had a cellar full of food, she had made so little. His gaze snagged on the numerous patches scattered on her sleeves. Obviously, Selina had come from poverty. Could that be why she had made so little breakfast? Because that was all she had been able to fix back home?

If that was the case, he didn't know what to do or how to handle the situation with delicacy. How could he let her know that it was okay to fix plenty here without hurting her feelings or acting like some rich boy throwing his wealth around?

Michael sighed inwardly. He silently prayed and asked God for wisdom concerning this situation. No answer came immediately, so in the meantime, he made do. He piled half of the eggs, three small biscuits and two pieces of bacon on his plate, then he moved the plate in front of her.

"Somethin' wrong with my cookin'?" She glanced at the center plate and then at his.

"I don't know. I haven't tried anything yet. But everything looks and smells real good. Why do you ask?"

"'Cause you only took half of what I fixed."

"Didn't you tell me you hadn't eaten yet?"

"Yeah. So?"

"Well, that's why I only took half."

Her forehead wrinkled, and her brown eyes narrowed.

Michael had no idea why she appeared so confused. Women. Who could figure out what they were thinking? No man, that's for sure.

He picked up his fork, scooped up a mound of eggs and shoved them into his mouth. Flavor, unlike any he had ever tasted before, burst through his mouth. "Umm. These are delicious, Selina. What did you do to them?" He spoke around the eggs, then gathered up another rounded forkful.

She smiled. "Fried them in butter and bacon fat. And

added the tops of those things I found down yonder." She pointed to the cellar. "They looked like the ramps back home, so I took a chance."

"What's a ramp?"

"An onion or a leek," she said as she added one piece of bacon, one biscuit and a small spoonful of the scrambled eggs onto her plate. "Come springtime, you can find them all over the Appalachian Mountains."

"I see. I'm sure it's beautiful there."

"Sure is." Her face brightened. The woman was definitely easy on the eyes.

"Do you miss home?"

Selina shrugged. "Don't know. Can't rightly say. I ain't been gone long enough to tell." With only a few bites, Selina finished her meager portion, hoping Michael had gotten enough.

"Have some more." Michael pushed the rest of the servings toward her.

"Thank you kindly, but I'm done," she said even though her stomach was pinched with hunger pain and wasn't near full enough. Then again, it never had been before. Now should be no different.

His eyes, soft and questioning, held hers as strong as a foot stuck in a mud hole. "Are you sure?"

Selina had made the decision, and she wasn't backing out now. "Yeah. I'm sure."

Michael's attention stayed on her face a spell before he heaped the rest of the food onto his plate and devoured it within minutes. He looked over at the stove with something akin to longing in his eyes before he averted his attention onto his coffee cup.

"Somethin' wrong?"

"Well, I was just wondering something. Before I took the rest of the food you said I only took half of what you'd made. Does that include biscuits, too?"

"Yeah. I wasn't sure how many to make. I wanted to stretch the food so we'd have plenty to eat. I'm sorry iffen I didn't make enough." She looked down at her hands, fiddling with the patch on her pants leg. She'd wanted to be such a good wife, and already she felt the pain of his disappointment.

Michael's finger rested under her chin, tugging it upward. "Selina, look at me." With the gentlest touch, he raised her head, forcing her to look at him, even though she wanted to look everywhere but at him for fear he would see the love she had for him in her eyes.

"I'm a big eater. I want you to know that we have more than enough food. So you can make plenty all the time. And…"

She watched him swallow and draw a breath.

"I want you to eat more, too. What you ate this morning wouldn't keep a baby chick alive."

She pulled her eyes away from his intense stare. It hurt to be so close to him, to feel he might care and yet know he didn't.

His finger dropped from her chin and rested in front her.

She wanted to snatch back his hand and cradle it against her cheek.

To hold it.

To feel its strength.

To enjoy the small pleasures a married woman like her ma had enjoyed.

But that would likely never happen, except in her dreams. And dream she would. No one could steal them from her. So when her head hit the pillow tonight, she'd dream of holding his hand.

Of him wrapping his arms about her and kissing her.

But until then, he was waiting for her answer. "Don't rightly know iffen I'd be able to. Food was mighty scarce back home. Always made sure my brothers and Pa had enough to eat first. Then I ate what was left. Which was never much. So, I'm used to not eatin' much. Even with you sayin' we have plenty, I still can't help but be scared that iffen I do eat too much more we might not have enough come winter time."

His eyes trailed over her face, her arms and her body. Well, what he could see of it with her sitting in a chair. Still, his studying her like that made her uncomfortable.

His attention ended on her eyes, and if she weren't mistaken, pity filled his. And she didn't like it. Not one little bit. She didn't want him feeling sorry for her and she'd let him know that. But before she had a chance to tell him so, he hitched his chair back and headed to the pantry.

When he came back he had a copper container with him, sat the thing down in front of her and raised the lid. He reached inside the jar and pulled out a handful of cookies and laid them on her plate and his.

He filled their coffee cups, something she should have thought to do, and then sat down. "Eat," he ordered with a smile. His face turned serious as he looked at her. "I don't want you ever worrying about food again, okay, Selina? We have ten dairy cows, a large herd of cattle and hogs, and plenty of chickens and eggs. We grow our own wheat so flour isn't a shortage, either. Plus, Mother, my sisters, and sisters-in-law all grow large gardens every year. And if something happens to any of the food or gardens, we can go to town and buy some. If worse comes to worst, we'll have it shipped in by train if necessary. Money is not an object."

Selina didn't know what to think. She'd never had such a mess of food before. She glanced at her plate and stared at the sandwiched cookies with the preserves in the middle. They looked mighty good and mighty tempting, too. Putting her fears aside, she decided that for once in her life her belly would take its fill.

Michael took a bite of one of his mother's syltkakor cookies. He thought about Selina not having enough to eat and how she had given her food to her brothers and her father first and then to some stranger on the train. A woman she'd just met. The very idea of that stirred something deep inside him. He wanted to provide for her and protect her from ever going hungry again.

As she continued to enjoy her cookie Michael used the opportunity to study her. Dark-brown eyelashes, long and full, almost touched the top of her high cheekbones. Her nose had a slight bump in the middle, and her lips were pink, with a few cookie crumbs sprinkled on them.

He reached over to wipe them off. The moment his thumb made contact with her lips, her eyes flew open and she jumped back. "What ya doin'?"

"You had crumbs on your lips." He flashed her a sheepish smile. "I was just wiping them off for you."

She swiped her mouth with her hands and then with her sleeve. With one eye slit, she tilted to the side. "Much obliged, I'm sure." She sat as far back into her kitchen chair as possible as if to get away from him.

"What kind a cookies are them anyways? They sure are good."

"They're syltkakors."

"Silt a whats?"

"Swedish sandwich cookies."

"Oh." That was all she said before taking another bite.

Watching her enjoy every morsel made him realize just how much he had taken for granted. He had always had plenty to eat, a roof over his head and an abundance of clothes. Never had he lacked for anything. But Selina had. And yet she didn't seem bitter, nor did she complain about her lack. He wondered just how many times in her life she had gone without so another would not. Knowing how poor she was, he was surprised by her generosity. And if he was willing to admit it even to himself, that generosity endeared her to him. Just how he felt about that, he wasn't sure. But he was sure about one thing. He would definitely find out. That thought both frightened and intrigued him.

Chapter Four

Five cookies later, Selina laid her hand against her gut. This was the first time she'd had a belly full of anything and it felt mighty nice. And scary. Her fears of running out of food stuck to her like caked-on mud. Would she ever get over that fear even after all Michael had said about having plenty?

Michael's eyes trailed to her mouth. Last time he'd touched her lips her belly and heart fluttered as if someone had released a thousand fireflies into them. So before he could brush the crumbs from off her lips again, she hurried up and did it herself.

"Well, I'd better go." He stood. "Thank you for breakfast, Selina." He headed to the front door and put on his jacket and hat.

Knowing he was heading out to do chores, she swigged down the last of her coffee and rushed to where he stood. She pushed her arms into her jacket and shoved her hat onto her head.

With his hand on the doorknob, Michael asked, "Where are you going?" He glanced at the breakfast mess on the table and stove.

"I'm goin' to help you with chores."

"Selina, we've been over this already. I know you want to help and I appreciate it, but it would help me a great deal for you to keep the house clean and have meals ready for me when I come in."

"I can do both. After I help you with the chores, I'll come back here and clean up this mess and get lunch ready for ya, too."

Michael rolled his eyes, swung the door open and stepped outside. His boots clunked on the steps as he tromped down them. That noise was meant to discourage her, but it wasn't going to work. Regardless of what he'd said about her being his wife and not having to earn her keep, she didn't want to be beholden to anyone, especially a man who didn't want her. She'd feel differently if Michael did want her, if he loved her, but he didn't. So, to her way of thinking that meant she was nothing more than a hired hand and a maid.

Selina struggled to stay alongside Michael, even though he paid her no mind. They rounded the bend that hid their house from the rest of the houses, into the main yard where the party had been the night before, and ended up at the barn.

Horses whinnied when they stepped inside. She breathed deeply the scent of horse and fresh-cut hay. Dust twirled in the sunlight and danced its way up her nose, tickling it. She sneezed loud and hard, not once but twice.

The horses snorted.

Michael whirled toward her.

"You sure you didn't blow your insides out, woman? Those are the loudest sneezes I've ever heard. Who would have thought something that noisy could come from someone as tiny as you."

She giggled. "Pa always told me I had the loudest sneezes ever. Said he never had to worry about my whereabouts 'cause my sneezes could be heard all over the mountain. And as long as he heard them, he knew right where I was at."

"I believe it." Michael chuckled.

She looked over at him. That was the first time she'd heard him laugh and she found it mighty pleasant. Something she could get used to.

She even got a glimpse of a little dip near one side of his mouth. Something she'd always been a sucker for.

Michael turned his back to her. He grabbed a pitchfork off of a nearby hook, rammed the fork into a mound of hay under the loft and tossed it into the first stall.

"I'm glad I caught you."

Selina twisted toward the voice and saw Abby.

"Mother saw you heading into the barn, Selina. She asked me to see if you would like to stop by this morning." Abby was a beautiful girl with her blond hair and blue eyes. She looked a lot like her handsome brother.

"That's mighty nice of her, but will you tell her I'm gonna help Michael with chores first, and that I'll stop by sometime today?"

"Sure will." Abby skittered off.

"You don't have to do chores. You can go visit with my mother."

"We done had this discussion. After chores I will." Selina searched for another hay fork and saw one hanging on a peg near the haystack. She filled it with hay and carried it to one of the stalls. The pretty chestnut mare with the white forehead and spotted rump dipped her head and swung it back and forth before diving into the pile.

"That's Macy's way of saying thanks," Michael spoke over Selina's shoulder.

"She sure is purty. Is she yours?" She tilted her head back so she could see his face.

He looked down at her and she forgot all about breathing.

He stared into Selina's eyes. He couldn't pull his attention away from them and the long lashes that framed them. Her irises were large, surrounded by a black ring. Their color was nothing like the solid brown he'd thought they were when he'd first met her. Instead they resembled a reddish-brown sorrel horse he once had.

All of a sudden she ripped her gaze away from him and onto something behind him.

"Why, hello there." Selina scurried over to Miss Piggy and scooped the gray-and-white barn cat into her arms. "Aren't you the purtiest little thing ever?" She stroked the feline's fur and stopped, then examined her hand. "Oh, no. You're bleedin'. You poor baby. Selina'll take care of you and make it all better."

Her words were long and drawn out in the same type of Southern drawl Rainee had. He had loved listening to Rainee talk and he had to admit, he enjoyed the Southern accent in Selina, too. And that surprised him.

Selina helped Michael feed and water the animals then gathered up Miss Piggy and headed for home. Did she really think of the Idaho Territory as her home? Not yet, but hopefully someday she would. Inside the house, she searched everywhere until she found what she needed. When she finished doctoring the cat, she placed the exhausted critter on Michael's bed and headed back into the kitchen.

With one glance at the breakfast mess, she rolled up her sleeves and washed the dishes and set things to right. Michael would have the chores done by now, so she decided to go visit Katherine. She stepped out onto the porch and stopped.

"Good morning, Selina." The very pregnant Rainee stood only a few yards away from her. Other than her belly, she was a tiny thing. Beautiful, too, with her honey-colored hair and matching eyes.

"Mornin', Rainee."

"I brought you some bread and cookies."

"Well, that's right neighborly of you." Selina rushed down the steps and took the basket from Rainee. "You didn't need to do that."

"I know. I wanted to." Rainee smiled.

"Can you come in and sit a spell?"

"I would love to."

As they made their way into the house, Selina said, "Would you like some tea or coffee?"

"Tea would be lovely. Thank you."

"Why don't you take a load off while I fetch ya some?"

"If you do not mind, I believe I shall." Rainee sat down while Selina commenced to making tea.

"Who would have ever thought having a baby would take so much out of a person?" Rainee spoke from the living room.

"Is this your first?"

"No. I have a nine-year-old daughter, Emilia, who we

call Emily, and a seven-year-old daughter, Rosella, who we call Rosie. They are visiting their grandmother."

"When's your baby due?" Selina asked as she came into the living room.

"In a few weeks." Concern skipped across the woman's face. "I hope and pray this baby survives."

Startled, Selina handed her a cup of tea and a small plate with a couple of cookies on the side, then sat down across from her. "What do ya mean?"

"In the eleven years Haydon and I have been married, I have been with child five times. The girls came along just fine, but after them, I lost the next two." Sadness filled her eyes.

Selina laid her hand on Rainee's. "I'm so sorry to hear that. Do you know why they didn't make it?"

"No. And neither did Doctor Berg." She took a sip of her tea. "Since I am being so honest with you I will also tell you I am quite scared to have this one. When Rosie was born, she almost did not make it."

"How come?" Selina hoped Rainee didn't mind her asking so many questions.

"I do not know. Haydon would never tell me. He did not want me worrying."

"I see. Well, don't you be worrin' none about this baby. I can help. I've birthed many a youngin'. Even troublesome ones. You just let me know when your time comes and I'll be there. Iffen you want me to, that is."

Rainee's eyes, the color of a fawn, brightened. "I would love to have you there. Thank you, Selina. I must admit, when I heard you telling our neighbors that you helped many a child into the world, I was quite relieved. Doctor Berg is our local doctor, but he is always so busy that I feared he would not be available when my time came."

"Well, I'll be here. You just let me know."

They sipped their tea, ate their cookies and visited as if they were old friends.

Rainee glanced at the clock. "Where did the time go? I have bread to bake and desserts to make to get lunch ready for Haydon and my girls."

She rose and put her tea cup and empty plate in the sink. "Thank you, Selina. I had a lovely time."

"I did, too. Come back again anytime."

Rainee grabbed Selina's hands. "You must come see me, too. I get quite bored sitting all day. Haydon will not let me do anything. I had to beg him to let me help with the cooking and care for my girls."

Selina's eyes widened. "What do ya mean, he won't *let* you?"

"Can you believe he hired me a maid?" Rainee rolled her eyes and sighed. "I sent her packing straightaway. But my husband brought her right back. I feel quite ill at ease with a maid. No one else has one and they have survived and I can, as well. But Haydon would hear nothing of it, so we finally came to an understanding. She could stay, but I would be allowed to help her some."

"Why'd ya let him tell you what you could or couldn't do?"

"Oh, I assure you, I do not. I just let him think he does." Rainee winked.

Selina smiled. "I knew I liked you." In the very next second a plan worked through Selina's mind. "Rainee, could I ask you somethin'?"

"Yes, you may."

"Do you think…" Selina looked down at the floor. "Do you think you could…" She pulled in her bottom lip and chewed on it. This was a might harder than she'd thought it would be.

"Selina, do not make yourself uneasy. Just ask."

Selina slowly raised her head. Seeing the sincerity in Rainee's eyes, she plucked up her courage. "I was wonderin' iffen you could teach me to talk good. And to read and to write. Iffen you have the time, that is."

"Sure I have time. But I see nothing wrong with the way you talk. I rather like it. Why do you want to change?"

"I have my reasons." Never before had she wanted to change for anyone, but now that she was married to Michael and loved him, she wanted to make him proud. If somehow she could do that, maybe he would come to love her, too.

"Please forgive me for asking, but if you cannot read nor write, how did you answer Michael's advertisement?"

"My friend Aimee did it for me." Boy did she ever. Selina still couldn't believe what Aimee had done to her and Michael. She had thought Aimee was different than the rest of those rich folks. Turned out she was just like them after all.

"I see."

No, she didn't see, but Selina didn't want to talk about that.

"I would be happy to help you. If you want to, come by after lunch, and we will start then."

"I'll be there." Selina walked her visitor to the door. "Thank you kindly, Rainee. That's mighty nice of you."

"You are most welcome. I am looking forward to it."

"Iffen you don't mind, I'll walk with you. Katherine invited me for a visit."

"I do not mind at all. I would love it."

They headed down the stairs. Rainee looped arms with Selina as they disappeared down the path in the trees.

In two shakes of a squirrel's tail, Selina climbed the steps to Michael's ma's house. Her ma now, too. That put a smile on her face. She raised her hand to knock on the door just before it swung open.

"Selina, I'm so happy you came. Please, come on in." For having money, everyone around here was sure friendly. Maybe Michael was right. She shouldn't clump all rich folks together.

Katherine stepped back and motioned Selina inside.

Two girls stood next to the kitchen table staring at her.

"Girls, stop that staring."

"Sorry, Grandmother," they both said.

The taller girl had blue eyes and blond hair and looked just like her pa. The shortest one had doe-colored hair and eyes like her ma. She glanced up at Selina. "You sure are pretty."

Selina squatted down to her eye level and smiled. "So are you. Anyone ever tell you ya look just like your mama?"

She tilted her head and lowered her eyelids. "Yes, ma'am, they have. Thank you."

Selina rose and turned her attention to the older one. "You look like your papa. And you're every bit as purty as your sister."

"Thank you." Her face brightened like the morning sun.

Katherine went and stood between the girls and faced Selina. "Selina, this is my granddaughter Emily." The oldest one squatted and rose. "And this one is Rosie."

The younger girl squatted like the older had. Selina wondered what that was all about.

"Nice to meet y'all."

"Nice to meet you, too," Emily said. Her sister repeated it.

"Okay, girls. Why don't you go back to working on your quilts now."

As the girls headed into the living room, Katherine asked, "Can I get you something to drink?"

"No, ma'am. But thank you anyway."

"Very well. Let's head to the living room where we can get comfortable."

Selina followed Katherine and sat down in one of the chairs.

"Don't mind the mess. I'm keeping the girls occupied by teaching them how to quilt."

Selina looked down at the girls sitting on the floor and the squares of material between them.

"I've never made a quilt before. Always wanted to learn, though."

"How come you didn't?" Rosie asked.

"My ma took sick when I was a youngin, and she died when I was ten, so I never got a chance."

"We'll teach you." Emily looked up at her grandma. "Won't we, Grandmother?"

"We sure will." Katherine smiled at Selina.

"Really? You'd do that?"

"Sure will. In fact," Katherine rose, "I'll be right back." She left the room.

"Are you making quilts for your beds?" Selina asked the girls.

"No, we're making them for our dollies," Rosie, the bubbly one of the two answered.

"What color you gonna make them?"

"Mine's going to be pink and yellow." Rosie puffed out her little chest.

"I'm making mine in two different shades of blue." Emily picked up the squares and showed them to Selina.

"Blue is my favorite color." Selina ran her fingers over the dark and light blue squares.

"I could make mine blue, too." The sad look on Rosie's face made Selina wonder what that was all about until she realized she'd made a big to-do over blue and Rosie's was pink.

Selina placed herself in a circle on the floor with them and looked at Rosie. "Rosie, I like pink and yellow right fine, too. Purple, orange, red—you name it and I like it. So don't you be changin' your mind 'cause someone else likes somethin' different. You just be yourself because the good Lord made you just the way you are. Perfect and just right."

With a big smile Rosie picked up the pink and yellow squares and got right back to work on her quilt.

Sitting with the girls, watching their faces, settled a longing deep inside her to have children of her own.

Katherine came into the room, carrying tied stacks of squared material. Selina leaped up and took part of them from her.

Her mother-in-law set her stack down. "Here you go, Selina. Take your pick of colors."

"Thank you kindly, Katherine."

"Please, I'd be honored if you would call me Mother."

Selina smiled. "I'd be right honored, too…Mother." It felt strange being all formal and calling her mother, but no one else called Katherine Ma, and neither would she. Selina whipped her attention away from Katherine so she wouldn't see the tears building in her eyes. No one could take her ma's place, but it felt nice to have a ma again.

She studied the stacks of squares. Each one had a different pattern. They were all so pretty, and not wanting to make the girls feel badly by choosing blue, she asked, "What's Michael's favorite color?"

"He doesn't have one. Says he likes them all," Katherine answered.

That made it easy. Selina chose a variety of colors. Then, Katherine, with the help of the girls, showed Selina how to sew the blocks together, something called piecing. Having Katherine show her how to do this made her miss her mama. Well, she wouldn't think about that now. She'd just enjoy her time with the girls and Katherine.

Two hours later, Selina excused herself so she could hurry home and fix lunch for Michael. She flew around the kitchen fixing lunch and had just finished when Michael came in the door holding his arm, blood staining his shirt sleeve and handkerchief. Selina's attention shot to him. She tossed the dish towel onto the table and bolted toward him. "Michael! What happened?"

Michael's arm throbbed. "I snagged it on a nail." Now he wished he would have gone ahead and fixed that stupid nail sticking out of the fence yesterday, but no, he'd been so excited about picking up his bride, he had forgotten all about it. Seemed he'd been doing a lot of things he regretted lately.

"Well, let me take a look at it." She unwrapped the blood-soaked handkerchief from around his arm. "This thing sure is deep. You're gonna need stitches. Got any thread and a needle?"

Needle and thread? You've got to be kidding. He yanked his arm back to his chest. No way would he let someone other than a doctor sew him up. "Yes. But I just dropped by to grab a bite and to let you know that I was heading into town to have Doc Berg take a look at it."

"Ain't no need to bother the doctor when I can take care of it for you."

Of course she could. "I'm sure you can, but after lunch I'll head into town just the same. Thank you."

Selina planted her hands on her small waist. "Nonsense. I been sewin' up cuts for as long as I can remember. I'm good at it, too. Fetch me that thread and needle or I'll find it myself. Got any clean rags? And some moonshine?"

"Moonshine? What's that?"

"Homemade corn liquor."

"The only alcohol I have is some whiskey for medicinal purposes."

"That'll work just fine. Fetch it, too."

"Bossy," he murmured under his breath as he headed to do her bidding.

"I heard that."

"Good." He grabbed the whiskey from the pantry and the needle and thread he used to sew up his tack.

He watched her burn the end of the needle with a match then pour whiskey over it. Using warm water, she sloshed a clean rag around the water then irrigated his wound by squeezing the water out of the rag. Gently, she dabbed the excess water and dirt from the laceration. He had to admit she was doing a nice job. She held a clean rag under his arm, tilted the whiskey jug above it and poured it into his cut.

"Ahhhh!" He yanked his arm from her. Whiskey ran onto his pant leg. "What did you do that for?"

"To kill any germs that might be in it."

"That stuff stings." The strong smell of whiskey singed his nose and made his eyes water.

"Oh, you big baby. Come here." She clasped his hand, raised it and started blowing on his cut, cooling the pain.

The contact did funny things to his insides and made him forget all about the stinging.

He stared at her, unable to peel his attention away from her beautiful face and puckered lips. What would it be like to caress those shapely lips with his own? Would they be warm or cool to the touch? Realizing where his thoughts were taking him, he yanked his focus and his mind back to reality. "Aren't you adding germs to it by blowing on it?"

"Oh, for pity's sake." She grabbed the whiskey jug and placed another clean rag under his arm and poured even more alcohol onto the wound. "There. Iffen any of my germs got in there, they're dead now. You happy?"

"No. It hurts. If I would have gone to the doctor, it wouldn't have hurt as much."

"Well, iffen you think that hurt, then you'd best be for backing up your horses, cowboy, and bear down on this." She all but shoved a piece of wood between his teeth and in the next breath she poked the needle through his skin.

He wanted to yell out in pain. Never was he one to handle needles very well. He bit into the wood, almost breaking it in half. What he really wanted to do was jump up and head straight into town to Doc Berg's office.

Pressure applied on his arm took his mind off of the needle. Minutes later, after a few more quick pokes and knots, she announced she was finished. While she made a bandage for it, he studied her work and found her stitches to be as good as any doctor's. Michael had to admit, he was impressed.

She bandaged his arm. "There. All done. Now that wasn't so bad, was it?"

"I hate to admit it, but no. It wasn't too bad. The alcohol was the worst part." He looked up at her and smiled. "Thank you, Selina."

"You're welcome. Now, let me get you some vittles." She put away the supplies she'd used and then set food on the table.

He smiled. This time she'd made plenty. After eating a big lunch, although there were still plenty of chores that needed tending to, having had very little sleep the night before, Michael decided to take a short nap to refresh himself. "Selina, I'm going to take a nap. Can you wake me up in about fifteen minutes?"

Her cheeks turned pink. He wondered what that was all about, but all she did was nod.

He stepped into his room and stopped. Sprawled across his pillows was Miss Piggy, the barn cat. "What are you doing in here, Miss Piggy?"

The cat raised her head, gazed at him a mere second, then laid her head back down.

"She needed a place to sleep," Selina said from behind him.

"There's a barn for that, you know. Animals do not belong in the house."

"This one does."

"No, she doesn't." He strode over to where Miss Piggy lay and stooped to pick her up. But before he had a chance to reach the cat, Selina grabbed his hand on his good arm, surprising him with how strong a grip she had for such a tiny woman.

"Don't you be disruptin' her. She needs to sleep so that cut can heal."

He stood to his full height, crossed his arms over his chest and spread his legs. "This is my bed, Selina, and I won't have animals sleeping on it or anywhere near it. Do I make myself clear?"

"Sure do. But you're forgettin' one thing. This here's my home now, too. You said so."

He did and it was. But there was no way he was allowing animals into his...their...house. He had worked his backside off to provide his wife with nice furniture and he'd be hanged if he'd let some animal that spent all day down at the barn rolling in only who knows what, come in and soil everything he'd worked so hard for. "That's true, but as your husband, I am the head of this house and what I say goes." He sounded like a bully even to his own ears, but he didn't know what else to say to keep Selina from bringing any more animals into the house.

"You may be the head over this house, but I ain't

never let a man boss me around or tell me what to do and I ain't aimin' to start now."

He had only himself to blame for not going to Kentucky and meeting Selina before getting married. Now he was stuck with the consequences of a headstrong woman. If he wasn't so frustrated over the whole mess, he would laugh. She couldn't be more than five-foot-three inches tall, yet here she stood, mere inches from him, glaring up at him and daring him to refute her.

And refute her he would. "That cat better be out of here by the time I get home, or I'll put her out myself." He whirled, changed his torn, bloody shirt, then stormed out of the house.

Chapter Five

The next morning, Michael was already gone when Selina woke up. The cookie jar sat on the table along with an empty milk glass. Selina wondered why he didn't wait for her. Surely he wasn't still upset with her. Yesterday, whenever the cat had woken from her nap and wanted outside, Selina had obliged her. So the animal wasn't in the house when Michael got home. Maybe she'd gotten up too late. She walked to the window and peeked outside. The sun wasn't even up yet and neither were the roosters, it was so early.

It bugged her that he hadn't woken her up to fix him some breakfast. Maybe with his arm hurt he wanted to get an early start, knowing it would take longer. Who knew. Either way, Selina wanted to help her husband with whatever chores needed to be done.

She grabbed a biscuit and gulped it down before heading out to the barn. Inside the barn, she found a lantern and lit it. Once the horses were fed and watered, the barn was mucked clean and the lantern was snuffed, she stepped outside just in time to watch the sunrise.

A long yellow streak outlined in orange rose above

the mountain. Shadowed puffs of clouds dotted the blue sky. "Mighty fine job Ya done there, Lord. Sure is purty." She watched it for a few more minutes, then turned toward the outbuildings in search of Michael.

Little things around her snagged her attention, though, and she forgot all about looking for Michael. God's creation was something to behold. She wandered around the ranch yard, stopping often to enjoy the good Lord's many pleasures. Like the smell of sweet apples filling the fresh air. Dew drops sparkling on the leaves of bushes, birds singing their morning song, squirrels chattering, probably telling something or someone that they were in their territory or taking their food. Yellow, fluffy baby chicks peeped, and chickens pecked away at the feed she'd just tossed them.

Time passed until she realized the sun had fully risen and had driven the morning chill from her body.

Standing near the woodshed, she turned when she heard footsteps brushing the grasses.

Leah came bustling toward her. "Hi, Selina. I've been looking all over for you. Michael asked me to take you into town to buy some material and some new boots. It sounds like so much fun, and I'm looking so forward to getting to know you better," the young woman said excitedly.

Selina looked down where Leah had linked arms with her as if they were old friends. To her delight, so far, everyone here was friendly. Made her feel welcome. She smiled at the pretty young lady whose blond hair shone like a halo. Field flowers surrounded the air about her. "You sure smell nice."

"Thank you." Leah smiled.

"Where is Michael anyways?" She allowed Leah to

lead her toward the barn. Leah's skirt swished as she walked.

"He's out doctoring and checking the cows."

"Maybe I should go help him. Can you show me what direction he went?"

Leah's voice and face fell. "He went up north. I could show you, but I was so looking forward to taking you shopping."

Selina could tell how much it meant to her, and she didn't want to disappoint Leah. "I can help him another day."

"Are you sure?" Her face lit up.

"I'm sure." Selina wanted to earn her keep, but Michael had asked his sister, her sister now, too, to take her, so she reckoned it was okay.

"Oh, goody. Let's go, then. I have the buggy all hitched and ready."

Leah led Selina to a fancy buggy with a half top. A black horse with a spotted rump was hitched to it. "That's a right purty horse. Ain't never seen horses like the ones y'all have before."

"They're palouse ponies. They are beautiful, aren't they?"

"Sure are."

They climbed into the buggy. Leah picked up the reins and gave the horse a light slap on the rump. "Giddyup, Lambie."

Lambie? As in lamb, the animal? That was a mighty strange name for a horse.

Hooves clip-clopped on the hard ground, and tack rattled like chains as they headed down the road toward town.

"You're going to love Marcel Mercantile. They have a nice selection of fabrics and shoes."

Selina was sure she would. She hadn't ever spent much time in a store before. No need to. Never had any money to buy anything. *Jumpin' crickets.* How was she going to pay for the material and shoes? Michael had to know she didn't have any money. Well, she wouldn't fret about that now. She'd wait until she got to the store, then she'd know what to do or what not to do.

"Michael said to tell you he set up an account for you to get whatever you wanted or needed and not to worry about how much it cost. Wasn't that sweet of him?"

Shock ran through her. "Sure is."

About a quarter mile up the road from the ranch, Selina spotted a large herd of cows on one side of the road and a large herd of pigs on the other. Michael and three other men were riding through the cows. She twisted in her seat, longing to join him, but that wasn't going to happen today. She was on her way into town to get new shoes and material to make new clothes.

Things she'd never had before.

Her and her brothers' clothes were made from other folk's hand-me-downs, and they never could afford new shoes. New shoes. Something she needed desperately. The ones on her feet were worn thinner than a moth's wings and about as fragile, too.

Up the road a ways, about two miles, she noticed a sawmill in the trees with several large stacks of wood and logs. And even farther up the road was a field filled with red poppies. "Can we stop a minute?"

Leah looked at her with surprise. "Um. Sure. Whoa, Lambie." She pulled the reins and the buggy came to a stop.

Selina hopped down and ran over to the red poppies. She stooped to take a look at them.

A few minutes later, Leah came up behind her.

"Ain't these purty? The edges of the petals look like the wrinkled skin of an old person. Just as beautiful, too." A bee buzzed around her, landing in the black center of the flower beside her. She watched, amazed at God's creation and how the bee's wings kept that little varmint in one spot while it worked on that flower. Selina turned to say something about it to Leah, but she was back in the buggy.

Selina gently held a flower in her hand and leaned over, breathing in deeply. Sweet honey was the only way to describe the wonderful scent. Not wanting to keep Leah any longer, she made her way back to the wagon, running her fingers lightly over a few of the petals along the way.

She climbed into the buggy. "Sorry to keep you waitin'."

"You weren't keeping me waiting. I hurried back here because I'm scared to death of bees."

"How come?"

"Well, one time, I got stung by a whole bunch of them all at once. Since then I've been deathly afraid of them."

"That's too bad. They're right pleasurable to watch."

"I'll just have to take your word for it." Leah laughed and Selina joined her.

The buggy shifted as it moved forward.

"Them poppies sure were purty." She looked around. "This place is a lot different from back home."

"You're from Kentucky, right?"

"Yes."

"Think you'll like living out here?"

"I reckon I will well enough."

"Were you scared to move so far from home? To marry a complete stranger?"

"Well, I never felt I was marryin' a stranger. Me and Michael had written so much, I felt as iffen I knew him already." She wouldn't tell Leah that things had gotten messed up in that area. She'd keep that information to herself.

"I'm thinking about placing an advertisement in some of the larger newspapers back east," Leah said, keeping her eyes straight ahead.

That shocked Selina. "Why would a purty gal like you need to place an ad?"

"Same reason as you." Leah smiled. "I'm looking for a nice man to marry. I'm not getting any younger."

"How old are ya?"

"Twenty-three. I'll be twenty-four in December. If you don't mind me asking, how old are you, Selina?"

"Just turned twenty-five." She shifted in her seat. "I know it ain't none a my business, but I was told there ain't many women out here even with the comin' of the train. So why would someone as purty and sweet as you have to place an ad? Ain't none of the men here tickled your fancy?"

"There's a few good men who have 'tickled my fancy,' as you say. But, I don't want to stay here. I want to move back to New York to live in the big city again. Years ago, when my father announced that he wanted to leave New York and move out west to the Idaho Territory, I asked Mother why. She said Father had an adventurous spirit. I can relate. I do, too. Just not for this place. The winters are just too long here and I really don't like living on a ranch." Leah sighed. "Even though I was young when we moved, I still remember wearing party dresses and going to balls. I know it sounds silly, but I want to do that again."

"Ain't never been to a ball myself before."

"Oh, you would love it." Leah brightened.

Selina glanced down at her dust-covered and patched clothes.

Leah's eyes followed.

"Don't reckon I'd fit in at a ball." Selina giggled. So did Leah.

"No, probably not. But you sure fit in with our family. Everybody already loves you."

Everybody except my husband.

"Are you sorry you came, Selina?"

"No. Not really."

"I can't wait to place an ad for a husband." The young woman's face brightened at the prospect of the dream.

Hope things work out better for her than they have for me. "Does your family know how ya feel?"

"No. I've been trying to figure out how to break it to them." The dream drained from Leah's eyes. Selina knew just exactly how the girl felt.

"Well, make sure you pray about it first, Leah. Things don't always turn out the way a person thinks they should." Realizing what she said, she quickly looked away and added, "Sure are a lot of wheat fields out here."

Leah looked at her, then at the wheat fields. "There sure are. Selina, what did you mean when you said things don't always turn out the way a person thinks they should?"

Ah, puppy's feet. She was hoping she'd leave that comment alone. Maybe she should tell Leah the truth so she wouldn't make the same mistake she had.

"Just make sure you meet the man you plan on marryin' in person first. That you spend time with him and get to know him real good. A person can only learn so much about someone from letters. The real thing might be a huge shock and a disappointment. Can be mighty hurtful."

"Is Michael different than what you were expecting?"

"No. I am."

Leah's brows rose, then creased with worry. Questions lingered in her eyes, but thank the good Lord she didn't ask them. How could she ever explain what she herself didn't understand?

Selina turned her face the other direction from Leah. They rode the rest of the short way in silence.

When they pulled into town, people gawked at Selina, whispering behind their hands. She didn't pay them any mind, though.

Leah reined the horse in front of a large building with a sign. They hopped down and stepped onto the boardwalk.

"Disgraceful. That's what it is. Disgraceful." A woman eyed Selina up and down, frowning.

"Good morning, Ethel. I'd like to present to you my sister-in-law, Selina Bowen."

"This person is your sister-in-law?"

Leah raised her chin. "Yes, ma'am. She is. This is Michael's wife."

"Michael's?" The woman turned pale. "This is Michael's wife?"

"Yes, ma'am, she is. Now, if you will excuse us, we're here to get some material to make some new clothes for my new sister."

Ethel bobbed her head. Even though she'd said mean things about Selina, Selina looked for the beauty in her.

"You sure have a nice smile, ma'am. And your dress is right purty, too."

"I—I," she stuttered. "I do? It—it is?" The woman Leah called Ethel looked down at her dress.

"Yes, ma'am." Selina smiled at her and Ethel's lips slowly curled upward.

"Thank you." She dropped her head and all but crawled away.

Leah looped arms with Selina and leaned close. "That was nice of you to say such sweet things to Ethel. Whatever you do, don't let what Ethel said bother you. She's just embarrassed because she had gone around town telling everyone that her daughter, Marybeth, had won Michael's affection and that it was only a matter of time before they got married."

"Did he want to marry her?"

"No. She's only fourteen."

"Fourteen?" Selina said loudly, then quickly glanced around, hoping no one heard her.

Leah nodded and they both belted with laughter. When they finally stopped, they stepped inside the store. Selina knew her eyes were bulging, but she couldn't help herself. She'd never seen such a large selection of stuff before in her life.

Just looking at all the different colored bolts of fabrics alone had her mind swimming. She ran her fingers over each one, enjoying the feel of new material. It took her forever to decide on the colors she wanted.

"Michael told me to make sure you got plenty," Leah said beside her. "He figured you'd purchase barely enough to get by and he didn't want you to do that. He said to tell you that he wanted you to have fun and not to think about the money. To get whatever you wanted in the entire store. Knowing my brother like I do, if you don't come home with a bunch of stuff he'll be disappointed."

Selina didn't know how to feel about this whole thing. Didn't quite know how to act, either. Finally, she chose a mixture of muslin and cotton materials in blue, pink and yellow. And enough blue, brown and black denim to make several pairs of trousers not only for herself but Michael, too. She also picked out matching thread and a package of needles.

Leah looped arms with her and led her to the shoe section. She picked up a pair of black lace-up shoes with small heels. "How about these? These are darling."

Selina glanced down at her cowboy boots and then over at the shelf next to the women's shoes. "I'd rather have a pair of those." She picked up a brand-new pair of brown cowboy boots that looked to be her size. New leather filled the air. She looked around to make sure no one would see her. The lady at the counter was busy helping the only other customer in the store, so Selina slipped her boots off and tried the new ones on. They fit perfectly. Felt right nice, too. "I'll take these." She smiled at Leah.

They laid all of her purchases on the counter where the other customer had been.

"Hi, Mrs. Marcel."

"Good morning, Leah. How are you?"

"I'm doing great. How about you?"

"If I were any better, the Lord would have to take me home because I wouldn't be able to handle so much joy." She smiled and more lines filled her beautiful skin.

The gray-haired woman looked over at Selina. Selina waited for the usual look of disgust, but none came. Instead, the lady's lips curled upward into a warm, welcoming smile as she extended her wrinkled hand toward Selina. "I'm Bertie. Bertie Marcel. And you are?"

Selina took her hand and shook it gently. "Selina Bowen, ma'am."

"Bowen?" Her gray brows rose. She looked over at Leah then back at Selina.

"This is my new sister-in-law, Mrs. Marcel. Michael's wife."

"Well, I'll be. That boy finally up and got married. About time. And to such a beauty, too. It's a pleasure to meet you, Selina. And please call me Bertie."

"Thank you kindly, ma'am. It's a pleasure to meet you, too." Selina had to fight back the tears burning the back of her eyes. These people here were sure different. Folks who owned the mercantile back home wouldn't even look at Selina, let alone be nice to her. The only thing they ever did was turn their noses down at her and ignore her as if she didn't exist. Money sure had a way of making people act un-Christian-like.

"Oh. Leah, some letters arrived for you yesterday. My, you sure have become popular lately." She chuckled. "I'll get them for you." Bertie went to a room with metal bars.

"Here, try this." Leah handed her a square piece of something brown.

"What is it?"

"Just try it. You'll love it." Leah bit into a piece and chewed slowly.

Selina turned the piece around in her hand and looked it over before taking a bite. Yum. Sweet and creamy. "What is this? It sure is mighty tasty."

"Chocolate."

"Ain't never heard of it before."

Leah offered her some more, but Selina didn't want to be greedy so she turned down the offer even though she sure did want another piece. She liked chocolate a whole lot.

Bertie returned and handed Leah a stack of letters held together with a string. Seeing all those letters reminded her of Michael and the stack he'd read her at the train station. Letters that had changed both of their lives forever. And not in a good way, either. Poor Michael. Well, she didn't want to think about that now. It was too depressing.

Selina finished getting what she needed, and then they headed home, laughing and talking a sow's ear off all the way back to the ranch.

They arrived home shortly before noon. Selina set her purchases down on the sofa. She noticed Michael had already eaten again. She'd have to talk to him about why he hadn't waited for her to fix him something. Until then, she had work to do. So she ate a biscuit with strawberry jam and a slice of ham on it, put on a pot of stew, then she got right to work sewing herself some new clothes.

Hours later, she held the trousers and shirt she'd made against her body.

"Where did you get those?"

Selina whirled at the sound of Michael's voice and the banging of the door. She'd been concentrating so hard, she hadn't even heard his footsteps echo on the porch, or the door squeak. It was nice seeing his handsome face again, warmed her like sunshine. She held the new outfit up proudly. "I made them." She smiled, knowing she had gotten all the money's worth possible out of the cloth.

But Michael didn't smile back. Instead, he looked over at the material sitting in a basket next to the rocking chair by the fireplace. "Is that all you made?"

She frowned. "For now. Ain't had time to make nothing else yet."

"But you plan on making some dresses, right?"

That was less of a question and more like an order. One she didn't take kindly to. "Michael Bowen, I told you, I ain't worn a dress since my ma died. A person can't hunt or do chores properlike in a dress. Iffen you think a body can, then you put one on and see for yourself that they can't."

He ran his hand over his face. Something he seemed to do a lot around her. "Selina, you know how I feel about you wearing pants. You're a woman, not a man. When are you going to get that through your thick head?"

She slammed her hands on her hips. "We've already been through this. Ain't no man or no woman gonna tell me what I can and can't wear. So when are *you* gonna get that through *your* thick skull? Just 'cause the good Lord made me a woman don't mean I have to wear a dress."

"I don't care what you say, woman. No wife of mine

is going to wear pants in my house. It's neither proper nor comely."

"Accordin' to who?" She crossed her arms in front of her. "Besides, you forget. This is my house now, too. *You* told me that, and I aim to take you at your word."

Michael closed his eyes and dropped his head back, blowing out a long breath at the same time. *Why me, Lord?* "We'll discuss this later. I'm famished. What's for supper?"

"Even iffen we discuss it later, my mind won't be changin'."

With a shake of his head, he went to the sink and pumped the handle harder than he needed to, taking his frustration out on it. When the wash bowl in the sink was full to the brim, he washed his hands, face and neck. The grime from the day ran down the drain. If only he could wash his problems away that easily and watch them all disappear down the drain, too. He grabbed a towel and dried himself off.

"I made stew for supper." She looked over at him as she stirred the pot. "Oh. I just remembered somethin'. How come you left so early this mornin' without lettin' me fix you some vittles? Same with lunch."

"I'm sorry. I forgot to tell you that me, Jess, Haydon, Smokey and the hired hands were going to get an early start. We had lots to do. As for lunch, couldn't wait till you got home. I was famished so I went ahead and ate. Oh, by the way. Thanks for taking care of the horses and chickens this morning and for cleaning out the stalls. That was a huge help." For a man who didn't want his wife doing chores, he had to admit he truly was grateful.

"You're welcome. Glad I could help." Her face beamed under his praise, making her pretty features even prettier. If only she'd learn to control her tongue. "Now sit down while I put supper on."

He obeyed like a good husband and sat down at the kitchen table. Selina flew around rattling dishes and silverware and clinking glasses as she set the table. Grabbing a couple of the crocheted potholders his mother had made, she picked up the stew pot and set it on the table, along with a pan of biscuits and some butter and jam, then poured milk into the glasses. He'd never seen anyone set pans on a table before.

His family always used serving dishes and put the biscuits in a covered basket. One more reminder of the huge gap in their lives to this point.

She raised the lid off the kettle and the savory smell of rich beef gravy reached his nose. His stomach growled. "Smells good, Selina."

"Tastes mighty good, too."

"Been sampling supper already, huh?" He laughed.

"Sure enough have. How else am I supposed to know iffen it tastes good?" A twinkle filled her eyes.

"You got a point there."

She grabbed his bowl, put a large portion of stew into it and handed it to him. He watched as she scooped one small ladle into her own bowl.

"Selina, do you remember what we talked about earlier?"

She looked over at him with a frown. "Not sure what you're referrin' to."

Reaching over, he dipped a full ladle of stew and put it into her bowl.

Surprise jumped to her face. "What did you do that for?"

"Because you won't."

She dropped her gaze and picked it back up, settling it on him. "Don't know iffen I'll ever get used to being able to take as much as I want."

His heart broke for her then. She might be a wild-cat, but she was his wife. And for some reason God had brought them together, so he'd try his best to take care of her. Even if she didn't want him to. And even if it killed him. And even if it was sure to drive him crazy. Which it just very well might.

This time he was careful not to grab her hand for prayers, and in a strange way he kind of missed it. So he laid it there for her to take.

She glanced down at his hand, then up at his face. He scooted his hand closer to her, offering it to her.

She inched her hand toward his until she finally rested her small one in his. They bowed their heads.

With prayers finished, he reached over and grabbed two biscuits, slathered them in butter, placed them on a small plate and set it in front of her. "Eat. That's an order."

"I told you, no man will ever tell me what to—"

Nonchalantly, he grabbed a buttery biscuit and shoved it into her mouth. "Hush up and eat."

Her eyes widened, then narrowed. She glared at him and bit down hard on the soft biscuit and chewed. He watched as she swallowed. "You think that's gonna shut me up, well you—"

Again, he shoved the biscuit into her mouth, leaving her no choice but to bite into it. "That's better." His chair moaned when he settled back into it.

Her eyes bore into him the whole time she chewed. At least the woman was mannerly enough to not talk with her mouth full. He was grateful to God for that much, anyway.

Crumbs stuck to her lips, but this time he wasn't about to wipe them off. If he did, she'd probably bite his fingers. Those flames shooting from her big brown eyes as she chewed the massive chunk he'd shoved into her mouth sent him a warning. One he was going to heed.

He scooped a spoonful of stew and put it into his mouth. While he chewed the best stew he'd ever tasted, he buttered several fresh-baked biscuits. The aroma of them reached his nose on the waves of steam. It was hard to enjoy it, though, with Selina staring him down while she ate. A keg of gunpowder ready to explode would have looked less dangerous. She tried to look mean, but she looked kind of cute, and he fought not to laugh.

He picked up a biscuit and brought it to his lips.

Quicker than a flash, Selina's hand shot out, mashing the biscuit against his mouth. She sat back with a smug look on her face, acting as if nothing had happened.

Michael wiped the butter from his face. "So you wanna play, huh?" He grabbed one of the biscuits and headed toward her face with it.

Selina's chair scraped across the wooden floor as she bolted upward and out the front door.

Michael flew after her, chased her through the woods, dodging pine trees and their prickly needles. Syringa bushes slapped his legs. Pine needles and broken branches crunched under his feet on the uneven ground as he pursued Selina through the woods.

Around the curve, he lost sight of her. It was as if she had disappeared into thin air.

Where could she have gone?

He stopped and panned the area but still caught no sight of her.

Stealthily he made his way through the pine and cottonwood trees and the thick underbrush. He held up the biscuit like a weapon, armed and ready. Each tree he approached with caution, quickly looking behind it before trudging onward.

He leaned forward to look behind another tree.

The next thing he knew, his body slammed on the grassy forest floor, mashing the biscuit he held into the side of his face. Selina's body straddled his shoulders, then bolted upward.

He shot out his hand, grabbed her pant leg and yanked on it.

She tugged and jerked to free herself, but he tossed his body onto his back and pulled her down on top of him.

Holding her tight with one hand he scraped some of the biscuits and butter from his face, pulled her down closer to him and raised his hand to smear it onto hers.

"No!" She yanked her head from one side to the other, giggling.

Her laugher was melodious, like a running brook.

He pulled her even closer. Their faces inches apart.

Their eyes connected, peering deeply into the other's.

Neither moved, as if they were frozen in that position.

His attention slid to her mouth. The temptation to kiss her lured him in, but he knew kissing her would be a huge mistake. He blinked, breaking the contact, and slowly released his hold on her shirt. "Yes, well—" he cleared his throat "—I guess we'd better get back to supper before it gets cold."

She leaned back, sitting on his belly, having no clue of the urges raging inside him. "You give then?"

"I give." Boy did he ever.

She crossed her arms. "I knew you would." Her smile spoke of her untamed spirit.

"Oh, yeah?" No way would he let her think he was that easy. He pressed his fingers around her waist and started tickling her.

"Ahh. No, no." She squirmed, giggling as she tried to get away. But she was no match for his firm grip. He tickled her more insistently, careful to keep his touch from hurting her.

"How's about we call it even?" she said between bouts of laughter and drawing in breaths.

"Will you behave?"

"I'll behave as best as I can." She smiled, then broke free of his grasp and darted back to the house.

He sat up and brushed the leaves and pine cones off of him. One thing he had to give Selina credit for: he never knew what she would do next. And that both frightened and excited him.

Selina rose before the sun and the roosters again. After a breakfast of flapjacks, fried taters and ham slices, she followed Michael from the hog pen as he headed toward the barn. Something butted her knee, almost knocking it out from under her. "What do you think—" She whirled and looked down, smiling. "Why, you little cutie. You wantin' some attention?" She knelt down on one knee and scratched the pink pig behind the ear with a small chunk out of it.

"That's Kitty," Michael said.

"Kitty?"

"Don't ask. Abby named her years ago."

"Y'all got a lotta animals with weird names. A cat named Miss Piggy. A pig named Kitty, and a horse named Lambie. Abby name them, too?" She played with the tip of Kitty's nose.

"Yes. None of us had the heart to say anything so we let her name them. But we were sure glad when she outgrew that stage. Having a horse named Raven and a bull named Taxt were…" He left the sentence hanging.

"Taxt? What's that?" She shifted her attention from Kitty onto Michael.

"A taxt is a mule deer fawn."

"Abby gave a bull a cute critter's name like that?" She stood, and Kitty leaned into her leg.

"Remind me to tell you a few of her other names sometime. Right now I need to go and check on the orchards."

"What kind of orchards?"

"Apple, plums and pears."

"Oh. I'd love to see them. Would ya mind iffen I tagged along? And after I've seen them, would you mind directin' me toward Sadie's house? I told her I'd come in a couple a days to help do her cannin'."

"Sadie lives on the other side of our orchards so that'll be fine. I'll saddle up Macy for you."

"That's mighty nice of you, but I don't use a saddle. And I can get Macy ready myself. All you have to do is show me which bridle to use."

"You don't use a saddle?" His eyebrows shifted above his blue eyes.

"No. Ain't never had one before. Never could afford one. We were lucky to have a horse. It was given to us by Mr. Clark. He couldn't take her with him when he moved so Pa ended up with her. Was right neighborly of Mr. Clark to think of us."

They stepped inside the barn and Kitty scooted on past the door.

Michael grabbed two halters from a room filled with tack. "I'll get the horses."

"No need to get mine. I can do it."

He looked at her as if questioning whether he should let her or not, then he nodded and handed her a halter.

He led Selina to one of the stalls. She stepped inside and closed the door. "Mornin', Macy. You wanna break outta this here cell and go for a ride?"

Michael stopped on his way to fetch his horse. "You act like she's in jail."

"She is. How would you like to be holed up here day after day?"

"Well, it's not like she can't go outside when she wants."

"Yeah, but it ain't the same. She can't up and leave whenever she wants to."

"Most horses can't."

"I know. I sure am glad I ain't a horse. Couldn't stand bein' cooped up all day. I gotta get out and go for a walk and enjoy all of God's creation. Why, did you know that there are a million different types of bugs alone? Some of them even prettier than a coon's face."

"A coon's face?"

"I guess y'all call them *rac*coons here."

That dip in his cheek made an appearance again even though his smile wasn't any bigger than a minute. "Never thought about all the different kind of bugs there are." Humor trickled through his voice and sparked his eyes.

"My mama used to say that beauty could be found anywhere and that the most beautiful things were often hidden. A person just had to look for them." She glanced over at Michael. "Ain't you never taken the time to notice how many different type of bugs there are? Or how the mornin' dew drops on flowers twinkle in the sun like night stars? Or how the stripes in the hundreds of kind of leaves are different? Why, there's a whole world out there with all kinds of beauty in it to see."

"Can't say that I have. I've usually got too much going on to take time for things like that."

She tsked. "That's a right shame, ya know. You don't know what you're missin'."

"That might be so, but right now what I'm missing is checking on our orchards. I'd better hurry and get to it."

"Mighty shame that you have to rush around here, there and yonder all the time."

"I'm sure it is. But I'll just have to take your word for it."

They readied their horses and led them out of the barn into the warm sun. A light breeze brushed across Michael's face.

He turned to help Selina mount but never got the chance. She grabbed a hunk of mane and swung her small form onto the horse's back. How she did it as small as she was, he wasn't quite sure, and he would have never believed it if he hadn't witnessed it for himself.

He shook his head, amazed, then mounted his own horse.

They rode through willows, white pine, cottonwood and fir trees. One thing was for sure—she hadn't been kidding him when she said she took time to enjoy God's creation.

Although he thought it was cute how her face lit up and her eyes sparkled when she stopped to study yellow buttercup flowers, white daisies, wild pink roses and even a few syringa bushes that weren't even blooming, did she have to do it now? At the pace they were going he would have to work twice as hard and twice as fast to get his work finished.

Not only did she point out every little detail, she had to stop and smell them all, too, closing her eyes as she did. Even placed a few under his nose. It had been a long time since he'd enjoyed the pleasant scent of roses or the sweet smell of a syringa bush. Someday he'd have to take the time to do it again, but right now he really needed to get back to work.

And yet, isn't that what had gotten him into this mess in the first place? Not taking time from work to check things out? Even now though, he still couldn't. There was too much to do and too little time to get it all done. So as much as he wanted to enjoy the things she was enjoying, he couldn't. He needed to hurry her along.

Finally, they reached the orchards. To his dismay, she did the same thing there. He gave up trying to hurry her and resigned himself to having to work late again.

Riding to one of the pear trees, he plucked a nice ripe one, reined his horse close to Selina's and handed the fruit to her. "Ever had a pear right from the tree?"

"No, can't say that I have. Don't know that I've ever had a pear before at all."

"Never?" That shocked him. "Well, you don't know what you've been missing. Here, try one."

She took it from him and studied it first. He should have known she would. She closed her eyes, her chest expanding as she breathed in its scent, and then she took a small, hesitant bite and chewed. Her eyes darted open. Her mouth parted and a big chunk disappeared out of the pear. Juice ran down her chin.

He reached over to wipe it away. When his fingers touched her, he noticed how smooth and soft and warm her skin felt under his fingers.

Their gazes connected, then hers dropped to where his fingers still lingered. He yanked his hand away, wishing he didn't have to, wishing he could run his finger over her cheeks and neck to see if they were as soft as the rest of her skin. A quick frown from her and he cast his urge aside and sat back straight in the saddle. "Well, this is where we part ways. Enjoy your pear. Eat as many as you'd like."

"What do ya mean 'this is where we part ways'?" From the fear that flashed through her eyes, he wondered if she had taken it the wrong way and forgotten she had asked him to point her toward Tom and Sadie's house.

He shifted in his saddle, and leather creaked under him. "Remember you wanted me to show you the way to Sadie's?"

Her mouth formed an O and the fear dissipated. He'd

been right. She had misconstrued what he had said. Relieved to put her fears at rest, he pointed the direction she needed to go and said, "You need to follow the dirt path over the hill and through the trees. It'll take you straight to their house. But be careful. Out there in Idaho Territory, you may run into wild animals." His sisters traveled alone all the time, but they were skilled in dealing with wild animals. He battled with what to do.

"What kind of wild animals?"

"Bears, coyotes, wolves."

Her eyes brightened. Not a trace of fear showed on her face. In fact, intrigue fluttered across it and that made him nervous. The woman had no idea what dangers lurked out there.

"I wish I would have thought to tell you to bring your rifle." This was one time he was glad the woman had one and knew how to use it.

"You think I'll need it?" Still no fear.

"Probably not. But it's always good to take one with you when you're traveling through the forest. Just be careful, okay?"

She nodded.

"Think you can find your way back home?"

"Yep. I can find my way back from just about anywhere. Now my brother, Jacob, he gets lost worse than a goose in a fog."

He chuckled at her analogy. "You're sure?" What if she didn't? Would he regret not taking her to Sadie's? He seemed to have a lot of those kinds of regrets lately.

Her deep sigh reached his ears. "Wouldn't have said so iffen I couldn't."

"What time you think you'll be home?"

"I reckon not till supper time. I didn't forget about your lunch iffen that's what you're worried about. I sliced some ham and put a fresh loaf of bread on the table for you."

"I wasn't worried about that. But thank you."

She waved him away. "You're welcome. Well, I'd better get iffen I'm going help Sadie with her cannin'. See you later, Michael. And thanks for showing me the orchards and for this here pear." She heeled Macy's sides and the mare started walking away.

Poor-decision regret snuck up on him again. The idea of her going alone tore at his conscience, making him rethink his plans for the day. He wanted, no *needed* to know that she got there and back safely. After all, he was the one who had brought her here to be his wife. She was his responsibility now. "Selina, wait!" He spurred his horse forward and caught up with her. "I'm going with you."

She reined her horse to a stop. "Michael, I know what you're thinkin'. But I really can take care of myself. Been doin' it all my life. I ain't scared of wild animals."

"I know. That's what worries me."

Her lips curled into a smile. "Well, it's sweet of you to worry about me, but I'll be just fine. You go tend to them orchards of yours, and I'll see you later." She kicked Macy into a trot. Her braid swished like a horse's tail as she headed up the hill and out of sight.

Hearing the confidence in her voice, he felt better about letting her go. "Lord, watch over Selina and keep her safe." The woman was starting to grow on him, and that made him nervous.

* * *

Toward dark, Michael's stomach growled. The sun was setting, leaving behind a sky painted orange with a few streaks of yellow. At the barn he unsaddled his horse and pitched him some hay, then walked toward his house.

Exhausted from a hard day of work, he couldn't wait to get home, clean up, eat and sit down on the sofa and read first his Bible, then start on *A Tale of Two Cities* by Charles Dickens.

The steps groaned under his weight as he climbed them. He opened the door and stopped short. His eyes all but popped out of their sockets at the sight. Curled up next to Selina on the sofa was a wolf pup.

"Selina! What are you doing?" he barked.

Selina bolted upward. Her eyes blinked rapidly and her gaze darted about the room wildly before landing on him. The pup stirred next to her.

"What are you thinking bringing a wolf into this house?"

"Jumpin' crickets. That's what all the hollerin's about? The pup?"

"That just isn't any pup. That's a wolf."

"I know that. But there ain't no way I was gonna just leave the little varmint there."

"Leave it where? What are you talking about, woman?"

"Poor little thing had its paw caught in a small animal trap. Ain't no way I was gonna leave it there to fend for itself and to keep on sufferin' like it was so I brought it home and doctored it."

"Se-li-na." He drew out her name and scrubbed his

hand over his face. "Don't you know how dangerous that is?"

"'Course I do. I ain't stupid, but I was born and raised in the hills of Kentucky and we got all sorta wild animals there, and I ain't never left one to die yet, and I ain't gonna start now. I've been tendin' to them ever since I was eight and found that baby coon without a mama."

"That—" he pointed to the pup still asleep on the sofa "—isn't a raccoon. Those things are dangerous. You're lucky its mama didn't attack you."

"I looked around for its mama. Besides, don't you know nothin'? Iffen I were in danger Macy would have warned me by gettin' all antsy, and the hair on the back of my head never rose so I knew I was safe."

"You can't go by Macy or the hair on your head rising."

"Sure I can. Been doin' it all my life and it's worked so far. I trust my instincts and the good Lord to keep me safe."

"You can't go by instincts, Selina. You have to use common sense. And saying you trust God to protect you when you're doing something ludicrous is ridiculous. It wouldn't be any different than me jumping out of a fifty-foot tree and saying that God will keep me safe because I trust Him. I'm either going to end up hurt really badly or killed. And most likely it will be the latter."

"Someone would have to be gone in the head to do somethin' that stupid."

He tilted his head and hiked a brow.

She slammed her hands on her hips. "You callin' me stupid?"

"No, I'm not calling you stupid, but what you did was stupid."

"You know, Michael, the way I see it is, the good Lord put me on this earth to help save them poor critters. Iffen He didn't, then He wouldn't have given me the knack for doctorin' them or the desire to."

"So now you're saying God is in this?"

"Yes, sir, I am."

"You're unbelievable, you know that?"

"Don't rightly know what you mean by unbelievable, but I know what's in my heart." She pressed her hand to her chest.

"There's no talking to you. No getting through to you, is there?"

She frowned. "Don't understand. Ain't that what we've been a doin' the last ten minutes? Talking? At least where I come from it is."

He sighed and shook his head. "I want that pup out of here tomorrow. I'll ride with you to put it back where you got it. And from now on, I don't want you bringing any more animals into this house. You understand me?" He kept his voice firm and hard, hoping she would get the message.

She stepped right up to him, leaving mere inches between them. Her head tilted back and she hooked his gaze and held it. "I understand you, but it don't mean I'm gonna do it. I'd rather move outta this here house than have someone tryin' to change who I am. What I live for. And that's doctorin' animals and helpin' people. Aside from all of that, I can't return it." She turned and sat down on the sofa and pulled the sleeping pup onto her lap and started stroking its fur. "I think her mama is dead."

"What makes you think that?"

"'Cause this pup raised an awful ruckus when I was

helpin' it, and the mama never did show up. Iffen she were alive, she would have protected that pup of hers."

Selina had a point. About a few things anyway. He was trying to change her. But he didn't see that as a bad thing. Someone had to protect this stubborn, head-strong woman from herself. Still, he glanced at the pup and back at her. Determination and compassion drifted from her.

What was he going to do?

He couldn't keep the wolf.

And he didn't want his wife moving out. That surprised him.

"I'll be gettin' my things now." She put the pup down and walked past him toward the stairs.

He caught up with her and grasped her arm, stopping her. "You don't have to do that, Selina."

"Yes, I do. I won't live where I can't be myself. For whatever reason the good Lord made me the way I am, and I won't be a changin' for you or anyone else. Iffen you're worried about me breakin' the vows we made before the Lord, don't be. I'll just bed down in the barn from now on." She shook off his arm and darted up the stairs, taking them two at a time with her short legs.

He hurried up the stairs after her. "You don't have to sleep in the barn. There's an old cage down in one of the sheds. I'll run and get it. The pup can sleep in it. But just for tonight. Do I make myself clear?"

She gave him that look. One he was coming to know well. That pup wasn't going anywhere.

"I'll be back. I'm going to get that cage now."

He hurried downstairs, lit a lantern, then headed down to the shed, mumbling all the way that the woman was going to be the death of him.

Chapter Six

Selina bolted up in bed to the sound of a man's scream. She tossed the covers aside, flew down the stairs into Michael's room and stopped. She pressed her hand over her mouth to hold in her laugh at the sight of Michael shoved up against the wall, staring at the wolf pup as if it was something to be feared. The pup's backside stood higher than its front and its tail was tucked between its legs. Selina hurried to the pup and gained its trust before picking it up and cradling it to her chest. "Poor baby. Did Michael scare you?"

"Me? Scare her? How would you like to open your eyes and see that face just inches from yours?"

"This face?" Using what little light there was in the dark room, she studied the gray wolf's features. "Nothing scary about it. Why it's as cute as two baby bunnies leapin' in the air at one another."

"How did it get out anyway?"

"I don't rightly know." Pup in hand, she scurried to the door.

"Where you going?"

"Iffen you must know, to put some clothes on." She

was wearing her thin nightgown. She still hadn't gotten around to making a new one yet.

She whirled and found herself face-to-face with Michael's chest. Tucking the pup closer to her, she covered her threadbare gown best as she could.

"Selina, we are married. You don't have to be embarrassed." His eyes held only kindness.

She didn't know what to say to that. They weren't like a real married couple. Her ma and pa shared the same bed. She and Michael didn't. The way he felt about her, she wasn't sure they ever would, neither.

"I know we don't share the same bed and all…"

Her attention flew to his face. Was the man a mind reader?

"But we do live in the same house. We're bound to see each other in, um, precarious situations now and then."

"Pre-care-ee-ous. What's that mean?"

"Delicate. Perplexing. Problematic."

"Probli what? Purple-lex-en what? You're confusin' me. Can't you just tell me what you're tryin' to say without all them big words?"

"Fine. Just remember you asked for it. So…brace yourself. There are bound to be times we're going to find one another not fully dressed and see things we are not used to seeing. But, we are married so it's perfectly proper and acceptable."

She glanced toward the ceiling and sighed, grateful he'd slept in his pants and not his britches. "I had to ask. Now. Iffen you'll excuse me, I'm gonna get myself out of this pre-care-ee-an situation." She raised her chin and headed toward the stairs, feeling Michael's eyes on her and hearing his deep chuckle.

* * *

Once again Michael had to admit, even to himself, that having Selina help with chores lightened the load for everyone. He stepped into the barn while Selina fed the chickens and collected the eggs. Horses crunched on grain and shuffled their hooves.

Jesse turned from saddling his horse and did a double take. "You look terrible. Like you haven't slept in a week."

"I haven't."

"How come?"

"Selina."

"What do you mean?"

"She's going to be the death of me yet."

"What did she do now?" His brother pulled the cinch tight and removed the stirrup from the top of the saddle, letting it drop to the horse's side before he faced Michael.

"You won't believe what she brought home."

"What?" Jesse's lips quivered and his nostrils flared as he struggled to hold back his smile as Michael had seen him do so many times before.

Michael glowered at him. "You're loving this, aren't you?"

Jesse held up his hands. "No, honest. From the few things you've told me, there seems to never be a dull moment at your house, and Selina is very unique."

"She's unique, all right."

"How do you feel about that?"

"I'm not sure. Sometimes she has me laughing at her backward ways and antics. Other times I want to find the nearest cave at Coeur d'Alene and hide out there rest of my life." Michael raised his hat, plowed his hand through his hair and replaced his hat. "Yesterday, on her way home from Sadie's, she found a wolf pup and brought it home."

"A wolf? You're kidding."

"No. In fact, when I woke up this morning, the wolf's face was only inches from mine. It about scared the life out of me."

His brother laughed.

"Glad you find this amusing. That thing scared ten years off of my life."

"I'm sure."

"I told her I didn't want her bringing any more critters home but she told me the good Lord made her that way and she would rather bed down here in the barn than stop doing that. I have no idea what to expect next. Or any idea what she might bring home next."

"Don't you think you're exaggerating a little bit, Michael? She only brought a cat and a wolf to your house."

"Only?" He dipped his head and hiked one brow toward Jesse. "The cat I could deal with. But the wolf?" He shook his head. "You know they can't be fully trusted. I wonder what she plans on doing with it once it's healed. She can't take it back because she says its mama is dead, and I refuse to share my house with a wolf, no matter what my wife says. That woman is as unpredictable and stubborn as a mule."

"Hmm. Just like someone else I know who's maybe not unpredictable but definitely stubborn." Jesse laid his hand on Michael's shoulder. "Look, Michael, what's done is done. You can't go back and change the past. The way I see it, you have two choices here. You can start embracing Selina and her uniqueness and pay attention to her good qualities, or you can continue to be miserable. The choice is yours."

"How can I embrace her when she's so different?"

"Different isn't always a bad thing. It can make for an interesting life."

"Interesting? That's one way to put it. But I'm not sure I want my life *that* interesting."

Jesse looked like he was about to laugh again. Michael felt his own laughter rising up in him. He let it out and Jesse joined him.

"Michael, have fun with it. See the humor in what she does. You're always too serious. You need to lighten up. Maybe that's why God sent Selina to you. To teach you to not take things so seriously all the time. To stop and enjoy life once in a while."

"That's what Selina said. Only she said it was a shame I was too busy to stop and enjoy the dew drops on flowers or something like that."

"Maybe you should listen to her." Jesse untied his horse. Dust motes kicked up from his horse's hooves as his brother led the animal toward the barn door.

"Whose side are you on, anyway?" Michael hollered after him. "Traitor."

The only response he got was laughter.

He was glad his brother found it funny. He didn't. Didn't Jesse know how hard this was on him? How he beat himself up on a regular basis for being so stupid? How hard it was for him to have all his dreams ripped from him in one moment?

That the person he had fallen in love with didn't exist.

Spotting a rock on the dirt floor of the barn, he took

his frustration out by kicking it with all his might. It crashed into the wall and echoed throughout the barn.

"You havin' a fit this mornin' or somethin'?"

He closed his eyes and pulled himself together before turning around and facing Selina. "Something like that."

"Anythin' I can help you with?"

"No. You've done enough already." Still put out with her over the pup and lack of sleep, he brushed past her and left the barn before he did or said something else he'd regret.

Selina watched Michael walk away. That man was strung tighter than a clothesline. He needed to learn to relax.

She looked around the barn. Chores were done here, so she decided to head over to Rainee's.

As she made her way across the large ranch yard, calves bawled for their mamas, hens balked and horses whinnied.

Under her booted feet, the boards echoed her arrival at Rainee and Haydon's. Selina knocked on the door.

Wasn't long before the door swung open. Rainee's wide smile made Selina feel welcome.

"Selina, I am so happy to see you."

"I ain't botherin' you or keepin' you from anything, am I?"

"No. Not at all. I was just knitting a blanket for the baby. Please, come in." Rainee stepped aside of the doorway and Selina walked inside.

She had expected to see fancy furniture and fine things, but there was no putting on airs here. Although the furnishings were nice, more than anything else they were downright homey.

"Would you like some tea?"

"Yes. That'd be mighty nice of you. Can I help?"

"No, no. I just finished brewing some." Rainee arranged five small plates on a wooden tray. She picked up a sugar bowl, pitcher and something that held cream in it that matched the rest of her well-used dishes. They sure were pretty with their pink and white roses, gold-colored handles, lids and spout. Chips and all.

Rainee opened a drawer and added spoons and cloth napkins on the tray, too.

Selina watched, wondering how she would ever fit in with these rich folks and their highfalutin ways. But Rainee wasn't anything like she thought she'd be. From the way the woman talked and carried herself, Rainee had come from money, too. Yet she was as friendly as Selina's neighbors back home.

"How have you been, Selina?" Rainee raised the cloth off a basket sitting on a cabinet in the corner. She added four triangle-shaped biscuits and placed them onto the biggest plate.

"Been fine as frog's hair. Yourself?"

"Quite well. Thank you." She smiled. "Shall we head into the living room?"

Selina took the tray and followed Rainee over to two wingback chairs with a small square table in between them. She set the tray on the table in front of the glass lamp and watched as Rainee picked up a small plate and placed a cup on it.

"Do you take it plain, or would you like cream and sugar with it?"

"Ain't never had cream nor sugar in it before. I reckon I'll just take it plain."

Rainee handed her a cup and started to put a biscuit on another plate.

"No need to dirty another dish. I can put it right here." She took it from Rainee and before she set it on the side of her cup, she took a bite. "This is right tasty. What is it?"

"A strawberry scone. Would you like some cream on it?"

"Thank you kindly, but it tastes mighty fine the way it is. Real buttery-like."

"Do you miss home?" Rainee asked.

"I sure do. I miss my family and the easy way of life back home. Here everythin' is rush, rush, rush. Why, you'd think a person was on fire with all that scurryin' about."

"They do keep rather busy, do they not?" If Selina wasn't mistaken that was sadness she saw in her sister-in-law's eyes.

"Do ya ever get lonely out here?" Steam rose toward Selina's nose as she raised the cup and took a sip of the strong brew and another bite of the scone.

"Only for my husband. He takes his leave early in the morning and does not arrive home until after the sun has set. So I scarcely see him. Before I became pregnant, the children and I went with him a lot, but as soon as he found I was with child again, he would not allow me to go with him anymore." Rainee set her cup back in the saucer and turned toward her. "Have you met Kitty yet?"

"I sure have. She introduced herself by buttin' the back of my legs."

Rainee laughed. "That sounds like Kitty. She was a bridesmaid at my wedding, you know."

"Did I just hear you say you had a pig as your bridesmaid?"

"Yes, you did."

Selina slapped her knee and guffawed. "I knew I liked you. I love animals, too. Why, Michael thinks I'm stubborn as an old mountain goat 'cause I'm always bringin' critters home. Last night I was fixin' to bed down in the barn 'cause…"

"The barn?" Rainee interrupted her.

"I brought home an injured wolf and you'd have thought it was a grizzly bear or somethin' worse with the way Michael carried on."

"A wolf." Rainee's delicate brows rose. "You brought home a wolf?"

"Yeah."

"May I see it?"

Selina smiled. The woman didn't make her feel crazy at all because she'd brought the animal home. She reckoned not everyone here was as set in their ways as Michael.

"If you do not have any plans for today, perhaps we could have a lesson and then go see that wolf of yours."

"I'd like that. Thank you kindly, Rainee."

"No, thank you. You have quite rescued me from boredom. Haydon has Abby take the children to the neighbors with her so they do not overtax me. I assure you they do not, but he thinks they do. I rather enjoy them and miss them when they are gone." Love for her children lit up her eyes. "Sometimes I feel as if I shall go mad cooped up inside all the time. I am used to keeping busy and not sitting around knitting all day."

"I ain't one for sittin' myself. Let's get that lesson done then I'll break ya outta here and take you to my place." Her place. Sure didn't feel like her place and she wondered if it ever would.

Exhausted, sore and ready to fall into bed, Michael dragged his body home, terrified at what he might come home to this time. Another animal? Or something worse? He really didn't want to find out, but he had no choice unless he wanted to sleep in the barn. Therefore, he forced one leg in front of the other and climbed the steps. Something smelled good. He opened the door and stepped inside.

Selina stood in front of the stove, flipping something over in the large black skillet. She turned and smiled. "Evenin', Michael."

"Good evening." Now, if this had been a real marriage, he would have stepped up behind his wife, turned her around, wrapped his arms around her and kissed her thoroughly.

But this wasn't a real marriage. Legally it was, but not emotionally. Disappointment sighed through him.

"Sit yourself down and I'll fetch you some vittles."

Michael removed his hat and hung it on a peg. "Thank you. I'll wash up."

Selina buzzed around, smiling and humming, a real bundle of energy. Did the woman ever tire?

He finished washing and sat down. As usual, Selina set the pans on the table, except for the one she'd fried the meat in. She put its contents on a platter.

She sat down and settled her hand close to his plate. He no longer had to ask for her hand—she now offered it. That small gesture pleased him. Why, he had no idea, but it did.

He clasped her hand in his. Warmth radiated through him as it did every time he touched her. "Selina, would you pray tonight? I'm tired."

"I'd be honored." She closed her eyes. "Dear Lord, thank You for a husband who works hard to put a roof over our heads, clothes on our bodies and food on the table. Thank You for Your provision. I pray that these here vittles provide what our bodies need so we might better serve You in all we do. And, Lord. Thank You for Michael. Amen."

To know that all his hard work and efforts were not taken for granted and that she appreciated all he had done to provide her with a nice home and plenty of food warmed him like hot coals on a cold winter's day. "Thank you, Selina."

She stopped dishing his plate and looked at him. "For what?"

"For your thoughtful and kind prayer."

She nodded, then went back to filling his plate.

"So, what did you do after chores today?" Michael took a long gulp of his milk.

She pushed his overfilled plate in front of him.

"Paid a visit to Rainee."

"How's she feeling?"

"Bored."

"I don't doubt it, being cooped up inside all the time like that. She's used to getting out and riding and helping Haydon."

"Before she got pregnant, did he ever mind her helpin'?" She raised the spoon from the bean pot.

"No, not at all."

Selina settled the spoon back into the pot of beans. "How come you do then?"

"I see things differently than Haydon. I believe a woman's place is in the home."

"In some ways you're just like most of the menfolk back home," she said on a sigh.

"What do you mean?"

"Well, they're always orderin' women about like big bullies. Showin' them very little respect. Don't let their wives have a mind a their own. The women that do speak up, they pay dearly for it with a whippin'. Years ago, I made up my mind that no man would ever boss me around like that."

"I know, I know. Boy do I know." He picked up the fried meat and bit into it, trying to discern what it was. Sort of tasted like chicken but wasn't shaped like chicken. It was rounder and the bones were closer together. Strange, he didn't remember anything that looked quite like this in the cellar. He took another bite, still unable to tell what it was. "What is this?" he finally asked around the bite.

"Snake."

"Snake!" Michael grabbed for a napkin and spit the lump of chewed up meat into it. He downed the rest of his milk, barely able to contain his revulsion as he did. "Selina, what were you thinking? People don't eat snake."

She looked like nothing in the world was amiss. "Sure they do. Why, back home we ate it all the time. And plenty of other critters, too."

"What do you mean?" He bore down on his teeth until they ached, waiting for her answer and dreading it at the same time.

"Oh, you know, squirrel, possum, groundhog, bear…"

"Squirrel? Possum?" He swallowed hard. The more she named, the more the snake shifted from his stomach into his throat. He waved his hands in the air in complete surrender. "Stop. I've heard enough."

He shoved his plate away from him, caught her gaze and held it firmly with a sternness she would not be able to misconstrue, "Listen to me. I don't *ever* want to eat any of the things you've just mentioned. There is no reason or need to. We have plenty of beef, pork and chicken." He emphasized each word to get his point across, then waited for her to tell him how she wouldn't let any man tell her what to do. Well, this was one area where *he* would not back down. She could go right ahead and sleep in the barn over that one.

He waited for anger to blow out from her like steam from a locomotive. Instead she put her head down. "I'm sorry, Michael. Where I come from, food is scarce. A body eats whatever it can find. I just couldn't throw the meat away." She spoke so softly that remorse darted through him.

He'd never been poor, so he had no idea what it was like to be hungry enough to eat snake, or possum, or squirrel. He shuddered just thinking about it. But she had, and he needed to remember that.

He reached for her hand. It felt so small in his. "I'm sorry for being so harsh, Selina. There was no way you could have known I don't eat things like snake. But next time, it's okay to leave it. It won't go to waste. Some animal who needs a meal will find it and eat it."

She yanked her gaze up to his and her eyes brightened. "I never thought of it that-a-way. You're right." Selina scraped her chair across the floor and stood.

"Where you going?"

"To fix you somethin' else."

"No need to do that. There's plenty of fried potatoes and biscuits and beans. I'll just eat them tonight." At least she had started making larger portions. For that he was grateful.

"You sure? I can cut you off a piece of ham."

"No, this is fine. Thanks. Now sit down and eat before your food gets cold." He smiled, and her lips tentatively curled upward as she lowered her small frame onto the chair.

She removed the snake from his plate and heaped more of everything else onto it.

"Thank you, Selina. I really am sorry if I hurt your feelings about the snake. Like I said, I'm just not used to things like that."

"I reckon you ain't used to a lot of things I do," she said while putting food onto her plate. Her portions were still small, but each day they were growing. "I know I'm different, Michael. And I know I ain't what you're used to and I understand."

"You're right. I'm not used to your ways. But that doesn't mean I can't learn." Did he just say that? He shoved a bite of potatoes into his mouth to keep it from saying anything else equally as stupid.

"You mean that?" Hope sparked in her beautiful brown eyes.

Knowing he'd put that sparkle there made his heart smile. Maybe he needed to open his mouth more often, after all. "I do." And he found he really meant it, too.

"I'll try and learn to do things the way you like them. But—" she held up her finger "—some things I ain't changin'." She glanced over toward the sofa at the wolf curled up in the old cage Michael had found in one of the sheds.

Her looking over at the pup had him working his jaw. For his sanity's sake, he hoped bringing strange, dangerous animals into the house was something she would try to change, too, but he had his doubts.

As they finished eating in silence, he was glad he hadn't given in to the thoughts of sending her back. For her sake, he would do whatever it took to make this work so she would never have to go back to the unimaginable poverty she had endured.

Selina stood. Dishes clanked and silverware rattled as she started clearing the table. He picked up his dishes and was getting ready to take them to the sink but Selina stopped him. "I can get these. You need to go lie down and rest a spell."

"Thank you, Selina."

"You're welcome. Now scoot." She gave him a light shove toward the living room.

He laid down onto his stomach on the sofa and within minutes felt himself drifting off to the sound of rustling soapy water and dishes quietly clinking.

In his slumbering state, he felt small but strong and gentle hands pressing against his shoulders and up and down his back, working in a circular motion. "Um. That feels nice," he slurred. The hands worked their way up his neck and massaged his scalp. Warmth spread through him. His eyes darted open and he rolled over onto his side with a start.

"What's wrong? Did I hurt you?"

"No. No. Not at all." A piece of her slipped into his soul. He bolted off the sofa with the need to put distance between them. "Listen, I'm tired. If you don't mind, I'm going to bed now."

Hurt flashed through her eyes, and again he felt instant remorse. She had no idea what had been running through his mind, and he had hurt her with his rash actions.

"Thank you, Selina, for working the kinks out of my muscles. They feel much better now."

She nodded.

"Good night."

"Night."

Leaving her standing there, he hurried to his room and closed the door, bracing his back against it. Not only was he starting to respond to Selina emotionally, but now even his heart had responded to her physical touch. Even though the woman was his wife, the whole idea of being connected to her scared him to the core.

Selina took the pup out of her cage and hugged the animal to her chest. She flopped on the sofa and stared at the closed door to Michael's bedroom. It stung that he had run from her like that.

Rubbing Michael's broad shoulders and back, running her fingers through his soft hair, had felt right and yet it had been all wrong. She had made her husband afraid of her. And just when they were starting to talk like normal married folk, too.

All she had wanted to do was draw the ache out of his muscles. But that had obviously been a mistake. In the future she'd be careful to keep her hands to herself. That was going to be mighty hard to do. She loved him. Loved how she felt when she touched him, when she was with him. Felt like she belonged to him, and she did, too. But in name only.

Lord, I want a real marriage. I'd be much obliged to You iffen You would work that out. Thank You kindly, Lord.

When she finished tending to the pup's needs, she pressed her ear against Michael's door, listening for any noise. Not hearing any, she went to the pantry and removed the books, the writing slate and the chalk from behind the canned food. She sat in one of the living room chairs and lit the lantern that was on the table between the chairs. She pulled her sewing basket closer so she could hide her learning stuff down in the material if Michael got up.

For a long time, she practiced writing her letters and silently pronouncing them.

Wood squeaking and feet padding across the floor snagged her attention. She shoved her things to the bottom of her sewing basket, picked up the nightgown she'd been making and commenced to sewing.

Michael stepped into the living room with his hair all rumpled, with nothing on his feet and wearing only a nightshirt that came just past his knees.

"You still up?"

"Nah. You're just dreamin'." She sent him a silly grin.

"It's kind of late for you to still be up, isn't it?"

She glanced over at the tall pendulum clock. A grandfather clock, Michael had called it. "I can't believe it's ten after midnight already." Telling time was one thing she had learned to do. She laid her sewing in her basket and rose. "I'd best get to bed so I can get up in the mornin'." She stopped in front of him. "How come you're up? Can I get you somethin'?"

"No. I just got up to get a drink and then I'm going right back to bed."

"Oh. All righty then." Selina turned to leave, but his arm reached out and snagged hers.

"Selina, thank you for getting the kinks out earlier. I wouldn't have been able to sleep at all if it hadn't been for you."

"You're welcome." Him saying that made her insides feel good.

Neither one moved.

His eyes roamed her face, stopping at her lips. She pulled in her bottom lip with her teeth.

The pup gave a short howl, yanking her attention away from Michael. She stepped past him and retrieved the pup from his pen. "I'd better take her outside for a spell."

From across the dimly lit room, Michael was still staring at her. She pulled the pup closer to her chest and made her way to the door. "G'night, Michael."

"Good night, Selina." His voice sounded deeper, broken even.

When she stepped outside out of earshot of Michael, she whispered, *I love you, Michael. And I'm praying that one day I'll be deservin' of you and that you'll love me back.*

Chapter Seven

Michael woke to banging on his door. He jumped up, pulled on his pants and headed to the front door, swinging it open. Dan, Tom Elder's seventeen-year-old son, stood there looking skittish. His shirt was untucked in several places and his red hair stood straight up.

"Dan, what are you doing here? What's all the ruckus about?"

"Ma's having her baby," Dan said between gasping breaths. "I went to Doc's house first, but he wasn't home. Ma told me to fetch your wife. Hurry. She said it won't be long now."

"I'll get her. Come in." Michael turned and almost bumped into Selina.

"Sadie havin' that baby now?"

"Yes, ma'am. She asked me to come fetch you."

"I'll get dressed and be right there."

"If you don't mind, ma'am, I'll wait. You can ride on the back of my horse."

"No need." Michael jumped in, not about to let his wife run all over the country in the dark with Dan, a boy who was known to get into mischief. "I'll get a couple horses ready and have them here by the time Selina gets dressed."

Selina laid her hand on his arm. "No need for you to do that, Michael. You need your rest. I'll be fine. Just go back to bed and I'll be back as soon as I can."

"No." He gently removed her hand. "I'm going with you."

She shrugged. "Suit yourself."

"I'll help," Dan said to Michael. The two of them ran to the barn and readied the horses.

Michael's intent had been to go back and get her, but Selina met them halfway. They mounted the horses and raced into the night.

When they arrived at Tom's place, Selina jumped down and ran to the house. Michael followed. Neither bothered to knock.

"Selina, am I glad to see you." Sadie stood in the main room with one hand on her stomach and the other on her back.

Tom paced the floor and stopped when he saw them. He rushed to Selina. "Do something, please."

"Calm yourself down, Tom. Everythin' will be just fine. Fetch me some hot water, clean sheets…" Selina continued to give orders.

Michael stood back and watched Selina take charge, calmly and with authority.

Pans clanked on the stove as Tom put water on to heat. When it was hot enough, he took it and everything else Selina asked for into the bedroom where she now had Sadie.

With the bedroom door closed, Michael watched Tom pace, then sit, then stand and pace some more.

This went on for more than two hours until a baby's cry reached their ears.

Tom burst into his bedroom while Michael stood back and listened.

"That's a mighty fine girl you have there, Tom."

A loud crash echoed through the small room.

"Tom!" Sadie's frail voice was soaked in fear.

Michael rushed inside to see what the commotion was all about. Tom lay on the floor next to a broken vase and a toppled table.

Selina knelt by him. "Got any smellin' salts, Sadie?"

"Yes, on the shelf above the wash basin."

"Michael, fetch me the salts, please."

He whirled, found the bottle, and rushed it back to Selina. She waved it under Tom's nose.

Tom moved his head from side to side and shoved Selina's hand away. "Get that stinky stuff away from me."

Michael wanted to step in and tell Tom not to treat his wife like that, and he would have until he reminded himself that the man was reeling from shock. With good reason, too. After nine boys, this was his first girl.

He offered Tom a hand up and shook his hand. "Congratulations, Tom. Can you believe it? You finally got yourself a girl."

Tom's face paled and he swayed, but Michael held him up.

Selina stuck the smelling salts under his nose again and Tom bolted alert. "I'm fine. I'm fine. I don't need any more of that stuff burning my nose hairs and lungs."

Selina moved it and chuckled. "Ain't the best smellin' stuff, is it?"

"That's for sure." Then, as if he remembered his wife, Tom dashed over to Sadie and dropped to his knees next to her on their bed. He reached for her hand. "Are you okay, Sadie? You don't feel dizzy or sick or anything, do you?" Panic rang through every word.

Selina looked up at Michael with a question in her eyes.

He leaned over and whispered. "Tom's first wife died giving birth to their last son. Tom didn't want any more children for fear of losing Sadie, too."

Selina left Michael's side, walked over to Tom and placed her hand on his shoulder. "Sadie's gonna be just fine, Tom. She's as healthy as a horse. Easiest delivery I ever done."

Tom looked up at her, and hope danced through his eyes. "You mean it?"

"Sure do. Now why don't you go fix some coffee or somethin' and let me clean up this mess?"

Tom looked at his wife. Sadie gave a weak nod.

"Thank you, Selina." After he righted the table, the two men headed toward the door. "That's some special wife you got there, Michael. I was so afraid when Dan said he couldn't find Doctor Berg, but Selina handled everything just fine."

"Including you." Michael grinned.

"Including me." Tom smiled. "Can't believe I fainted."

"Well, I'd have fainted too if I found out my wife just gave birth to a girl after all those boys." Michael had hoped someday to have a whole houseful of children. He didn't know if that would happen now. Unless he and Selina could find common ground, he refused to bring children into a world where neither mother nor father loved the other.

Tom fixed coffee and the two of them had just sat down at the table when Selina came into the room with her arms loaded with soiled sheets and bed clothes, looking more worn out than Michael had ever seen her before. Strands of hair stuck out of her long braid and brown circles hung under her eyes. Michael knew he needed to get her home so she could get some sleep.

Selina stood in front of the wash tub, filling it with soap and hot water from the stove.

"Those need to soak," he said, standing over her shoulder. "I need to get you home so you can get some rest."

Selina looked up at him. "I'll be fine. Ain't no way I'm leavin' Sadie to wash these and to fix breakfast for her family. You don't mind, do ya?"

"Has that ever stopped you before?" He couldn't hold back the grin.

She smiled, too, although it was weak. "Nope."

"Listen, I'm going to head home, then. Don't wear yourself out, okay?"

"I won't. Thank you for carin'." She reached up and kissed his cheek. Her eyes bolted open, then her attention swung behind him.

He turned and found they were alone. Tom must have slipped away to Sadie.

"I—I'm sorry, Michael. I shouldn't have done that. It was only—"

Without thinking it through, Michael pulled her to him and shut her words up with his mouth. Sweet honeysuckle and spring met his advance, and in one second he was falling through time and space into her arms and charms.

A knock sounded at the Elder's front door. "Tom, it's me, Doctor Berg."

Michael jerked his head up and quickly released her, nearly sending her crashing to the floor with his suddenness. He should have never kissed her. He whirled and headed to the door, taking with him the memory of her soft lips, lips that had never even responded to his kiss.

Dead tired, Selina headed for home. Cleaning Sadie's house, along with washing her clothes and fixing enough food to last Sadie's family for a couple of days, had plumb worn her out.

Head hung low, she shifted and swayed with her mare's movement. Her head gave a yank, then she raised it and tried to hold it upright. Struggling to stay awake so she wouldn't fall off the horse and break her neck, she turned her mind to her surroundings and back to Michael's kiss. When he had grabbed her and kissed her like that, she'd been so shocked all she could do was stand there.

Her fingers found their way to her lips. She wished Michael would kiss her like that again, but that wasn't likely to happen. From the way he tore out of the house, he must have regretted kissing her. Had it been that awful for him? It sure hadn't been for her. When his lips had touched hers, it was as if the heat of the noon sun had found its way into her body, warming it through with liquid love.

The breeze lifted the strands of hair from around her face and swung them across her cheeks. It took what little energy she had left to brush them away. She wished she could brush the broken pieces of her heart away as easily and let the breeze carry them far away so it wouldn't hurt so bad.

Selina rode into the ranch yard and up to the barn door. She closed her eyes for a moment, then swung her leg over the horse's back.

Before she so much as saw him there, Michael's spicy musk scent surrounded her and his hands went about her waist. She tilted her head backward, and her back brushed against Michael's chest as he lowered her. Her feet touched the ground, but because she was worn out, her legs wilted and she swayed.

Michael's arm wrapped around her, holding her strong and steady. "Thank you, Michael," she whispered through a yawn. She took a half step away from him. Her eyelids felt like someone had tied rocks to them and was pulling them downward.

"I'll take care of Macy. You need to get her home." Jesse's voice reached her ears.

Selina wobbled her attention onto Jesse and offered him a smile.

The next thing she knew, strong arms were scooping her up.

Michael's body shifted underneath her with each step he took. "I'm carrying you home and no arguing with me, you hear?"

She heard, and she wanted to protest but was too tired.

So just this once she'd let him have his way.

And just this once she laid her head into his chest.

And just this once she pretended they were man and wife in every way.

Tomorrow, things would be back to normal.

Tomorrow she would remember that he didn't love her and that he was only doing his duty by her, but tonight she didn't care to remember.

Michael's peppermint breath drifted around her as his breathing increased with each step toward home. His soothing heartbeat swept through his arms and against her back where he held her. Her eyes slid shut and sweet dreams of Michael carrying her floated through her mind.

Selina felt herself being lowered and her eyes bobbed open. "We home?"

"We're home." Michael's voice was as soothing as the birds singing in the trees and the river waters back home.

She pulled up from the couch and dragged her body toward the stove.

"What are you doing?" Michael asked from behind her.

"You ask me that a lot, don't ya?" She tried to laugh but couldn't find enough get-up-and-go to do so. "I'm gonna fix you some vittles then head to bed."

Michael laid his large hands on her shoulders. He turned her around and gently nudged her toward the sofa. "You don't have to do that. Mother made dinner for us tonight. All we have to do is eat."

Relief pushed through her. "That was mighty sweet of her."

"She figured you'd be exhausted after being up all night and gone all day so she made extra and sent it over."

She stopped resisting him and allowed Michael to lead her into the living room.

He gently pressed on her shoulders, forcing her to sit. Her eyes followed him as he walked back into the kitchen. The man sure came from some mighty fine stock.

Michael brought her a plate full of food and a glass of warm buttermilk. She thanked him, then picked up a piece of fried chicken and tore off a chunk. Chewing took more strength than she had, so she put it back down and set the plate aside. She curled into a ball on the sofa and closed her eyes.

Michael filled his plate and headed over to join Selina. His heart melted seeing her curled on the sofa and her food barely touched.

He set his plate next to hers, slid his arms under her shoulders and legs and carried her up the stairs. The woman weighed next to nothing. Selina might act tough, but she felt fragile in his arms, and he could feel her ribs she was so thin. She was eating more than when she had arrived, but not much more. On top of not eating enough, she worked harder than their draft horses during wheat harvest.

He laid her small, sleeping frame on the bed. Poor thing was so tired she didn't even arouse. He looked at her trousers, her belt and her boots, wishing he could put her into something more comfortable. But even though they were married, he wouldn't feel right changing her clothes. Instead, he removed her boots and laid a blanket over her.

Tendrils of hair feathered against her pillow. Her lips parted. He wondered what it would be like to kiss her as often as he liked without restraint.

To hold her in his arms whenever he wanted.
To have a real marriage with her.
To love her.

Chapter Eight

Michael headed downstairs. He picked up his plate and sat down at the table, alone. His attention trailed upstairs to where Selina was sleeping. He'd gotten used to eating with her and it felt weird not to. Funny how the woman was starting to grow on him.

He finished his dinner and cleaned up so Selina wouldn't have to. When he finally headed to his bedroom the wolf howled from his cage near the sofa, making the hair on Michael's neck and arms rise. Before the thing woke up Selina, he hurried and snatched it out of its cage, rushed it outside and set it down on the ground.

The second he let it go, he realized his mistake. The pup took off running into the thick woods. Michael ran after it, dodging trees and branches. He struggled to keep his eyes on where it was heading, but before long the pup had disappeared from his line of vision.

If it were a dog, he would holler its name, but it wasn't, and the animal had no name. Pushing back thick brush, he searched frantically for the wolf, but it was too dark to see. He knew by the time he got back to the house and grabbed a lantern, the thing would be long gone, if it wasn't already. As much as he didn't want the wolf around, he felt like a louse that it was his fault the animal was gone. He should have paid more attention to what he was doing.

How was he going to tell Selina what he had done?

And would she believe him after all the fuss he'd made about having the wolf in the first place?

Selina squinted and placed her hand over her face to block out the light coming in through her bedroom window.

Light?

She bolted up and looked around. What time was it, anyway? She threw the covers back and, since she was already dressed, flew down the stairs and glanced at the grandfather clock. Fifteen minutes after eight. *Jumpin' crickets.* She had way overslept.

The house was quiet. Michael had already gone to work, and that poor wolf pup hadn't been fed or tended to since last night. Her attention drifted to the empty cage.

Empty? Her heart flew to her toes. She ran through the house in search of the pup, but he was nowhere to be found.

She rushed outside, checking all around the house, under the porch, through the trees, under every bush, all the way down to the barn, and still no sign of the young critter.

She bridled Macy and then rode off, widening her search. A rider headed her way. Relieved to see it was Michael, she galloped to him and leaped off her horse.

So did Michael. "Have you seen the wolf pup, Michael? He's gone. I can't find him anywhere."

Michael's eyelids dropped.

Oh, no. "Where is he?"

Michael raised his head but wouldn't look at her. "Last night when you were sleeping he started howling, so I took him outside. When I set him down, he darted off into the woods. I tried to find him, but it was too dark to see where he went. I'm really sorry, Selina."

Anger bit through her. Was he? The man never did like the idea of her having the wolf pup in the house. Had he let him go on purpose?

"I know what you're thinking, Selina. I can see it in your eyes, but I didn't do it on purpose. I wasn't thinking. I was so concerned he'd wake you up that I forgot to put the rope on him."

She looked into his eyes. There was truth there. She glanced away, toward the place where she'd found the pup, and sadness drizzled over her heart. She hadn't realized she'd gotten so attached to the little critter.

"Did you get some rest?"

She pulled her attention back onto Michael and the concern in his voice. "Sure did. I slept like a bear in hibernation. Much obliged to you for lettin' me sleep. I'll hurry back home now and get cleaned up so I can come back and help with the chores."

"The chores are all finished. Why don't you go home and rest, sew or do something that isn't too tiring for you?"

"I'm fine. But I think I'll go check on Sadie. See iffen she needs any more help."

"Mother and Leah went to help her today."

"Well, that was right nice of them. What are you fixin' to do now?"

"Head back to the barn to get ready to start harvesting the wheat tomorrow."

"Oh. Anything I can do to help?"

"No. But, I'll tell you what. Why don't we head over to Jake Lure's first? He had a litter of pups he's trying to get rid of."

Her eyes shot up toward him. "You mean it, Michael? You don't mind? I thought you didn't want animals in the house."

He held his hand up. "Wait a minute. Wait a minute. I didn't say anything about it coming into the house. The dog will have to say outside."

The instant the words left his mouth, Michael knew that pup wasn't going to live outside. What had he done? Why had he offered to get her a puppy? Who was he kidding? He knew the answer to that question. When he'd told her about the runaway wolf pup, the heartbreak that had dashed across her face crushed him. To ease her hurt, he was willing to go over to Jake's house. Jake. The man who jeered people by insulting them and had heckled Michael about Selina's trousers. Maybe going over there wasn't such a good idea.

Then he made the mistake of looking at Selina again. Seeing the joy on her face, he knew he would have to follow through with the puppy idea. "Before we go and look at the puppies, you have to promise me it will stay outside."

She weaved her head back and forth. "Sorry. Can't do that. 'Cause once I give my word, I keep it, and

I can't promise I won't feel sorry for the little critter whenever it looks up at me outside the door all sadlike."

The woman was honest if nothing else. And she really did love animals.

Now what should he do?

He hated the idea of animals in the house he had spent months building and furnishing—with expensive, quality furniture—so everything would be perfect for his new wife. Whether he liked it or not, Selina was that wife, and it was her home now, too.

All he could do was hope and pray the puppy didn't tear up the place the same way Jesse's puppy had chewed up Michael's favorite toy when he was younger. Or soil anything like when Abby had let one of the barn cats loose in the house and it had a litter of kittens on his father's shirt folded on a shelf in the closet. As a young boy, whenever Michael wore that shirt it was like having his father with him wherever he went, and made him less lonely for him. An animal in the house had ruined that for Michael. But, he wasn't a boy anymore. It was time to let that go. "Okay. You win. Let's go see if Jake has any more pups left."

Selina threw her arms around his waist and pressed her head against his chest. "Thank you, Michael. I'm so happy I could kiss you." She yanked from his arms and looked up at him like a frightened fawn. "I didn't mean I would up and kiss you or nothin'. I just meant that I was so happy I could. But no need to fret, I won't," she prattled on.

Michael placed his fingertips gently over her mouth. "I know what you meant, Selina."

She nodded. "Can we go get that puppy now?"

He moved his hand away and laughed. "Yes. Let's go."

Standing next to Selina's horse, Michael bent one knee, intertwined his fingers and laid them on top of his knee. Selina placed her foot in his hands and, using it like a stirrup, swung herself onto Macy's back. A breeze of soap stirred in the air as Selina moved.

"You must be excited. You actually let me help you up this time."

She laughed and it sounded like soft thunder and a misty rainfall combined. He mounted his horse and they headed toward Jake's.

When they rode through the bunchgrass, a rabbit skittered out of its hiding place, startling not only them but also their horses. Their mounts snorted and side-stepped.

Selina hung on and calmed Macy down.

Very impressive. Bareback, anyone else would have been thrown.

"Oh, iffen only I'd a had my rifle with me. I'd have shot that little critter and made us some rabbit stew."

Leather creaked as Michael shifted in his saddle. "I don't understand you, Selina. You love animals. You're always doctoring them and here you are wanting to shoot something as cute as a rabbit."

"Oh, I don't enjoy it iffen that's what you're thinkin'. It's a matter of survival, and I know the good Lord put certain things on this earth to provide food for our bellies. I could never shoot somethin' just to be shootin' it. And, it does bother me. But when you see your brothers hungry, you'll shoot just about anything to provide for them."

Michael couldn't even imagine what the woman and

her family had gone through. Couldn't imagine what it was like to go hungry, and he prayed he never would. Hearing her comments hurt enough. "Did everyone in your family go hunting?" Side by side, they followed the wide trail through the trees.

"Not when they were younger. When my ma took sick and died, my pa loved her so much he plumb gave up. Forgot all about us youngins. But I didn't. I couldn't bear seein' them beg for somethin' to eat. So, I taught myself how to shoot and hunt and look for plants and other things that were edible."

"How old were you when your ma died?"

"Ten."

"Ten?" Michael felt the shock clear to his toes. What kind of a father let his ten-year-old daughter hunt? He couldn't fathom letting his sixteen-year-old sister Abby go hungry or hunt for food. "How old was your brother?"

"Seven. Ma lost two babies after she had me."

"How many brothers and sisters do you have?"

"Ain't got no sisters. Only six brothers."

"How old were they when your mother died?"

"Jacob was seven. Peter and Eli were five, Matthew was three, and Zeke and Zachary were almost two. Jacob, Peter and Eli are married now. And Doc's payin' for Matthew to go to school to become a doctor so he can take over his practice one day. Zeke and Zachary live with Jacob and his wife, Sarah. Even though they're seventeen now, I could a never let myself get hitched iffen I thought they wasn't being taken care of."

His admiration toward her went up another notch, although he wondered how someone so young could raise a family, especially two sets of twins. "So you basically raised them by yourself then." It was a statement, not a question.

"Had to. My brothers helped when they got older, but it still took a lot of work to gather food and all."

"Why didn't your father help?"

"Like I told you, Pa gave up when Ma died. He just sat around, starin' into the air most of the time until his muscles no longer worked. It got to where we had to carry him everywhere. Sure hurt watchin' him suffer like that."

"What about the suffering you and your siblings endured because he gave up? Didn't you ever resent him for basically dying then, too?"

Even though his own father's death was an accident, Michael had felt that way when the man had died. But, Selina's pa, well, he had just given up and that wasn't right.

His horse shook his head, trying to rid its neck of a pesky horsefly. Michael leaned over and took care of it for him.

"No, I never did resent my pa for that, Michael. He loved my ma something fierce. And before my ma died, Pa used to read to us, tell us stories, hugged us a lot and told us how much he loved us. Pa was a good provider up until then. But his heart broke when Ma died. He said it was as iffen he'd died that day, too. And in a way, I reckon he had."

"My father died a long time ago." Michael still felt his father's death as if it had just happened instead of eons ago.

"What was your pa like?"

"He was a strong man who loved the Lord and loved to spend time with his family. That's one of the reasons why he moved us out here, to spend more time with us. Business took too much of his time back in New York. And even though he worked hard, long hours out here, we were all together and could go with him anytime."

"How'd your pa die?"

"A tree fell on him. Crushed his chest. He died instantly. I never got to say goodbye."

"You still can, you know."

Michael glanced over at Selina, frowning. "What do you mean? He's gone."

"Well, I never got a chance to say goodbye to my ma. Always felt like somethin' was left undone, iffen you know what I mean."

He understood exactly what she meant.

"So, before I came here, I went to Ma's grave and had myself a long chat with her. Told her I was sorry I never got a chance to say a proper goodbye and all. Told her I loved her. And that I'd see her again whenever I went to meet my maker. I had me a right fine talk with her and all that weight I'd been carryin' with me all them years plumb lifted."

Michael wondered if it would work for him, too. He'd give it a try when no one was around. After all, he didn't want anyone to think he'd lost his mind by talking to the deceased.

Suddenly Selina stopped her horse and jumped off.

"What are you doing?"

"Oh! Did you ever see anythin' so beautiful before in your life?"

He strained to see what she'd found so beautiful, but he didn't see a thing.

Selina squatted and when she stood, a caterpillar crawled up the length of her forefinger.

That's what she'd found so beautiful?

"Can you believe the good Lord took the time to make each of these here caterpillars different? And iffen that weren't enough, He turns them into beautiful butterflies, makin' them even purtier."

Michael looked at the black hair on the caterpillar. Why hadn't he ever noticed the fuzzy hair before? Or, for that matter, a caterpillar before? Seeing them through Selina's eyes, the thing really was almost beautiful.

"Wanna hold it?" She turned toward him and raised her finger upward.

"Sure. Why not?"

Selina pressed her fingertip to his.

The insect inched onto his finger and onto the back of his hand, tickling Michael's skin. He had to admit, it really was something to see. He glanced to where she'd found it and then to Selina. "How did you ever see this minuscule thing from on top of your horse?"

"Mini school?"

"Sorry. Minuscule—small thing."

She gave a quick nod. "When you're lookin' for it, it's easy."

"You were looking for a caterpillar?" Incredulousness filled his voice.

"No." She gazed upward into the tree. Michael's gaze followed hers.

"See that bird nest?"

He strained, peering through the branches until he finally saw the small nest.

"A long time ago, I learned there's hidden treasures everywhere. You just gotta look for them. See that web?"

"What web?"

She pointed to it. Sunlight captured it in its spell, making the spider web glisten, revealing the intricate pattern. Why had he never noticed how uniform the web was? How silky it looked?

He glanced around, wondering what other "treasures" he had missed because he'd never taken the time to look. A rush of excitement skittered through him. Maybe someday Selina could show him even more of the things he'd missed. Right now, though, he needed to hurry up and get a puppy so he could get back to work. "We'd better go." He glanced at the insect still exploring his hand. "What do I do with this?"

"You can let it loose on one of them leaves."

Michael leaned over and waited as it left his hand and crawled onto a large leaf.

They mounted their horses and hurried to Jake's house.

Everything was quiet when they pulled into Jake's yard. No dogs came to greet them.

"Somethin' wrong?" Selina stopped her horse next to his.

"Shh." He placed his finger to his lips. "Do you hear that?"

Selina tilted her head. "The only thing I hear is a dog barkin'. Sounds mighty upset."

"Wait here. I'll go see what's going on."

"I'm comin' with you."

Michael stopped Selina's horse by grabbing a rein near the bit. "No. I want you to stay here. Until I know how bad it is, I want you to stay."

"I'm used to seein' all kind of bad stuff. Nothin' bothers me."

"You really are a stubborn little thing, you know that?" He let go of her horse. "Don't say I didn't warn you."

"I won't."

They wove their way through the fir trees.

The barking got louder. At the top of the hill they looked down. Banjo, Jake's dog, was next to his master's body, which was lying face down at the bottom of the hill. The thin, loose rock was too dangerous to take the horses down, so Michael looked around for a safe place. "Let's go around that way."

They followed the hill until they found a spot where they could safely go down. As they neared Jake, Banjo bared her teeth, growling low and menacing, placing herself between Jake and them.

"It's okay, Banjo. We're here to help."

The dog stopped growling and tilted her head sideways.

"You remember me, don't you, girl?"

Banjo dipped her head the opposite direction.

Michael dismounted and so did Selina.

He loosely wrapped the reins around a bush and took two steps toward Jake and stopped. "Wait here." He glanced back at her. "Please?"

She looked at the dog and nodded.

Michael was grateful she listened to him this time. Unsure what Banjo would do, he didn't want her getting hurt.

He extended his hand toward the dog and slowly approached him, talking to her in a calm voice. When he reached Banjo, he let the dog sniff his hand. "I'm here to help him, girl."

Keeping his eye on the dog, which still looked uncertain, he slowly knelt beside Jake and laid a hand on him. His body was warm—he was alive. Michael eased Jake over onto his back.

Blood and dirt covered one side of his face and forehead where a nasty cut oozed. "Jake, can you hear me?" Michael looked over at Selina standing near the horses. "Grab my water canteen from off my saddle."

Selina tied Macy's reins to the same bush as Michael's horse and grabbed his canteen. Michael turned his attention back onto Jake and continued to call the man's name.

She handed him the open canteen, then squatted on the opposite side of Michael.

"That's a mighty nasty cut he's got there. I reckon he's got a concussion."

Hearing her say the word concussion, he wondered how she'd ever learned such a big word.

"We need to take him to his house so I can clean that up." She examined the cut. "It's deep. He's gonna need stitches."

"I think what he needs is a doctor. Would you mind riding into town and getting Doctor Berg?"

"No need for that. I can fix him up just fine."

"I know you can. What I'm concerned about is his unconscious state." Michael laid his canteen against Jake's lips and let the water run into the man's mouth.

Jake stirred and groaned.

"Can you hear me, Jake?" Under his closed eyelids Michael could see Jake's eyes shifting and rolling before they fluttered open.

"Michael? What are you doing here?" he rasped. Jake started to sit up but stopped. He clutched his head and lay back onto the uneven ground.

"I'm going to take you to your house, Jake. Do you think you can handle riding my horse?"

Jake managed a nod. "Nice to see you again, Selina," he slurred, then turned mocking eyes up at Michael. Remembering Jake's jeering comments about Selina when he'd first met her, Michael darted a warning glance at the man.

Jake turned a slow but cocky grin toward Michael. Even injured, he never stopped his jesting, only this time he'd done it with his eyes and his smirk-laden grin.

Michael had half a mind to leave the man here.

"We'd better get you to the house so I can clean that up."

"You ain't touching me," Jake groused.

"I ain't gonna leave you like this." Selina stared at Jake.

Michael knew that look well. It meant she was going to do what she was going to do and nothing or no one would stop her.

Look out, Jake, he thought, then he remembered Jake telling him that he knew who would be wearing the pants in his family.

Was Jake right?

"Help me get him up, Michael."

Jake again sent him a smirk.

"No. I say we just leave him here. I'm sure some bear or coyote needs something to eat for dinner tonight." Michael stood and looked down at him.

Jake's eyes widened with fear. He glanced up at Selina, then back at Michael. "You heard the lady," Jake said, and no smirk covered his face this time.

Selina and Michael helped put Jake atop Michael's

horse. Up the hill and to the house they went, Michael leading the way.

Inside Jake's house, they settled him onto his mattress.

"What happened anyway?" Michael asked.

"I heard the dogs barking and wolves howling. Figured the wolves were after Banjo's pups, so I thought I'd take my shotgun and scare them off. Never got a chance, though. Went looking for Banjo's puppies. Slipped on a piece of rock and tumbled down the hill. Last thing I remember was hitting my head on something hard." His words were strained.

"When was that?"

"Before sunrise." He rubbed his wound, staining his fingers with blood and dirt. "Don't know what would have happened if you hadn't come along. I'd still be down there." He frowned, then flinched, then reached to touch the wound again, but Selina moved his hand away and placed it at his side. "Why did you two come over here anyway?"

"To see if you had any more pups left."

"Oh. Had two females but they're gone. I think the wolves got them or they're running with them. Not even sure if that sort of thing happens, all I know is they're gone."

Selina looked over at Michael. He was certain she was remembering the wolf pup. Again, he wanted to ease her heartbreak by getting her a puppy, but it looked like that wasn't going to happen. Not today anyway. But he'd keep his ears open.

Selina went about heating water, cleaning, stitching and bandaging Jake's wound. "Want me to fetch Doc on account of that concussion?" she asked when she was done.

"No. I'll be fine. Had one before. He'll just tell me to rest and to make sure someone wakes me up every so often." Jake smiled, then grimaced.

"Well, who's gonna wake you and take care of you?" Her concern didn't slip past Michael. He saw it in her eyes.

"Could you stop by Tom's on your way and see if he'll let Dan come stay with me a couple of days?" he asked Michael.

"Sure. If we're going to do that, though, we'd better leave now," he added to Selina.

"I ain't leavin' here until I fix him some vittles first."

Michael's gaze flew to Jake. He waited for the smirk, but it never came. In fact, Jake's face was blank from shock, no doubt.

"Thank you, Selina, for helping me." He looked back at Michael. "That's one fine woman you've got yourself there, buddy."

He knew Jake meant it, too.

Through the green and gold clusters of tall, thin-bladed grass they headed for home. Mosquitoes buzzed and hovered around them, landing on their arms and faces. Selina kept swatting at them, trying to keep them away from her, but the little varmints were not to be stopped.

Their horses swished their tails hard and fast, shifted their pointy ears and shook their heads trying to rid themselves of the pests, too, but they wouldn't leave. "This sure is interestin' grass. Has to be almost three feet tall. Does it have a name?"

"It's bunchgrass."

The stuff grew in bunches, but Selina wasn't sure if Michael was teasing her or not. Judging from the serious look on his face, she reckoned he wasn't.

"Sorry about the puppy."

"Wasn't meant to be I reckon."

"I'll see if I can find you one somewhere else."

"Okay." Her legs dangled as she rocked with the rhythm of the horse. Macy's tail brushed against her pant leg as she continued to swat at not only the mosquitoes but also a huge fly that kept hanging round. "When we get back home, do you need help gettin' things ready for tomorrow?"

"Tomorrow?"

"Yeah. Earlier you said you had to get things ready for harvestin' the wheat."

"Yes, I do. But there isn't anything you can do to help."

"Oh. Well, I reckon I'll rid the garden of weeds before I go see Rainee, then."

"Do you go there often?"

"I do. I like Rainee. She's good folk."

"She sure is."

"Rainee's from the South, too, so how did she meet Haydon?"

"She placed an advertisement for a husband and Jesse answered it."

"Jesse answered it? He's been married to Hannah a long time. Why would he go and answer an ad for a wife?"

"For Haydon."

"Huh? That don't make a lick of sense."

"It's a long story."

"Well, we got time before we get back to the ranch." She watched his chest rise and fall.

"Rainee's brother wanted to sell her to the neighbor man next door. A man who had murdered his wife."

Selina gasped. "That's horrible. Why?"

"He needed money. Anyway, Rainee found out and so she placed an ad and Jesse sent for her to be Haydon's wife."

"Haydon know about it?"

"No. Boy was he angry when he did find out. Haydon didn't want anything to do with her, but then she rescued him and he fell in love with her. Now they're happily married with another child on the way."

Leave it to a man to give the short version. She wanted to hear more, but she'd ask Rainee sometime instead.

As they rode home in silence, one thing kept buzzing through Selina's mind like the pesky mosquitoes around them. She knew for certain Michael really didn't want anything to do with her, either, but he was stuck with her because they were married.

If only their situation would turn out as well as Rainee and Haydon's. She doubted it ever would, though. And that ripped the heart right out of her. Each day she spent with him, she loved him more and more. In fact, she'd fallen in love with him round about the fourth or fifth letter he'd sent her, and even coming here hadn't changed that.

They rode through the Bowen's ranch yard to the barn. After taking care of her horse, Selina turned to Michael. "You want me to bring you some lunch out here or you wanna come home and eat?"

"It would be great if you brought it here today. I have lots to do."

"I can do that. I'll be back quicker than it takes to cook frog legs."

"Frog legs? You eat frog legs?" Michael's eyes were wider than a purple ironweed bloom.

She wondered if they had any ironweed around here. Sure helped a lot of stomach ailments and the pain after birthing a baby. "Sure do. They're mighty tasty. Ain't you had any before?"

Michael's hand shot up. "No. And I don't ever plan on it, either. So don't get any ideas about ever fixing me any, okay? Promise."

Selina giggled.

"I don't like the sound of that laugh."

He really looked worried now. She giggled harder.

"Se-li-na. You said once you promised you wouldn't go back on your word, so I'm pleading with you to promise me you won't ever fix me frog legs." He scrunched his handsome face as if that was the worst thing that could happen to him.

Selina burst out laughing while Michael continued to look like a coon caught in a live trap.

"I need to get busy. When you're done laughing, would you bring me something to eat, please? And no frog legs, either." He whirled, mumbling something about eating at his mother's house from now on.

She chuckled all the way to the house.

While she threw together two roast beef sandwiches, she imagined what Michael's face would look like if she really did serve him a helping of frog legs. For pure orneriness, she'd do it just to see. Nah. That would be too cruel.

She wondered if he liked crawdad tails. Were there even any around here? She'd have to find out and fix him a plate of those. After all, he didn't say anything about crawdad tails.

Chapter Nine

Selina stood on Rainee's porch and knocked on the door.

Footsteps drew nearer and it swung open. Selina blinked. A woman with red hair answered the door.

"Is Rainee home?"

"Yes, ma'am, she is. Won't you please come in?"

Selina stepped inside and looked around.

"Excuse me. I'll be right back." The tall woman who looked to be in her early twenties disappeared through the back door.

The woman must be the maid Haydon had hired to help Rainee. She didn't need a maid. Selina would be glad to help her.

Voices drifted from the direction the woman had gone.

Within minutes Rainee appeared, hair all sweaty, her calico sleeves rolled up and the front of her white apron soaked. "Hi, Selina." Rainee waddled up to her and gave her a hug but was careful not to get too close. "Forgive my appearance. I have been helping Esther with the laundry." Rainee pressed her finger to her lips. "Shhh. Must not tell Haydon, okay?" She giggled.

"Should you be a doin' that in your condition?"

Rainee waved her off. "I feel fine. Truth is, I feel better when I am working than when I am not. Sometimes it is most vexing having a husband who will not allow me to do these things myself. But—" she sighed "—he loves me and is worried about me."

"You're mighty lucky."

Rainee frowned, then turned toward Esther. "Esther, would you please fix us some tea and bring a few of the cookies we baked this morning?"

"Yes, ma'am."

"And, Esther. There are only a few pieces of laundry left. Would you mind finishing them? And while you are outside hanging them, would you please keep an eye on the children? When you finish, please send the girls in and then you may go home, and I will pay you for the whole day." Rainee smiled.

The pretty woman's big green eyes lit up. "Thank you, ma'am."

"You are most welcome. And thank you, Esther, for all your hard work."

Esther's face glowed. She turned and headed into the kitchen.

Rainee motioned for them to head into the living room. As they sat across from each other, Rainee lowered her voice. "Is something wrong between you and Michael?"

Selina didn't know what to say. She didn't want to disgrace her husband, but it sure would be nice to have someone to talk to about it. Then Michael's words from earlier came to mind. "Michael told me when you got here Haydon didn't want you. Do you mind iffen I ask why?"

Esther brought their drinks and cookies. It felt strange being waited on.

As Esther left, they both took a drink of their tea. Rainee set her small plate with the cup on it on her lap so Selina did the same.

"Michael is right. When I first arrived here, Haydon did not want anything to do with me. I was so hurt and confused I did not know what to do. I had no money and no place to go. I could not go home, either, because my brother had beaten me until I could no longer bear it. That is when I placed the advertisement. I thought I was coming here to a man who really wanted me. Was I ever shocked to discover that not only did he not send for me, but he did not want me, either."

"I know the feelin'," Selina whispered, staring at the cup in her lap.

"What do you mean?"

Selina drew in a deep breath. Gathering up as much courage as she could, she caught Rainee's eye. "I need someone to talk to about this. Promise me you won't say anythin' to anybody about what I'm fixin' to tell you, okay?"

"It will not leave this room. I assure you."

Did Selina dare trust her? The last person she trusted had done her dirty and now she and Michael were paying for it.

Then again, Rainee hadn't told anyone about their reading and writing lessons, so maybe she could trust her about this, too. Besides, the woman knew what it was like not to be wanted by the man she'd come to marry.

"Remember when I told you that my friend Aimee wrote those letters to Michael for me?"

"Yes."

"Well, Aimee didn't write what I'd told her to. But I didn't know that until after I got here and had Michael read the letters to me that Aimee sent him. Aimee had stretched the truth about some things. Plus, most things were what she'd say and do, not me. And she left out a lot of things, too. Michael was mighty shocked when he saw me." Selina tore her eyes away from Rainee. "Aimee never did tell him I couldn't read or write and that I carried a rifle and hunted. Or that I wore a cowboy hat and boots and trousers."

Rainee giggled.

Selina yanked her eyes toward her sister-in-law, frowning and wondering if she was making fun of her.

Rainee stopped laughing. "I am sorry, Selina. I am not laughing at you. It is just that I have always wanted to dress like you."

Selina's mouth dropped open. "You did? Are you joshin' me?"

Rainee shook her head. "No, no. I always have."

"Well, I'll be. Ain't never heard anyone like you say somethin' like that before. They usually make fun of me."

"What do you mean 'like me'?"

"Someone who's got money. I ain't had the best of luck with rich folks."

"Neither have I."

Again, Selina's jaw fell open. "What do you mean?"

"Most people who come from wealth are such snobs and can be quite hateful."

Selina didn't know what to say to that.

"I really do envy you, Selina. I would love to wear a pair of trousers. Dresses are so binding. I would love to be like you. Free. A breath of fresh air."

The back of Selina's eyes stung. "Thank you kindly, Rainee. Nobody's ever said anythin' like that to me before, either."

Rainee laid her hand on top of Selina's. "I really do mean it, Selina." She sat back. "The closest thing I ever got to wearing pants was my riding skirt."

"What's that?"

"Basically a pair of pants that look like a skirt."

"Would you show me how to make some?"

"Sure will."

Then Selina glanced at her lap. "Rainee, I know you said ya envy me and all, but could you help me to become a lady like you?" She looked up at Rainee, hoping with all her might her friend would say yes.

"Why do you want to change who you are, Selina? Everyone loves you just the way you are."

"Not everyone."

"Michael?" Rainee asked softly.

Selina nodded.

"I am so sorry, Selina. Of course I will help you. But, I wish you would reconsider."

Oh, how Selina wanted to. She loved who she was and didn't want to change for anyone. But she loved Michael. And if he wanted someone like Rainee and Aimee, then that's what she'd give him. Her gut ached just thinking about being someone she wasn't, though.

"Selina."

Selina shifted her attention back onto Rainee.

"Please pray about this first, okay? I can see this is truly vexing you. But God did not make you to be like someone else. He made you the way you are for a reason. Did you ever think that perhaps God wants to use who you are to do something in Michael?"

The weight in her gut lifted. "I never thought of that before. Maybe you're right. I'll pray about it first." She smiled, feeling much better.

"Selina!" Emily and Rosie ran over to her.

Selina jumped up and gave the girls a hug. She pulled back and looked at the wet spot on the front of her dress and smiled. "Looks like you two have been helpin' with the laundry."

"Yes, we have," Emily said.

Rosie hung her head.

"What's the matter, Rosie?" Selina asked.

"I didn't get to help because I dropped the clean pieces on the ground and Miss Esther had to rewash them."

"Oh, sugarplum. I'm sure you didn't mean to." Selina wanted to make the girl feel better.

"She didn't." Emily stood up for her sister. "She was just trying to help."

Selina wished she'd had a sister to stand up for her growing up. Even more so, she wished she had girls of her own. At bedtime, she'd have another long talk with the Lord about that among other things, too.

She visited with the girls a spell, finished her tea and the gingersnap cookies, then hurried home. After spending a few hours sewing clothes for her and Michael, she went in search of something that would work as a net for catching fish—and maybe some crawdad tails. She smiled. Being herself felt mighty nice.

Close to home, the strong smell of food reached Michael's stomach. Hungry enough to eat the side of a barn, he hurried up the steps, slung the door open and froze in the doorway. "What is she doing in here? Get that pig out of here right now!"

Sitting next to his wife at the kitchen table was Kitty.

"Well, hello to you, too. She followed me home so I let her in to visit with me." Selina patted the pig's head.

"To visit with you?" Michael stepped inside, letting the door slam shut behind him. Was this woman for real? "Just look at her. She's covered in mud and who knows what else."

Selina glanced down at Kitty. "It's dry. Besides, don't worry. She ain't hurtin' your fancy furniture."

"My fancy…" He expelled a long breath of frustration. "I don't know how to get through to you. What is wrong with you, woman?"

"Ain't a thing wrong with me. Rainee said so."

He'd never seen Selina look so smug before. "Rainee? What does she have to do with this?"

"She likes me just the way I am."

"Yes, well, she doesn't have to live with you. I do."

"Ain't you lucky?" She smiled.

"Lucky?"

"Yes. God is teachin' you somethin', Michael. And any time the good Lord teaches us somethin', it's always an adventure."

"Living with you is an adventure. I never know what I'm going to come home to."

"Well, at least I ain't borin'."

"That's for sure." He could do with some boredom.

"See."

Michael's chest heaved as he let out another heavy sigh. There was no winning with this woman. "Please. Just put Kitty outside and please, please don't bring

her in here again. I'm going to clean up for supper."
He turned and headed toward the sink. With his back
to Selina, he asked, "What are we having?"

"Fried taters and onions, greens cooked in bacon fat
and salt pork, fried fish and crawdad tails."

Michael froze. Did she just say crawdad tails?
He wrinkled his nose and shook his head. Nah. She
couldn't have. Crawdad tails were only used as fish
bait. He must have misunderstood. He finished washing his face and hands while Selina set the table.

He sat down at the end of the table. A table loaded
with a covered Dutch oven pan, two cast iron skillets, a
covered bowl, a plate of butter, a jar of strawberry preserves and a pie pan with a few pieces of apples slices
sticking out of the lattice top crust. His mouth watered
just looking at it.

Selina filled their milk glasses and sat down in the
chair on his left. As was their ritual, he reached for her
hand, ignoring the usual warmth that spread up his arm.

They bowed their heads. "Father, we thank You for
this day and for all that we got accomplished. Thank
You for sending us to Jake's today and for using Selina
to help him. We thank You for Your bountiful provi-
sions, in Christ's name, Amen."

"Amen." Selina reached for his bowl, raised the lid
on the Dutch oven kettle and spooned some green,
wilted-looking vegetables with chunks of bacon into
it. That must be the greens she was talking about. He
had to admit, they looked good. He forked a bite and
ate it. Salt exploded into his mouth, along with the taste
of bacon. Aside from the shock of how salty they were,
they were really delicious. "These are really good."

"Thanks."

"What are they?"

"Mustard greens and mountain sorrel."

Mountain sorrel? Wasn't that a weed? And what were mustard greens anyway? He didn't dare ask what they were. He was better off not knowing.

She grabbed his plate and raised a lid off one of the frying pans.

The fried potatoes and onions looked delicious.

She spooned a large mound onto his plate. Then she raised the lid on another skillet and scooped out a large fish, trout if he wasn't mistaken, and laid it next to the potatoes.

"Where did you get the fish?"

"I caught them down at the crick this afternoon."

"*You* caught them? Down at the *what?*"

She held the covered plate midair and looked at him with a confused frown. "That's what I said, didn't I? I caught them down at the crick. Crick, as in, you know, a small stream a runnin' water."

"Oh, you mean *creek.*"

She set the lid down on the table and looked over at him. "That's what I said. Crick."

"No, you're saying crick, not creek."

"Crick, creek, who cares? I caught us a mess a fish to eat for supper and they're gettin' cold with you sittin' there arguin'."

"I can't believe you went fishing. Did you clean them, too?"

"Well, who else woulda done it, Michael? Ain't you ever heard of a woman fishin' before?"

"Only one. Rainee. But—" he shook his head "—a lot of the things you do, I've never heard of any other woman doing. In fact, I've never met anyone like you before."

"That's 'cause there ain't no one like me. God made me one of a kind. Just like He does everyone. There's no two people alike."

For that, Michael was grateful. He couldn't handle another one like Selina.

She pulled the cloth off of the covered plate. Small mounds of deep-fried something was on them. She placed a pile on his plate and then fixed her own plate.

Michael tried everything except for the little fried bits. That was next. Using his fingers, he picked one up and put it in his mouth and bit down. The texture was a little tough, the flavor different. Good, actually. He popped another one into his mouth, and then another. "These are really good. What are they?"

"I told you we were having crawdad tails."

Michael froze. He'd forgotten all about her saying that because he was certain he hadn't heard her correctly. But he had and now he wished he hadn't. Suddenly the piece in his mouth grew and his stomach roiled.

Weeds and fish bait? The woman was trying to kill him. Against his better judgment, he allowed his manners to take over and swallowed the ball of fish bait. He leaned back in his chair and eyed Selina. "Selina, we've had this discussion before, but it bears repeating. We have plenty of food. You do not need to go hunting for it. If you wanted fish, you only had to ask me, and I would have gotten you some. Do not—I repeat, do not—ever feed me fish bait again."

"Fish bait? You callin' my cookin' fish bait?" Her chair scraped against the hardwood floor as she leaped

We'd like to send you two free books to introduce you to the Love Inspired® Historical series. Your two books have a combined cover price of $11.50 in the U.S. and $13.50 in Canada, but they are yours free! We'll even send you two wonderful surprise gifts. You can't lose!

Love Inspired HISTORICAL

An Honorable Gentleman

Love Inspired HISTORICAL
VICTORIA BYLIN
Marrying the Major

Love Inspired HISTORICAL
ANNA SCHMIDT
Family Blessings

Love Inspired HISTORICAL
LAURIE KINGERY
Could love blossom before the spring?
The Rancher's Courtship

Love Inspired HISTORICAL
NOELLE MARCHAND
Unlawfully Wedded Bride
Married—by mistake!

Each of your **FREE** books is filled with romance, adventure and faith set in various historical periods from biblic times to World Wa

GET 2 FREE BOOKS!

Love Inspired HISTORICAL

YES! *Please send me the 2 FREE Love Inspired® Historical books and 2 FREE gifts for which I qualify. I understand that I am under no obligation to purchase anything further, as explained on the back of this card.*

affix free books sticker here

102/302 IDL FMHT

FIRST NAME	LAST NAME

ADDRESS

APT.#	CITY

STATE/PROV.	ZIP/POSTAL CODE

▲ DETACH AND MAIL CARD TODAY!

® and ™ are trademarks owned and used by the trademark owner and/or its licensee. © 2011 HARLEQUIN ENTERPRISES LIMITED. Printed in the U.S.A.

LIH-FL-12

If offer card is missing write to: The Reader Service, P. O. Box 1867, Buffalo, NY 14240-1867 or visit: www.ReaderService.com

NO POSTAGE
NECESSARY
IF MAILED
IN THE
UNITED STATES

BUSINESS REPLY MAIL
FIRST-CLASS MAIL   PERMIT NO. 717   BUFFALO, NY

POSTAGE WILL BE PAID BY ADDRESSEE

THE READER SERVICE
PO BOX 1867
BUFFALO NY 14240-9952

up. Flames shot from her big brown eyes as she mashed her hands onto her hips.

Michael held up his hands. "Sit down, Selina. That's not what I meant."

"Then just what did you mean?" She plopped onto her chair, never taking her fiery eyes off of him.

"We use crawdad tails for fish bait. We don't eat them."

"Back home we do both." She crossed her arms over her chest and made no motion to go back to eating.

Michael rested his arms on the table. "Look, I understand that you were poor and had to hunt and fish for your food. But you don't have to do that here. Trust me. We have plenty of food."

"I know that, Michael." Her voice softened. "Did ya ever think I might like to fish and that I might like to eat some of them foods I grew up with?"

Knives of understanding ripped into him. No, he hadn't. Not even for a half second. Right then he suddenly realized that she actually enjoyed eating those things. She wasn't trying to be obstinate. She was trying to bring a little of her old home here.

"Truth is I miss home." Her eyes fell downcast. "And sometimes when I find things that remind me of Kentucky, it helps me to be less lonely for my family." She roughly wiped away a tear that trailed down her cheek, and sniffed.

Now he'd done it. He'd made her cry with his insensitivity. Wishing he could take it all back, he reached over and laid his hand on top of hers.

Her gaze slowly slid to where his hand rested.

"I'm sorry, Selina. Of course you miss your home. Oh, speaking of your home, I almost forgot. Some letters came for you today." Maybe that would help ease her homesickness.

Homesickness. Fear tore into him at that one word.

When Haydon and Melanie had moved here, it wasn't long before Melanie had become restless and the vicious fighting began, destroying Haydon, Melanie and those who loved them. Before Michael would allow himself and Selina to go through something like that, he would get their marriage annulled. But not until he did everything he possibly could to make this marriage work, and to make Selina happy and to help ease her homesickness.

"Letters? For me?" Her eyes brightened.

He pulled them out of his vest pocket and handed them to her.

Sadness replaced the joy he'd seen only seconds ago.

"I can't read, remember?"

How could he have been so foolish? "I'm sorry, I forgot. I can read them to you, if you'd like."

"I'd like that very much. But can we do it after supper? I'm mighty hungry."

"Sure."

"Thank you kindly, Michael. And I'm sorry about the crawdad tails. You made me promise not to fix frog legs but you didn't say anything about these so I figured it was okay. From now on, I'll just fix enough for myself and make you somethin' else. Is that all right with you?"

"That's fine. Thank you for understanding."

"Didn't say I understood." She smiled and winked at him.

That playful wink felt as if one of those fried fish had come to life and was flopping around inside his stomach. To get his mind off the effect she had on him, an effect he wasn't ready to deal with, he picked up his fork and shoved a bite of potatoes into his mouth. They really were good the way she fixed them. The craw-dads, however...

Chapter Ten

Selina finished the dishes. She couldn't wait to see who had written her from back home. Home. She missed her brothers and the Appalachian Mountains. There, she could be herself and no one thought anything of it. No one cared if she fixed frog legs, crawdad tails or greens. In fact, they loved and appreciated all her hard work.

Here, nothing she did was ever right, and she sure didn't feel needed or wanted.

Back home, she had a sense of belonging, too. Well, with the exception of rich folks. But the only time she had to be around them was when she went to pick up their mending and laundry.

The last pan clinked when she hung it on the nail off to the side of the cook stove. She draped the towels on a peg above the sink and turned toward the fireplace and to Michael, who was watching her as she made her way toward him. She sat in the chair next to his.

"You ready?"

"Sure am. Can't wait to see who wrote me." She

watched eagerly as Michael opened the first envelope and pulled out a piece of paper.

Selina,
We sure do miss you around here, but we's awful glad you found yourself a good man. Things is the same round here. Well, except for no pa. Still hard to believe he's gone. But he's with ma now, and that's what he was wanting all along. Everyone here is a doing good. The boys are growing like weeds and stronger than oxes. Afore long they'll be able to beat me at arm wrestling. They all send their love. Sarah too. She's gonna have a baby come first part of the year. We're sure excited about it. Can you imagine me a pa? I kinda like the idea. How bout you? You fixin to have any youngins anytime soon?

Selina's face burned hotter than the coals in the fireplace.

Michael looked at her from the corner of his eye.

Logs popped and crackled, filling in the quietness. If only it would fill in the awkwardness, too. But nothing could. The way things were betwixt them right now, there wasn't much chance for her and Michael to have any children. They were just two people living under the same roof, pretending to be married.

"Selina, I don't want to offend you or anything so please don't take this the wrong way, but how come your brother knows how to read and write and you don't?"

"None taken. Weren't any teachers around when I was younger. Two years after Ma died, one came to the mountains from some big city back east. I was too busy providin' for my brothers and pa to go to school, but I made sure they went. Jacob didn't wanna go. He wanted to help. But I made him go." She leaned closer to Michael, anxious to hear more. "Now, is that all he said?"

Michael's eyes dropped to the paper.

We sure would appreciate hearing from you. So, Michael, if you are reading this, would you drop a line, letting us know how our sister is doin? We'd be mighty grateful. Thank you kindly.

    Zeke and Zach said to tell you hi and that they love you and miss you.

    We love you too, Selina, and miss you heaps. Come for a visit whenever you can.

Love,

Jacob and Sarah and the boys

"Do you want to reply to it now?" Michael asked.

"No. I want you to read me the others first."

She listened as he read the letter from Eli and his wife, Bobby Sue, and now from Peter and his wife, Bella.

Dear Selina,

I just wanted to let you know that Pastor Hickens and I were thinking about you and praying that all is well with you. Mrs. Jenkins and Mrs. Albin send their love. Just so you know, you can stop worrying about both of them now because they are being taken care of almost as well as when you were taking care of them. Aimee has been helping them. She...

At the mention of Aimee's name, she jerked her attention onto Michael to see his reaction. Wrinkles lined his forehead but he kept right on a reading. Only Selina didn't hear another word, she was too busy wondering what he was feeling.

There was one letter left. She watched as Michael ran his finger under the seal and removed the letter from its envelope. The muscle in his jaw worked back and forth and his brows furrowed. Whoever it was from had him mighty worked up. Only she couldn't tell if it was anger or something else. He excused himself to get some firewood and was gone for almost an hour. She could hardly wait to see who the letter was from.

Ever since Selina had arrived, Michael had shoveled his anger at himself and her friend into a deep hole, burying and hiding it as well as he could. But seeing the signature on the letter he held, all the bitterness, resentment and anger resurfaced.

He sucked in a deep breath and willed none of those things to show while he read to Selina. Selina felt bad enough about the whole situation and he didn't want her feeling worse. Living with her had proved she wasn't capable of the deception that had led to their ill-begotten marriage.

To deal with the anger he had toward himself and Aimee, he had taken it out on the firewood when he split it, pounded harder than necessary on the nails when he repaired the corrals, and shoveled the muck in the barn with a vengeance. The stench of it was as bad as the stench of his anger, anger that needed to be purged like the dung in the barn. When none of those things worked, and actually exacerbated things, he had finally turned to prayer. That was the only thing that helped him deal with it enough to go back inside the house. He offered up a quick prayer and then turned to the letter.

My dearest friend,
I hope you and Michael are settled into your new life together. I'm so happy for you, Selina. I only wish I could find someone as wonderful as your Michael seems to be. You are so blessed to have someone like him, as is he to have someone like you. Both you and he deserve the best, and I wish you both all the happiness in the world.

Michael continued to read, his voice monotone even though a gamut of emotions stirred inside him. Emotions he couldn't quite put his finger on.

Things are not the same around here without you. Rather boring, actually. Father is planning another party. I so hate those things. Everyone here is so phony. Unlike you, Selina. You are the one and only genuine person I know. Don't ever change. For anyone. You hear me. Oh, before I forget, Bosley had her puppies. Seven of them. I think of you every time I look at them. They're so sweet and loving and accepting. Just like you, my dear friend. You are truly one of a kind. I am planning a visit real soon as

I cannot wait to see you again. I love you and miss you terribly.

Give Michael my love.

No thanks. He wanted no part of the deceptive woman.

Your forever friend,
Aimee

Michael folded the letter and put it back into the envelope. Though the room was quiet, the ticking of the grandfather clock and Selina's breathing roared like a violent stampede.

Selina set the rocking chair into motion. "I sure don't understand her." He barely heard her, her voice was so soft.

"You don't understand what?" he asked equally as quiet.

"She acts like she ain't done nothin' wrong."

That's what he was thinking, too. Aimee seemed to think that he and Selina deserved each other. Why would the woman think he would like Selina? He'd told her what type of woman he was looking for. And Selina was far from it.

Would he ever be able to truly forgive Aimee for deceiving them?

And would he ever be able to love Selina the way he had loved who he'd thought she was?

Selina struggled with Aimee's letter. It surprised Selina that Aimee acted like Michael and Selina belonged together. If only she had kept Michael's letters, then she'd have asked Rainee to read them to her. To find out what they really said. But she hadn't kept them because she couldn't read them herself anyway.

Aimee said she was coming for a visit. Truth was,

Selina didn't want her to come. The very thought of it tied her stomach into knots. Especially after all those words about how wonderful Aimee thought Michael was. Sounded as if Aimee loved him, too.

Like a flung rock to the head, reality smacked her. *Dear Lord. She is, isn't she? Aimee's in love with Michael.*

Selina pondered how Aimee was more Michael's type than she was. Aimee was unmarried and a real looker, too. Would Michael fall for her once he laid eyes on her and saw how sweet and kind she acted?

With Michael and her being married in name only, would Michael get their marriage annulled so he could marry Aimee? That thought frightened her more than anything ever had in her life before. Well, there was no way she would let that happen. She had to figure out a way to win Michael's heart—and fast. She'd have to work harder to learn how to write so she could write Aimee and tell her she wasn't welcome here. If not, she feared she would lose Michael forever.

That night Selina wrestled with her sheets. Long before the sun peeked over the mountain, she got up, flew through breakfast and chores and then hurried over to Rainee's.

A surprised Rainee greeted her at the door.

"What am I gonna do, Rainee?" Selina blurted before she even stepped inside. "I can't have her show up now…"

Rainee opened the door to let her in.

Emily and Rosie looked up from the table and their puzzle, then rushed over to Selina and hugged her.

"You want to help us put our puzzle together?" Rosie asked.

Selina glanced at the wooden puzzle pieces scattered on the kitchen table. Normally she would love to spend time with the girls, but today she had too much on her mind and really wanted to talk to Rainee.

"Not today, girls," Rainee said. "I want you to go find Esther and stay with her until I tell you it is okay to come back inside, okay?"

"Yes, Mother," they both said with disappointment.

Selina hated disappointing them like that, but she'd make it up to them later.

When the girls were out of sight, Rainee looped arms with Selina and led her to the living room. A tray with a pot of tea, cups, the small plates she learned were called saucers, and all the fixings for tea were set on the round table between them.

Rainee fixed them both a cup of the dark brew. "Now, tell me what this is all about. Who is coming to see you?" She held the cup to her lips.

"Aimee. She says she's comin' for a visit. She's real purty, Rainee. And Michael fell in love with the woman in them letters. The letters were more her than me. I'm so afraid when he meets her and gets to know her, he'll send my hide packin'."

"Michael would never do that, Selina. He is a man of his word."

"Maybe so, but I ain't takin' any chances."

Rainee seemed to be studying Selina for a moment. Her tea cup tinkled when she set it down. "I have an idea. Come with me."

Selina followed Rainee into one of the rooms. There stood the same kind of treadle sewing machine that Selina had at her house but didn't know how to use.

Rainee showed her how to use the machine. Selina

caught on fast, and the two of them commenced to sewing.

That evening, Selina couldn't wait until Michael got home. With supper on the stove, she sat on the sofa, watching the door.

The boards on the steps creaked.

Selina hurried to stand in front of the fireplace.

Footsteps sounded on the porch, then stopped at the door.

Selina held her breath.

The door squeaked opened.

Michael stepped inside and stopped when his attention landed on her. His eyes almost popped out of their sockets. "Se-Selina? Is that—is that you?"

Michael was certain his heart had stopped beating. The vision in front of him could not be his wife. "What happened?"

She frowned. "What do you mean, what happened? Ya told me you wanted me to make dresses, so I did. Well, one at least anyways."

"That was days ago, and you made it clear you weren't going to wear dresses."

"A woman can change her mind, can't she?"

"Guess so. But, you said you weren't changing for anyone."

"Ain't changin' *who* I am, just what I'm wearin'."

Boy was he ever glad she did. She looked great in a dress. He ran his eyes down the length of her. Her molasses, copper-and-honey-colored hair hung to her waist in waves. The woman really did have a shape to be envied by any woman.

The vision of loveliness standing in front of the fireplace was more of what he had in mind when he pictured the woman he had married.

His heart picked up its pace as she glided toward him, looking and walking every bit the lady. Her pink skirt swished with each step she took, and he found he couldn't peel his eyes away from her.

Only a foot separated them now.

He got a whiff of something sweet.

Her brown eyes sparkled as she looked up at him. "What do you think?"

"I think I like it. You—you look beautiful. I could get used to coming home to this."

"Could you?"

He slid his attention to her hopeful, beautiful eyes.

Eyes that suddenly seemed to be pulling him into their depths.

He inched his body closer to her.

She took a small step toward him.

His heart beat faster, and his body trembled.

She looked up at him, blinking.

His arms reached out to her, pulling her to him.

His gaze lowered to her slightly parted lips, lips that invited his to join them.

But just to make sure he wasn't mistaken, when he leaned his head down, he searched her face for permission.

Her eyes slid shut. That was all the permission he needed. He covered her lips with his, drinking in their softness, enjoying the feel of her. His heart yearned to draw her even closer, so he did.

"Anybody home?"

Michael whipped his head toward the door, letting Selina go. "Jake? What are you doing here?" Michael's insides groaned. Of all the times Jake had to stop by, why did he have to pick now?

"I was on my way home from town and thought I'd stop by and tell Selina thanks again for saving my life."

"Come on in," Michael said, even though he really wanted to ask him to come back another time.

The screen door squeaked as it opened and closed. Jake stepped inside and his eyes bulged. "Woo wee. You sure look beautiful this evening, Selina."

"Thank you kindly." Selina glowed under his praise.

The look of approval on Jake's face bothered Michael, so he tucked Selina under his arm. "She sure does."

"Would ya like to stay for supper?"

Please, please say no.

"I'd love to."

Michael inwardly groaned again.

"Well, have a seat and I'll fetch another plate."

Jake sat in the chair across from Selina's. Michael noticed Jake was well-groomed and smelled of soap and shaving cream. Even his clothes were pressed, not very well, but they were pressed nonetheless. Just who was he trying to impress? Selina?

Selina brought an extra plate and glass and set it in front of Jake. He followed her with his eyes as she headed to the stove. "She sure looks nice, Michael," Jake whispered. "I'm sorry about what I said about her when she first came. I was wrong."

Those words meant a lot coming from the one person who never seemed to speak a kind word about anyone.

Selina's shiny mane shifted from side to side at her waist as she headed back to the cook stove. He'd never seen her hair down before and it was definitely a sight to see. She was a sight to see. He only hoped she would wear her hair down more often and start wearing dresses all the time.

She brought a covered basket, a plate covered with a towel, a saucepan, and the Dutch oven kettle and set them down.

His heart stopped, fearful of what was in the pan. Some bizarre food?

He held his breath when she removed a lid exposing creamy mashed potatoes.

Michael breathed a sigh of relief. So far so good.

She filled both men's plate with a generous portion and a small portion for herself.

Anxiously he watched as she raised the lid on the saucepan. Steam and the smell of gravy rose.

Whew. Thank You, Lord. Michael kept his smile hidden.

She filled a ladle and made a hole in their mounds of potatoes and filled it with the smooth, rich, brown gravy.

He glanced at the towel-covered basket—he wasn't worried about that one. It either had biscuits or bread. As for the covered plate, that one had him worried. Who knew what was under that cloth? Just so it wasn't crawdad tails, fried snake or some other crazy food.

She raised the cloth to reveal something fried.

His breath held. It sort of looked like chicken, but he wasn't sure.

"What piece of quail would you like, Jake?"

"Quail? That's quail?" Michael asked somewhat relieved.

"Sure is."

"Where did you get quail?" Michael asked.

"Killed it myself."

"You hunt?" Admiration filled Jake's eyes.

"Been huntin' most of my life."

"I'm impressed." Jake seemed to be impressed with a lot of the things Selina did. And that bothered Michael.

Selina tilted her head and looked surprised. A piece of hair fell across her cheek. Michael longed to move it out of the way just so he could feel her soft skin underneath.

She loaded their plates with quail. "Y'all want regular biscuits or cornbread ones?"

"I love cornbread," Michael said. "I'll take three of them and two of the regular biscuits."

"Me, too," Jake added eagerly.

After she handed them out, they bowed their heads and prayed.

"What else can you do?" Jake scooped a large forkful of mashed potatoes and shoved it into his mouth, then put a slab of butter on his biscuit.

"The same stuff everyone else does, I reckon."

"No, not everyone. I don't know anyone other than Doc who can sew cuts like you. And this food is delicious. As delicious as the meal you cooked for me. That was the best meal I'd had in a long time." He looked at Michael. "Your wife is one fine cook."

"She sure is." *That is, if a person didn't count the fried snake and crawdad tails,* but Michael kept that thought to himself.

"Thank you for your kind words about my vittles. How's the head doing?"

Jake smiled. "I'm doing well, thanks to you."

Hey, I was there, too. If it weren't for me taking her over to get a puppy, she wouldn't have even seen you to help you. Just where did that come from? It wasn't like him to be jealous. Especially over Selina.

"Iffen you want me to, I can check it and change your bandage before you go."

"That'd be great. Thanks." Jake drank half a glass of milk and wiped his mouth. "I was wondering something. Out here, you need to be a strong woman to survive. You got any friends back home just like you?"

Michael sucked in a piece of quail, completely blocking off his air supply. He grabbed his throat. Selina jumped up and shoved his head to his knees. Air whooshed from his lungs and a piece of quail flew from his throat and landed on the floor.

He rasped and wheezed, "Thank you, Selina."

"You're welcome." Her eyes raked over him with fear. "You all right now?"

He took a generous drink of his milk. "Yes. Thanks to you." Hadn't he just heard those same words from Jake?

Michael couldn't believe that the man, whose main goal in life was to taunt people, actually wanted someone just like Selina.

They went back to eating and Jake and Selina talked the whole time, leaving Michael to wonder why he and Selina didn't have conversations like that.

Jake hung on Selina's every word as she talked about Kentucky and the Appalachian Mountains.

Michael watched her eyes light up, heard the sweetness in her melodic voice. His gaze fell to her lips as she talked.

Those same lips he had enjoyed kissing earlier.

Seeing how easily she and Jake carried on a conversation, he wondered if he could ever enjoy talking to her like that. If he could ever love her.

Jesse said love was a choice. Michael had willingly made that choice once and look where it had gotten him. He had married a woman he thought he knew extremely well. A woman he loved and had given his heart to. Yet, here he was married to a complete stranger he did not love. Just like Haydon had done.

Thoughts of the horror of his older brother's first marriage stormed over him. The image of Haydon carrying Melanie back to the ranch that last, fateful day when she had fallen to her death, memories of his brother—silent, sorrowful, angry, inconsolable.

There were rumors afterward. Michael had heard Melanie was unfaithful, that Haydon blamed himself for not being attentive enough, for keeping her here when she so wanted to leave. And now she was dead.

But those were only ghosts in his memory now, the bits and pieces a young man gathers as his family struggles to live through a crisis. Try as he may, he couldn't shake any of them as he listened to Selina talk to Jake. Was he stepping right into the trap he had sworn he would never go near?

All he knew was his heart was in his throat and his mind was spinning around so fast he couldn't catch it. Everywhere he looked was the possibility of ending up just like his brother, and he had no idea how to avoid the fate that seemed to lie in wait to swallow him whole.

Selina dried the dishes and put them away. Over and over she pondered Michael's kiss. She wanted more. But until she was certain it was her he was thinking of and not Aimee or some woman who didn't exist, she wouldn't share his bed no matter how much she wanted to. It was a good thing Jake showed up when he did. She wasn't sure what would've happened if he hadn't. And that would not have been good.

Tomorrow she'd get busy and make herself a few more dresses and she'd wear her hair down more often, just because Michael liked it that way.

She still couldn't believe she was wearing a dress just to please a man. But Michael was worth it, so she would do whatever it took to win his heart and to hold on to him. She wasn't going to let Aimee steal her man.

Finished with cleaning up the kitchen, she wiped her hands on the towel and hung it on the peg above the sink, then headed over to where Michael was sitting in the living room with his Bible.

She sat down.

"Why didn't you tell me you could draw?"

Selina yanked her head toward him.

"The first I heard of it was when you told Jake. What else should I know about you?"

"Ain't much else to tell."

"Where did you learn to doctor people?"

"Doc taught me." Selina chuckled. "With six brothers who always had cuts and broken bones, Doc said it would save him a heap of trouble iffen I learned. When the boys got older, every free chance I got I went with either Doc or Josephine, the midwife back home, to learn not only how to doctor, but how to birth babies. I just wished I would have learned before it was too late."

"Too late for what?"

"My cousin Lou Ellen. She died givin' birth. Wouldn't have happened iffen there had been someone there to help her."

"Earlier you said you miss your home. What do you miss about it?"

"My family mostly."

"Would you mind drawing me something?"

"Now?"

"Yes. Now."

"I ain't got no paper or pencil."

"I do." Michael walked over to his desk, and when he came back, he handed her a thin square board with a stack of papers on it and two sharpened pencils.

"What do you want me to draw?"

"Something about Kentucky that means something to you."

She nodded.

Michael read his Bible while she drew.

The picture in her mind slowly came to life on the paper. When it was just the way she wanted it, she smiled, then looked over at Michael. "I'm done."

Michael stood behind her. "Selina, it's beautiful."

"That's the house I grew up in. On the porch are the rockers my pa made before my ma died. Hangin' from the tree over yonder is a swing he'd made for all of us. It's ratty now, but I drew it as I recollected it when it was new. All them trees—" she pointed to the ones in the drawing "—they're hickory nut trees. And that's the river we drew water from and caught fish from. It's a whole lot bigger than the ones y'all have here."

She continued to describe the boulders nearby, the different kinds of bushes and flowers. "Well, that's it. That's my home. Old home, anyways."

"It's very pretty. You are one talented, gifted lady."

"Gifted? I ain't gifted. Talents and gifts come from the Lord. The Holy Spirit does the drawin'. I just sit down and let Him use my fingers. Speakin' of gifts and the Holy Spirit, would you read to me outta the Good Book? It's been a long time since anyone has."

"Of course. I'd love to. What would you like to hear?"

"Didn't get much Bible readin' back home, so I'd be mighty thankful for anythin' you read." She set her drawing, the rest of the paper and her pencils on the coffee table.

Paper rustled as he turned the Bible pages. "I'll start in the book of James. 'James, a servant of God and of the Lord Jesus Christ, to the twelve tribes which are scattered abroad, greeting. My brethren, count it all joy when ye fall into diverse temptations, knowing this, that the trying of your faith worketh patience.'"

"What's that mean? Diverse?"

"It means a great deal of variety. Or in this verse, many temptations."

She nodded. "I see."

"'But let patience have her perfect work, that ye may be perfect and entire, wanting nothing.'"

"I sure do struggle with patience sometimes."

"Me, too. Actually, I think we all do—otherwise the Lord wouldn't have bothered putting it in His Word."

"So what's it say we're to do when we're tempted?"

"Well…" The pages rustled as he turned them some more. He ran his finger down the page. "Here it is. It says here in James 4:7, 'Submit yourselves, then, to God. Resist the devil and he will flee.'"

"Submit? What does that mean?"

"Well, the way I understand it is, when we're tempted, we're supposed to turn to God. In doing that, we set ourselves up to receive His transforming, saving power. If we simply try to resist the devil without turning to God, then we're depending on our own strength and our own willpower. And our strength and willpower are in no way sufficient."

She frowned and tilted her head.

"Not sufficient means it isn't enough."

He must be getting to know the look she gave because he'd explained that word without her even asking.

"We need God's grace and His mercy to help us resist the devil and flee temptation."

"I see. I'll have to ponder on that. Thank you, Michael."

"You're welcome." He covered his mouth when he yawned.

"It's gettin' late. You'd better get to bed."

"Yes. I'd better. It's going to be a long day tomorrow. Actually, for the next few weeks, too. I want to warn you, you won't be seeing much of me during that time. We'll be doing our best to get the wheat in."

"I understand. Iffen there's anything I can do to help, let me know, okay?"

"The best thing you can do to help is to take care of things around here. Laundry, mending, meals, stuff like that. If I don't have to deal with any of that, it makes a huge difference."

"I can do that. I'm gonna do of heap a sewin', too. And I'll make sure you have plenty of vittles and water to take with you."

"Sounds good." He rose, then looked down at her. "Just don't send me any crawdad tails or frog legs, okay?" His eyes had a twinkle when he said it.

She giggled. "I won't." She stood. "Michael? Could we pray together before you go to bed?"

"Sure." He reached for her hands and bowed his head. He started to pray and when he got to the part about thanking God for her wearing a dress, she couldn't help but laugh.

Michael opened his eyes and looked at her, his expression serious.

"Sorry. I just found it funny."

"I mean it, Selina. You wearing a dress means a lot to me." His blue eyes roamed over her face.

She tilted her head. "How come?"

"I don't know. I just know that it does." He still held her hands. That meant a lot to her. She was grateful for any touch or any affection he gave her. And as much as she wanted to share a bed with him, she was grateful he wasn't forcing his husbandly rights on her, instead giving them time to get to know each other before they did. If they ever did, that is.

Suddenly she felt the need to ask, "What did you want in a wife, Michael?"

Selina's question sent Michael backward. "You really want to know?"

"Wouldn't have asked iffen I didn't."

He dropped her hands and stepped to the fireplace. With one hand on the mantel, he stared into the dwindling fire, deciding what he would say. The truth was always best. "I wanted someone like Rainee. *Not* Rainee, but someone *like* her," he hastened to add lest Selina get the wrong idea that he was in love with his sister-in-law. Yes, he loved Rainee, but like a sister now.

"And…" Selina interjected.

"Someone who's confident, genteel, educated. A real Southern lady, who could hold her own in any type of situation whether it be here on the ranch, or at a dinner theater, or entertaining prospective business clients. I wanted someone to take care of my home and children. Someone who supports me in what I do. Someone who isn't afraid of jumping in and helping, even getting dirty when the need arises. Someone with spit and fire. Who challenges me. Who's willing to fight for what she believes."

As soon as the words left his mouth, he realized Selina fit that part of his dream wife perfectly. And today, she was dressed every bit a lady. A beautiful lady at that. One who had walked with dignity and grace. The other missing attributes he could learn to deal with. The one he couldn't was love.

"Go on," she whispered.

"Someone to come home to. But most of all someone I can love with all my heart and who loves me back the same."

"I love you, Michael," she whispered.

Michael stopped breathing and his heart stopped beating.

The air in the room suddenly vanished.

He had no idea how to respond to that because he didn't love her back.

"You don't gotta say nothin', Michael. I know you don't love me. I just wanted you to know that someone does love you. And that someone is me." She didn't look at him.

If she was the woman he'd fallen in love with, those words would have thrilled him. With a little hope and a lot of prayer, perhaps someday they would. "Thank you, Selina, for letting me know." He kissed her on the cheek. Her skin felt soft against his lips. Before he got carried away again, he stepped back. "And now, I really must get to bed, or in the morning I'll regret it." He brushed past her and headed to the bedroom. Without looking back he said, "Good night, Selina," and stepped through the door and shut it.

He propped his back against the solid wood and closed his eyes. When he opened them, they landed on the empty bed. A bed he longed to fill with love.

Shoving away from the door, he removed his clothes and climbed into bed. "God, I know You don't make mistakes and that there's a reason You put Selina and me together. Therefore, I'm asking You, Lord, to fill both of our hearts and home with love. Selina deserves no less."

Selina sank into the chair. The things he wanted in a wife trailed through her mind.

She pondered each one.

Confusion coiled in her mind. Wasn't she everything he'd said he wanted? Well, except for the genteel part. Nothing genteel about her. As for the lady part, she could work a little harder on that. She could wear dresses more often to please her husband, and she'd keep reminding herself to walk like Rainee had showed her, with something she'd called poise. Nothing more than walking slower with your head up straight and your shoulders back.

As for the rest of his list, it definitely described her. No. No it didn't. He said he wanted someone to entertain potential business clients and who could handle themselves at a theater. Could Rainee teach her how to do that? After all, he wanted someone like her. Selina didn't blame him—Rainee was wonderful.

He said he wanted someone who could educate his children, too. That wasn't her yet. But it could be. She'd work harder to learn to read and write. With that thought in mind, she pulled out her lessons and got to work. As for the rest of Michael's list, well, he wanted a fighter. *Well, sugah, you got one.*

Chapter Eleven

For almost three weeks Selina worked hard at keeping the house clean, making Michael's favorite foods and sewing shirts and pants for him and new dresses for herself. She'd finished making her first quilt, too.

Every time she saw Michael's smile and the approval on his face when she wore a dress and left her hair down, it pushed her to work harder at changing. She was even trying to learn to talk better, too, but that part wasn't going too well. Rainee thought it unnecessary anyway, but she still helped and understood.

No kisses had been shared between Selina and Michael since the last one, but Selina felt it was only a matter of time before he came around again. After all, he'd been dogged tired every night when he came home from the fields.

Today was the last day of harvesting. Michael's footsteps on their porch didn't have their normal spring. He walked like a man in his nineties, shuffling as he came in the door, more tired than she'd ever seen him before. "Evenin', Michael."

He nodded.

Selina grabbed the lunch bucket and water jug from him and set them on the round table next to the door.

His smile barely curled his lips.

"You okay?"

"I'm fine."

"Sure you are," she said mockingly as she pressed her hand against his forehead. "You're burnin' up. Why don't you clean up and head to bed, and I'll bring dinner to you there?"

"I'll be fine." His voice sounded weak.

She slammed her hands on her hips. "You ain't fine, Michael. Your skin feels hotter than white flames." She stepped behind him, placed her hands on his shoulders and gave him a push toward his bedroom.

He didn't fight her but shuffled his way slowly to his room. Inside, he flopped on the bed and sat there, staring at the wall.

"You need help gettin' undressed?" When she realized what she had asked him, her face flooded with heat. She hadn't thought before she spoke. For years she'd helped her pa undress down to his underclothes. But this was different.

Michael slowly raised his head toward her. "I could use some help."

Selina swallowed. The man really was sick. He never let her help him. And this time he was going to let her undress him. She wasn't sure how she felt about that now that he'd said yes. But she reckoned it was fitting because, after all, he was her husband.

She stepped in front of him and slipped his suspenders over his shoulders, then undid his buttons and tugged the shirttail out of his trousers. She climbed on the bed behind him and pulled his shirt off.

His broad-shouldered body was a sight to behold. God had really outdone himself on Michael. She wanted to run her hands over his smooth back to feel the hard muscles underneath her fingers. But now was not that time.

She removed his shirtsleeves by running her hands down his arms. Arms that bulged, that were as solid as rocks, only warm. She needed to hurry and get him cooled down. Hopping off the bed, she came around to the front of him.

A blond lock of hair fell across his forehead, touching his eyebrows and almost his eye.

Without thinking, she reached out and brushed it away. Halfway through, her attention snagged onto Michael's blue eyes.

He was watching her.

She should move away but she was as stiff and unmovable as a frozen pond.

Her mouth turned dry as hard bread.

Michael watched her every move.

She wondered if he was going to kiss her again.

"You're so beautiful, Selina," he whispered.

"So are you," she whispered back. Then catching her slip-up, she said, "I meant you're mighty handsome yourself."

He raised his hand and slid it behind her neck, tugging gently on it until her lips touched his. She melted into them, wanted to melt into him, but his lips were hot under hers. Even though she wanted more of his tender kisses, that would have to wait. Michael had a fever, and she needed to doctor him back to health. There would be time for kissing later. She hoped. Reluctantly, she raised her head.

"What's wrong?" His eyes looked droopy, tired.

"Nothin's wrong. It's just that you're hotter than the sun in July. You need to rest, Michael. Why don't you finish undressin' while I fetch you some vittles?" Her eyes wandered to his bare chest. "I'll—I'll be right back." She fled the room.

Seeing his bare chest, she had a yearning to press her head against it, to hear Michael's heartbeat in her ear, to be held next to it. To him. "Dear Lord, help me," she prayed on the way to the kitchen. "Temptation is a mighty powerful thing. And right now, I'm being mighty tempted."

Michael sat on the edge of the bed, dazed. The gentle feel of her hands as she ministered to him touched him deeply. He wanted to pull her into his arms and kiss her until he had no breath left. But he wouldn't. Only deep, abiding love would induce him to go further. So if and when that happened, he wanted the moment to be special. For both of them.

It took every ounce of energy he had to remove his pants, climb into bed and bury himself under the covers. Selina said he had a fever, but a chill drove clear down into his bones.

Selina stepped into his bedroom holding a tray. She set it on the stand next to him before reaching over and grabbing the extra pillow. The one meant for his wife.

"Sit up a minute."

He raised himself up.

As she placed the pillow behind him, Selina was mere inches from him. The verse he had read about temptation and fleeing it flashed through his mind. He closed his eyes to blot out the temptation before him.

The bed dipped. He opened his eyes.

"Here, sip some of this."

"What is it?"

"Just drink it, Michael. I promise it will help break that fever of yours. Trust me."

He took a sip and pushed it away, frowning. "Does this have alcohol in it?"

"Whiskey. Didn't have moonshine or I'd have used it instead. Whiskey'll have to do."

Not being a drinking man, he hated the taste of whiskey, but she asked him to trust her, so he decided he would. He'd seen enough of her doctoring skills to believe she knew what she was doing.

"What else is in it?" He took another sip, cringing inside at the bittersweet taste.

"Tea, ginger and honey."

Michael finished drinking the tea, feeling the warmth of it spreading into his body. Exhausted, he let his head flop back against the pillow.

"Ready to eat now?"

He didn't have the strength to raise his arms, but he needed to eat to get his energy back. "Yes."

"Tell you what. Why don't ya let me feed you so you can save your strength."

It had been a long time since someone had pampered him when he was sick, so he lay back and thanked God for the help and compassion Selina showered on him.

Selina reached for the bowl and spoon on the tray and settled the bowl under his chin before she laid the spoon to his lips. He opened his mouth and let her feed him.

Delicious was the only way he could think to describe the food. "What is that?"

"Chicken 'n' dumplins. Looks like I picked a right fine day to fix it, too. It'll help ya heal."

She fed him one spoonful at a time. It didn't take him long to fill up. Now all he wanted to do was sleep. His eyes drifted shut.

The bed shifted. His eyes opened to a slit.

Selina tucked the blanket around him and under his chin. "Sleep well, Michael." She leaned down and kissed his cheek. Her lips felt cool next to his hot skin. "Iffen you need anything, you holler. Don't you be gettin' up, you hear?"

He nodded and closed his eyes.

Hours later, Michael woke up. His blanket was damp and he no longer felt hot. He let his eyes adjust to the dark room, wondering what time it was.

In a rocking chair next to his bed, Selina sat sound asleep. How long had she been there?

He took the opportunity to study her.

Her hair, gathered to one side, flowed down the chair, revealing a sleek neck, a graceful, feminine one.

His gaze slid to her heart-shaped face, her high cheekbones and her nice lips. The woman was not only beautiful, she was compassionate, nurturing and unselfish, as well.

"Michael? You okay?" Selina asked through a sleepy voice.

"I'm fine. I actually feel pretty good."

She sat up in the chair.

"You were right. That stuff you gave me broke my fever. And now I need to get out of these wet nightclothes and sheets. They're soaked."

"I'll get you some dry clothes." She lit the lantern next to his bed and then rummaged through his bureau and then the trunk at the end of the bed. She came back with a clean nightshirt, sheets and blankets.

Michael tossed the blankets off. Selina whirled, turning her back to him.

He stood, and she put her arm behind her back, offering him the shirt. "Soon as you get that other one off and this one on, I'll make up your bed."

He smiled. Last night she had seen his bare chest and run her hands slowly over his arms. Now, she was bashful. He found it rather endearing.

Michael slid the damp nightshirt off and put the dry one on. "I'm finished. You can turn around now."

She turned, reached for a pitcher and glass sitting on his night stand, filled it with water and handed it to him. "Why don't you sit over yonder—" she pointed to the rocking chair she'd been sleeping in just minutes before "—while I make your bed up?"

He did as he was told and watched as she hurried to change his bedding. She really was a sweet little thing. He pulled his pocket watch out of his vest pocket and looked at it. Three in the morning. "Selina, why don't you head on up to bed now? I'll be fine."

"You sure? I hate leavin' you to yourself."

"I'll be fine. I feel a lot better. Go on and get some sleep."

She nodded. "Iffen you need me, don't you hesitate to call me, okay?"

"I won't. Good night. Or should I say good morning?"

She smiled and headed out of his room.

Michael woke to the smell of bacon and coffee. Sunlight peeked through the windows. He checked his watch again. Eight-thirty. He groaned, unable to believe he'd overslept. Chores needed to be done. He dressed, then hurried out into the kitchen.

Selina stood at the stove wearing her trousers again. He refused to let his disappointment show. "Morning."

She kept her back to him but turned her head. "Mornin'. Sit yourself down. I'm almost finished heatin' things up. How you feelin' this mornin'?"

"Good. Just a little tired from working the last few weeks from sunup to sundown."

"I'm sure you are. I know I would be." She poured him a steaming cup of coffee and handed him a plate filled with pancakes, bacon strips and scrambled eggs.

"Aren't you having any?"

"Already ate."

"How long you been up?"

"Long enough to do chores and fix you breakfast. I told Jess you probably wouldn't work today 'cause you had a fever last night. He was mighty worried about you, but I told him you were doin' all right. He said to tell you to stay home, that he would do chores today. I told him I took care of most of them and I would finish after I checked on you. He put up a mighty big fuss about that. But I didn't let him stop me."

"I can believe that," he whispered.

"I heard that."

Michael smiled. "Just what time did you get up?"

"Never went to bed after I left your room. I came in here and fixed me some vittles, then headed to the barn."

Michael was speechless. She spent all night sleeping in a chair, making sure she was there if he woke up and needed anything, and then she did all of his chores so he could sleep. "You're something else, you know that?"

Spoon in hand, she turned and looked at him, frowning. "What do you mean, 'I'm somethin' else'?"

"Just what I said."

"Is being 'somethin' else' a good thing or a bad thing?"

"Depends."

"On what?"

"On what the circumstances are. In this case being something else is a good thing."

"Oh, I see." She nodded and smiled. "Then I'm glad I'm somethin' else."

Michael chuckled. One thing for sure, there was never a dull moment with Selina around.

He picked up his fork and started eating. "What are you doing anyway?"

"Making you chicken soup for lunch in case I ain't home."

He stopped his fork midway to his mouth. "Where you going?"

"To Rainee's. Yesterday she wasn't feelin' so good. I think that baby's fixin' to enter the world anytime now. I want to see iffen she needs my help."

"You think she's going to have it today?"

"I do. I feel it in my gut." She faced him again. "You don't mind that I go there and leave you alone for a spell today, do you? Iffen I thought you needed me, I'd stay. But, you said you were feelin' better, so…"

"No, no. You go ahead. I'm going down to the barn to help clean up the harvester and stuff."

"You don't need to do that. Jess said him and the

boys would handle it. I really think you should rest. Give your body a chance to recover completely."

"We'll see. I might just go down and help for a bit and then maybe I'll meet you at Rainee's and see how she's doing."

Selina placed the lid on the pot she was stirring and set it off to the side. "Well, I'd better change my clothes and head on over there."

She was going to change her clothes. That meant she'd only worn the trousers to do chores in. He knew what she was up to. She was wearing dresses because she knew how much it meant to him. Well, if she could give up her stubborn ways, so could he. From now on, he'd try a lot harder to be a better, more understanding husband. He remembered the gift he had for her in his vest pocket. "Wait, before you go. I have something for you."

She stopped and watched him as he headed over to her. "Hold out your hand."

He placed the rock on her palm, wondering why he was so nervous all of a sudden.

When she looked down at it, her eyes widened. "Oh, Michael. That's so purty. What kind of rock is this?"

"An opal. When I saw it, I thought of you and the hidden beauties you spoke of."

As she examined the pearly white rock her eyes grew wider and her smile broadened. "Just look at them shiny pinks and blues and greens. They sparkle like broken glass in the sun." She looked up at him and hugged the rock to her chest. "Thank you, Michael. I'll treasure this for the rest of my life."

She reached up, kissed his cheek and smiled before heading up the stairs.

Seeing the pleasure that small gesture had given her brought a smile to his face. Sure didn't take much to please her. And for some reason, that pleased him.

Selina knocked on Rainee's door and Esther answered it. "I came to see how Rainee is today," Selina said.

Concern wrinkled the corners of Esther's eyes.

"Somethin' the matter?"

"She's in bed. Says she's not feeling very well."

"Is that Selina?" Rainee's voice sounded from her bedroom. "Send her in, please."

Selina followed Esther to Rainee's bedroom and the rich brownish-red four-poster bed with spindly posts and light purple bedding.

"How you feelin' today. Any better?"

"No. I believe my time is here." Rainee rubbed her hand over her rounded belly. "I am so glad you are here. I feel much better already."

"Well, don't you fret none. Back home I helped Doc birth over a hundred babies."

Haydon stepped into the room, looking all nervous and worried. "I sent Smokey to get Doc. Do you need anything? Can I do something? Do you need another pillow? Something to drink?"

Selina smiled to herself, knowing things were the same everywhere.

Two hours and lots of contractions later, Selina shooed Haydon out of the room. Doc still hadn't shown up, but this baby wasn't waiting for him any longer.

She checked and saw the baby's head crowning. "Okay, Rainee, push." The second Selina saw the cord wrapped around the baby's neck she ordered Rainee to stop pushing. Her cousin had died because of the very same thing. Well, she wouldn't let Rainee or this baby die. She'd helped Doc back home enough to know what to do now.

"I am not sure I can stop," Rainee lamented.

"Rainee, you have to," Selina said calmly. "Draw in a deep breath and listen to me. You *have* to stop pushin'."

"What is the matter?" Rainee asked, fear running through her voice.

As much as Selina didn't want to tell Rainee what the matter was, Rainee needed to know how important it was for her to stop pushing. "The cord is wrapped around the baby's neck."

"Dear God, no."

"Don't panic. I can unwrap it, but you have to stop pushin', okay?" She had to get it unwrapped as fast as she could to save not only the baby's life, but Rainee's, too.

"Okay. I shall try." Rainee stopped pushing, her breathing came hard and uneven.

"You're doin' good, Rainee. Now, be ready to push as soon as I tell you to, and don't stop until I say it's okay, ya hear?"

"Y-yes." Rainee gasped for air.

Holding on to the slippery head as best she could, Selina ran her hand under the cord and carefully slid it over the baby's head. Selina silently praised God that the cord had stayed attached and in one piece. If it had broken, Rainee could have bled to death. "Okay, now push, Rainee. And don't stop until I tell you to."

Rainee pushed and pushed and in moments the baby was in Selina's hands.

The doctor burst into the room and without asking took the baby from Selina. Within seconds, the baby howled. Selina went to Rainee's side and dipped a cloth into the cool water and blotted the moisture from her face and neck.

"Thank you, Selina." Rainee reached for her hand and gave it a weak squeeze.

"You're welcome."

Knowing Rainee was in good hands with Doc Berg, Selina washed up and then slipped out of the room. Her nerves were plumb worn out just thinking about what could have happened to Rainee if that cord had broken. That thought set her body to shaking again.

Michael sat on his mother's porch swing with his niece Rosie. Yards away from them, Emily visited with her grandmother, who was watching the girls while Rainee had her baby.

Michael wondered how things were going with Rainee. In a few minutes he'd go and see, but for now he was just enjoying the sunshine and spending time with the bubbly child sitting next to him.

"Did you see what I made, Uncle Michael?"

He glanced down at his niece and the doll she held up for him to see, all wrapped in a handmade, large-stitched and slightly crooked quilt.

"You sure did a nice job on it, Rosie. It's very pretty."

"It sure is." She toyed with the quilt around her doll for several long moments before she looked up at him. "Aunty Selina's favorite color is blue, you know."

"Yes, I know it is." Did he ever. That was why he had ordered blue-patterned china, and had their...his... bedroom decorated in blue.

"Mine's pink. And that's okay. 'Cause Aunty Selina said it was."

"What do you mean Aunty Selina said it was?" Michael couldn't wait to hear this one.

"Well, when she came to visit Grandmother, she really liked the blue squares Emily had picked. Made me feel a little sad. Like I didn't choose a pretty color or something. But then Aunty told me God made all different kinds of colors for us so we could each have our favorite. That He made each of us different, too. And that I was perfect and just right like I am." Rosie's little chest puffed out.

"You sure are, munchkin." He kissed her on top of the head.

"Know what else she said?"

"No. What else did she say?"

"She said that it was okay to like different things and to be different. I like that." The smile beamed like the bright sunshine around them. "You wanna know why, Uncle Michael?"

"Yes, I do."

"'Cause, I always wanted to be like Emily, that's why. She's so smart and pretty. Always does things just right and I don't. But after Aunty Selina told me that, I know it's okay to not do things the same way Emily does. Doesn't mean I'm not as good as Emily, just different. And that's okay."

Out of the mouths of babes. "It sure is." This was a lesson he needed to learn, too. It was okay if Selina was different. He just needed to learn how to live with those differences.

Sitting here, listening to his niece chatter on, the desire to have children of his own overpowered his emotions. He glanced over at Haydon's house. He couldn't sit there any longer, wondering how things were going.

He excused himself and went to Haydon's. When he stepped inside, Selina was closing Rainee and Haydon's bedroom door. One look at the worry lines on his wife's face and her tired eyes sent concern rushing through Michael. Concern not only for his wife, but also for Rainee. He went to her side. "You're trembling. Is everything okay in there?"

Selina nodded. "Everythin's fine now. It was a good thing I was here, Michael, or things could've been really bad for Rainee. Doc Berg only just arrived a minute ago."

"What do you mean? What happened?"

"The cord was wrapped around the baby's neck."

Michael gasped.

"Iffen that cord had broke, Rainee could've bled to death, just like my cousin." She shuddered.

"Thank God you were here to help." Michael opened his arms and Selina sank against him. "Thank you for saving them." He hugged her to his chest.

"No. Thank the Good Lord. All I did was what He told me to do." She stepped back from his arms, and he wondered why.

"I think you need to go home and get some rest, Selina. You've had a long night and day."

"I'm fine." She slumped in a nearby chair.

"You don't look fine. Your eyes are barely open and you look like you could fall asleep any second. I'm taking you home. Now."

She yanked herself up straight in the chair. "I ain't going home just yet. I need to be here to help Rainee."

"Yes, you are going home. Rainee's fine, the baby's fine. But you're not. Besides, Doc Berg is with her now. There's nothing else to be done here."

"I said I was fine. Just tired is all."

"All the more reason for you to go home and get some rest."

"Michael's right." Haydon stepped into the living room. His hair was rumpled and he looked like he'd aged ten years. "Doc Berg is finished. He said Rainee and the baby are doing well and that you did a very good job." Haydon stepped up to Selina and clasped her hands. "Rainee told him the cord was around the baby's neck. Doc said you saved my wife and son's lives. How can I ever thank you enough, Selina?"

"You just did. Besides, I was glad I could help."

"I'm so glad Michael brought you into our lives, Selina." He gave Selina a quick hug. "Now, go do what your husband says. Go home and get some sleep."

"Yes. You heard the man. Do what your husband says," Michael ordered, winking at her.

She pursed her lips and narrowed her gaze at him. Michael stood and took her arm. "Come on, sweetheart. It's time to go home." Had he just called her sweetheart? He glanced down at her. Judging by the way her eyebrows were raised, he must have. Well, what was done was done. He turned his attention to his brother. "Congratulations on your new son, Haydon."

Haydon stood up straighter. "I have a son. Can you believe it?"

"Did you name him yet?" Michael asked.

"Yes. We sure did. His name's Haydon. Haydon Junior."

Michael didn't think it was possible, but his brother's chest puffed out even further.

They headed to the door and stopped.

"Tell Rainee I'll check in on her tomorrow. Unless she needs somethin' tonight. Iffen she does, you come get me, you hear?"

"Will do. Thanks again, Selina."

"Take care of little Haydon Junior," Michael told his brother.

"You can count on it."

They slipped outside into the darkness and headed for home. All the way, Michael's heart ached with envy. Would he ever know what it felt like to be a father? To hold a son or a daughter in his arms. To watch them grow up. Take their first step. Call him Father.

He darted a sideways glance at Selina. Over the past several weeks his affection toward her had been growing. There was more to his wife than her strange attire, her lack of education and her different way of talking. And it was time to find out even more about her. Maybe it was time to start courting his wife.

Chapter Twelve

Selina stretched in her bed. Sunlight lit her room. She wondered what time it was, so she tossed the covers aside to check.

"Oh, no you don't. Stay right where you are."

Selina froze with her hand holding the blanket midair.

Michael stepped into her bedroom carrying a tray and smiling. His blue eyes sparkled and so did his teeth. No stubble dotted his manly chin. He wore one of the new blue shirts she'd made and pressed for him.

He set the tray on the nightstand close to her bed. "I brought you breakfast. So sit up, okay?"

She eyed him warily.

He folded the blue blanket down around her lap.

He grabbed the extra pillow on her bed, gently shifted her shoulders forward and slid it behind her back. "There. That's better."

He set the tray on her lap and turned. With a single yank, he spun the chair around, set it down by her bed and sat. "I hope you like them. It's about the only thing I know how to make." His eyes held hope.

Selina glanced at the huge pile of flapjacks. "Where's your plate?"

"I already ate. Those are yours. The coffee's a little on the strong side. Isn't as good as yours, but it isn't bad."

Selina kept watching him, shifting one eyebrow and then the other. "Okay, Michael. What are you up to?"

"Up to? What do you mean? Can't a husband bring his wife breakfast in bed? You did it for me yesterday."

"Ain't the same. You were sick. I ain't."

"Do you have to be sick for me to do something nice for you?"

She dipped her head sideways, but her eyes stayed on him.

"Look, I know you're wondering what I'm up to, but please, just eat your breakfast. See, I even heated the syrup." He lifted the small pitcher and poured it over the stack of flapjacks with a large chunk of butter melting in the center. He cut a triangle out of the hot cakes, and brought it to her lips.

She opened her mouth, keeping her eyes on Michael.

His eyes slid to hers. She ate, staring into his beautiful blue eyes. "These are right tasty." She took the fork from him and dove into the stack.

Michael chuckled. "That good, huh?"

"Sure are."

"When you're done eating, get dressed. You can even wear your trousers if you want."

Her eyes darted open. She slammed her fork down on the tray. The dishes rattled and coffee sloshed over the side of her cup. "Okay, what's goin' on? You can't stand my trousers."

"I know. But I thought we'd go for a ride today and

I figured you'd probably be more comfortable wearing pants instead of a dress."

"Goin' for a ride? Where?"

"It's a surprise. Now finish eating and get dressed. I'll see you downstairs." He pushed the chair back near the window and headed out the door.

Selina watched him disappear.

He was acting mighty strange. She'd better hurry and eat and get dressed so she could find out what that polecat of a husband of hers was up to.

Michael whistled while he tossed two apples, a chunk of cheese, leftover biscuits, ham slices and gingersnap cookies into a flour sack. He had just finished filling the canteens with water when Selina glided down the stairs. Shock barreled through him. The woman wasn't wearing trousers, but a lavender skirt, a yellow blouse and cowboy boots. Cowboy boots. He shook his head and chuckled. Now that was what he was used to seeing.

He met her at the bottom of the stairs and took her hand.

Just like she had when he served her breakfast in bed, she eyed him suspiciously. Well, let her be suspicious. She had every right to be because he was up to something. But he wasn't telling her what—he'd show her instead.

"Sure you don't want to wear your pants? We'll be doing a lot of riding today."

"Nope. See." She pulled one side of her skirt off to the side, revealing the split down the middle. "They're as good as britches. Rainee told me about them. Showed me hers. She even helped me make them."

Michael laughed. He should have known. "Well, they look very nice on you, Selina."

"Thank you. That's mighty nice of you to say so."

"Well, I have everything ready. So let's go."

"Don't you have chores to do?"

"Nope. I already did them. Sound familiar?"

She frowned. "Oh, so that's why you're doin' this. To pay me back. Well, I don't want to be paid back. I did it 'cause I love you." She gasped and slammed her hand over her mouth. "Um, we'd better go iffen we're a goin'." She darted away from him, slapped her cowboy hat on her head and grabbed her rifle, which was leaning against the bench near the door. Then she was out of the house before he could even pick up the canteens and flour sack filled with their lunches.

When he neared the door, he heard her mumbling. "Can't believe I up and said that. The man doesn't love you, so why're you tellin' him you love him, Selina girl? Ain't you got no pride left? Or did you throw it all away on that man?"

While Michael smiled at her antics, at the same time he felt bad that he did not reciprocate her sentiment. All he could do was keep praying someday he would. He walked up beside her. "I didn't get the horses ready yet. We'll have to do that first."

"Where we goin'?"

"Now, what did I read the other day about patience and letting it have its perfect work?"

"And what did I say about not havin' any?" she shot back.

Was she ever fast at those comebacks. "You got me there. Come on. Let's hurry."

"Michael." She laid her small hand on his arm and

warmth spread through it, landing in his heart. "Can we check on Rainee first?"

"Already did. Haydon said she was resting and that she was doing very well. We'll go by and see her later, okay?"

"Okay."

He could tell she was disappointed, but he didn't want to wake Rainee.

They hustled down to the barn. The familiar smell of horse, grain, hay and dust greeted his nose.

"Hi there, Abbers."

Abby whirled and tossed her hip-length braid behind her. "Selina! Hi."

His little sister hugged Selina.

"What about me?"

"Oh. Hi, Michael." Abby hugged him with less enthusiasm than she did Selina.

"Hi yourself. I see how I rate." He winked at Abby and she wrinkled her nose up at him.

Leah stepped out of the stall, leading her horse.

"Hi, Selina. Boy don't you look nice."

"Thank you kindly. So do you."

"Hi to you, too, sis."

Leah gave him a quick wave.

"Where are you two heading off to?" Michael asked.

"We're going into town. You want to come with us, Selina?"

Michael blurted, "No!"

Leah lips curled upward. "I see. And just where are you two going?" She waggled her eyebrows.

"That's none of your business." He smiled.

"A surprise," Abby chimed in. "Ooo, I love surprises." She walked over to him and cupped her ear with her hand. "Whisper to me what it is. I won't tell."

Michael leaned down near her ear. "No."

Abby yanked her head back. "Oh, you. You're so mean."

He tweaked her on the nose. "And don't you forget it."

"Come on, Abby," Leah said. "Help me get Lambie ready so we can go. I don't want to miss…" She stopped and yanked her gaze over at Michael.

"You don't want to miss what?"

"Nothing."

"Le-ah. Who is he?"

Leah shook her head. "No one, Michael. I'm teasing you. Do you think I would take my little sister with me if I were going to see someone?"

"Yes."

Leah blushed.

Something wasn't right. He wanted to follow her to see what she was up to, but Abby was going with her, so the thought of her meeting someone did seem pretty far-fetched. Still.

"We goin' ridin' or what?" Selina tossed him a halter.

They readied their horses and rode off, making their way down the Palouse River into the deep woods. Michael followed the tracks until they came to a grove of trees. There they were, just as he had hoped.

He dismounted and held up his arms to her, waiting for her to refuse his help and jump down by herself like she always did. This time, however, she accepted his help, which pleased and surprised him. She swung her right leg over the horse's withers and placed her arms on his shoulders.

He held on to her even when her feet touched the green grass below their boots.

She gazed up at him, and his lips curled upward. "You smell nice, Selina."

"It's that lavender water Rainee give me."

He smelled her neck, letting his breath brush the hollow of her throat.

She swallowed. "What—what'cha doin'?"

"Enjoying my wife's perfume." He breathed deeply, his senses coming to full alert.

"I—I see."

He raised his head, and when their eyes connected, the sun suddenly seemed brighter in spite of the clouds covering most of it.

Selina stared up at him.

He leaned and lightly touched his mouth to hers, whispering, "Your lips are so soft."

She said nothing.

He pulled back and stars sparkled through her eyes. The urge to kiss her floated over him like the clouds above, but he wanted to take things slowly with her. "I brought you here because there's something I want to show you."

"O-Okay."

Leaving her nearly speechless was something that rarely happened.

From out of his saddle bag he grabbed his spy glass and gazed through the trees with it. "Look." He handed it to Selina and stood behind her. "Hold it up to your eye and look over there." He reached his arm around her and pointed to a place in the midst of the trees. The scent of lavender and soap swirled around him like the air from a crisp spring day. He needed to concentrate on showing her what he'd found. *Focus, Michael, focus. And not on Selina and how nice she smells and how good she feels in your arms.*

Selina held the spy glass against her right eye and shifted her head one way and then the other. Michael knew the exact moment she spotted it. "Is that—is that who I think it is?"

"Yes. It's your wolf pup."

She turned to glance up at him. The surprised innocence of a child on Christmas morning clothed her features. "How—how did you find her?"

Those lips of hers so close to his were tempting.

Slow, Michael, slow, remember?

He forced his gaze from her mouth and onto the woods where the pup was. "I noticed the wolf pack the other day. I wondered if the pup you doctored was among them, so I kept track of their whereabouts until I could show you that she's back with her family and doing well."

"You—you did that for me?" She blinked.

"Yes."

"Thank you, Michael. That was mighty nice of you. I'm much obliged." She walked in the direction of the pack of wolves.

Michael caught up to her and clasped her upper arm, halting her. "Stay here. It's too dangerous. We're taking a chance by being this close as it is." Although his voice was but a whisper, he kept it stern along with the look he sent her.

"I just want to see if her leg is healed."

"It is. If you want to see for yourself, then take a look through the glass."

She held it up to her eye again. "Can't see it. The others are in the way."

"Just wait."

"There's that ole patience thing again." She sighed.

"Sure is." He chuckled. "They're starting to get restless. We'd better go."

She nodded. "Thank you, Michael, for bringin' me here. It means a lot to me."

"I know. That's why I did it."

"You sure can be sweet when you wanna be, you know that?"

"When I want to be, huh?" Mirth inched his lips into an upward curl.

"Didn't mean it like that."

"I know what you meant. It's okay. You can be pretty sweet yourself…when you want to be." He winked. "Now let's go."

They mounted their horses and rode through the woods. Wind foraged through the trees, rustling through the branches and finding its way to them.

Michael gazed up at the sky, wondering when it had turned so dark. Being in Selina's presence and seeing her joy and surprise had him shutting out everything else around him.

Lightning flashed in the distance. Thunder rumbled above them within seconds.

"We'd better hurry and take cover. That storm's moving in here fast. We'll never make it home in time. Follow me."

Branches and pine needles crunched under the

horses' hooves as they rode swiftly through the trees, bushes and foliage. She followed the path he cut.

The wind blew harder, lifting Selina's hair, tangling the strands with its rising fury.

"Hurry, Selina." The coolness of the storm descended on them. Lightning struck again and again and each clap of thunder grew louder and quicker.

The sky opened and rain pelted down on them, soaking their clothing.

Michael led Selina through the trees to a hidden cave he'd discovered deep in the hillside when he and his family had first arrived in the Idaho Territory. It had been dug years ago by an old prospector looking for gold.

They stopped at the large cavern's opening and dismounted. Both Macy and Michael's horse Bobcat were used to being in closed-in spaces, so he grabbed the reins from Selina and led them inside the dimly lit cave. Just inside the opening, he dropped their reins, knowing they would stand still as long as their restraints were in that position. Haydon had trained them well.

Wet horse and leather and a hint of sulfur filled the damp interior of the cave.

Chills rippled through Michael's body.

Selina loosened the stampede string on her hat and let it fall against her back. She stood, rubbing her arms. He removed the blanket from one side of his saddle bags and draped it around her shoulders, closing it snug against her neck.

"Thank you kindly."

He nodded.

"Aren't you cold?"

"A little."

"Well, here." She moved one arm out in a gesture for him to join her under the blanket.

He nodded and she removed the blanket, draped it around him, tucked herself under his arm and pulled the ends of the blanket together.

"This is rather cozy, don't you think?" Michael gazed down at her.

"Sure is." She smiled up at him.

They stood there, staring outside.

Thunder rumbled above them.

Wind whistled through the trees.

But the sound Michael heard most was his own heartbeat pulsating in his ears. What was it about being so close to her that set his heart racing? Was this what love felt like, or was this just some physical attraction because of Selina's beauty? Isn't that what had lured Haydon to Melanie? *Lord, help me to not make the same mistake. Guide me where Selina's concerned, Father.*

He continued to silently pray about the situation and for his wife until peace filled his soul.

Selina laid her head against Michael's chest. His soothing heartbeat drew her soul further into his. She wanted him to kiss her again. She loved the feel of his lips on hers. And every time he kissed her, her toes curled and her knees turned to mush. Each day she was around him, she loved him more. If she wasn't mistaken, he seemed to be caring for her more and more, too—and trying to make this marriage work. She sure hoped so, hoped it wasn't just some fancy on her part.

The hankering to kiss him settled into her chilled bones. His body heat warmed her outsides, but his kisses would warm her insides. Of that she was certain. *Wonder what he'd think if I kissed him.* Only one way to find out.

Selina slid her head up his chest and raised it to meet his eyes. Smiling eyes that pulled her in faster than quicksand, only not nearly as dangerous. Or maybe they were. A heap of courage was what she needed to follow through with her plan to kiss him. Willing some into herself, she pushed forward, "Michael, would you mind kissin' me again?"

His lips slowly curved into a smile, and his eyes sparkled like sun on water. "Don't mind if I do."

He shifted her body around until she faced him. Strong arms wrapped around her, cocooning her with them and the blanket.

His face leaned toward hers at the same time hers raised upward. Lips soft, yet firm, took hold of hers in the gentlest way.

Being wrapped in his arms felt right and good.

After what seemed like forever, he raised his head. "Somethin' wrong?"

"No. Nothing's wrong." He smiled and his voice sounded breathless and croaky. "It's stopped raining. We'd better head for home."

She wasn't ready to leave, though. "What about the lunch you packed? I'm mighty hungry."

"I am, too," he whispered, his eyes swirled with emotion. "Let's eat, first."

Could it be that Michael was falling in love with her? For the first time since she got here, she had hope for just that. And that hope set her stomach and heart to fluttering as much as it did when Michael kissed her. *Lord, have my prayers been answered?*

Chapter Thirteen

The next day, Selina went to check on Rainee. Afterward, she went home, changed from her dress into some trousers, grabbed her rifle, placed the sling around her neck and went for a long walk through the trees.

She took in a deep breath, enjoying every little aroma that mid-September in the Idaho Territory brought her way—moist leaves, pine, forest dirt and a hint of rain.

Stems of light filtered down through the trees from the bright afternoon sun. She walked higher and higher up the mountain. She stopped between two cedar trees and slowly followed their trunks upward with her eyes. Those giants sure made a person feel small. They were so tall that it looked like they could reach up with their branches and touch the few clouds speckling the sky.

"God, You sure outdone Yourself with these. They're mighty pretty to behold. Thank You, Lord, for allowin' me to be a part of somethin' so wonderful. I just love it here, Lord. And Lord, iffen there's any way, could You help me and Michael to become a real family someday? I'd sure be beholden to You. Thank You kindly, Lord."

She continued walking. Every once in a while, she stopped to smell and to feel the softness of the wild pink rose petals, to admire the brown center in wild daisies, the fine bright yellow color of buttercup flowers and the different kinds of bush berries. Some berries she hadn't seen before. She wondered if they were something she could eat. But not knowing for sure, it was best to leave them alone.

She walked through fields of grass that almost reached her waist. Her eyes took in the green-and-gold rolling hills of Paradise Haven. A name most fitting.

Birds entertained her with their happy songs as she continued to take in the area Michael had called the Palouse.

Snuggled against a hillside with dirt patches, grass and bushes stood an old broken-down house and a barn. Curiosity got the best of her.

She headed toward the buildings, running her hands over the top of the tall grass blades and enjoying the soft yet stiff feel of them against her fingertips.

Off to the right of the house stood a large cottonwood tree and on its left a grove of green bushes.

No glass filled the windows or doors. Part of the roof had caved in and the chimney was in mighty poor shape, broken into all kinds of pieces.

She stepped up to the door and peeked inside. A broken drop-leaf table lay on the floor along with a heap of broken boards.

She strained to see everything from the doorway but couldn't, so she placed one foot on the wooden floor to make sure it was safe before she placed the other one, too. The planked floor was solid as a rock, so she took a look around, imagining what the place had been like before being deserted.

In one bedroom sat a rusty bed frame and an old broken-down dresser with only one drawer that hung as if it were fixing to fall at any minute.

She looked at the staircase, wondering what was up there. Should she go see? Was it safe? She tested the first step. It creaked under her weight but felt pretty solid to her.

Careful not to get in too big a rush, she tested each step as she made her way up.

At the third step from the top she could see what was in the open space. Besides busted-up chimney bricks and broken boards, the only other thing here was a wooden box in the corner. From what she could tell, it looked like it wasn't in too bad of shape. She wondered what might be in it.

The boards groaned as she slowly made her way toward it.

Holding her rifle back out of the way with one hand, she leaned over and raised the lid.

A mouse darted out from behind it, startling her.

Selina screamed and jumped back.

The crunching sound of splintering wood echoed loudly in the empty space.

The floor disappeared under Selina's feet, dropping her through it hard and fast.

Her legs buckled when they hit a pile of broken boards below, and her head slammed against the iron bed frame.

Then everything went black.

Dragging from exhaustion, Michael lugged his body up the darkened steps to his house. No lights shone through the windows and no food aromas greeted him. "That's strange." His words floated into the black pitch of night. The only sounds he heard were the squeaks of the screen door and front door as he stepped inside.

No food waited on the stove or the table. No lit lanterns. And no Selina in sight. "Selina!" he hollered.

Silence.

"Now where could she be?" He searched the house, checking each room, including the pantry and cellar, calling her name as he did. By the time he reached the last room, he was starting to panic.

His attention trailed to where her rifle usually rested, but it wasn't there. He quickly lit a lantern and flew outside, yelling her name and listening for a response.

Coyotes yapped in the distance.

Crickets chirped.

He rounded the house, searching for her. When he couldn't find her, he hurried to his brother's house and knocked on the door. He hated to bother Haydon, having a new baby and all, but Jesse and his family were having dinner with some of the neighbors.

The door swung open. "Michael? What's the matter?" Haydon asked as Rainee walked over.

"I can't find Selina." Michael stepped inside. "Did she come by and see you today, Rainee?"

"Yes, she did. But that was hours ago." Wrinkles lined her forehead.

"She's not home and I can't find her anywhere. Did she say where she was going after she left here?"

"She said it was such a lovely day that she wanted to go for a walk and explore the ranch. You think she got lost?" Rainee turned fearful eyes on him and then up at Haydon.

Haydon slipped his arm around Rainee and pulled her to his side. "I'm sure she's fine, darling." He smiled, but even Michael could tell it was forced.

"I'm going looking for her." Michael whirled around.

"Wait. I'll go with you." Haydon looked behind him at their maid, Esther. "Esther, will you throw together some food and water in case we're gone all night?"

"Yes, sir."

"I'll go saddle up the horses. Will you run and get Smokey?" Michael asked. "If anyone can find her, he can."

"That's right. He found Rainee." Haydon lovingly looked down at Rainee and gave her a quick kiss.

He sure had. Their family would be lost without the man who was more like a father to them than a long time friend and employee.

"Meet you at the barn," Michael said.

"Be careful," he heard Rainee say to Haydon, and his gut twisted.

"I will." Haydon sprinted toward Smokey's small cabin, and Michael ran to the barn, the lantern swinging in front of him.

Worry had now escalated into panic.

In the short six weeks Selina had been there, he realized only now how much she had come to mean to him. He admired her free spirit. How she took the time to enjoy the little things in life. How she helped anyone who had need and asked for nothing in return. He admired her spunk and her love for animals. Well, except when she brought them into the house. So far, he'd come home to a cat, a wolf and a pig, and during wheat harvest, a raccoon, a bird and a squirrel, which he immediately shooed out despite Selina's protests.

He stepped inside the barn. His shadow danced against the wall as he lit another lantern and hung them on the hooks on the wall.

Michael finished saddling the last horse, then tied a couple of rolled blankets onto each one. Smokey stepped inside the barn with his bloodhound, Skeeter, a gift from Haydon. Haydon had brought Skeeter back from his trip to Rainee's place in Little Rock, Arkansas. Said it was the perfect gift for the man who eleven years ago had used his tracking skills to help find Rainee when she'd fled into the woods to escape her evil brother's plans to sell her to a murderer.

"Thanks for coming, Smokey."

Gray completely covered his head and more wrinkles lined his tanned, leathery face, but the man could just about outdo all of them when it came to working. "Anytime, boss."

"How many times have we told you to stop calling us boss? You're family, remember?"

"No, he doesn't," Haydon said, stepping into the barn. He had three canteens in one hand and an overstuffed sack of food in the other. Michael's brother handed each of them a canteen, then tied the bag of food onto his horse's saddle. Haydon's horse, Rebel, danced, ready to go. So was Michael.

"Thanks, Smokey. Haydon." Michael eyed each one. "Let's go."

They blew out the lanterns and led their horses from the barn.

"You have anything of Selina's with you for Skeeter to track?" Smokey asked.

"No. But I need to stop at the house and get a jacket. I'll grab something then."

Smokey gave a quick nod. "A hairbrush or anything will do."

They mounted their horses and headed to his house. Michael ran inside and up the stairs. His attention fell to Selina's hairbrush. What was left of the old thing, anyway. Instantly he felt horrible. Why hadn't he made sure all of her needs were met? As he ran down the stairs he wondered what else she needed that he didn't know about. He made a mental note to find out.

Michael grabbed his jacket, shoved a few candles and a box of matches in his pockets and raced out the door.

Smokey and his dog stood next to his horse. The older man stepped forward and took the brush from Michael and placed it under Skeeter's nose. "Find her, Skeeter."

The bloodhound bayed and headed into the trees. Michael and Smokey quickly mounted and took off after Skeeter and Haydon, who was right behind the dog.

An hour later they topped a hill and saw McCreedy's abandoned house. Skeeter bayed, ran down the hill and disappeared inside the house.

"Heeya!" Michael tucked his legs tight into Bobcat's sides. He leaned back as the horse jarred his way down the hill.

The hound continued to bay.

Michael reached the house first. Before his horse even stopped, Michael dismounted and rushed inside the broken-down house. "Selina!" He followed Skeeter's bark. It was only when he got closer that he noticed a small form lying on the floor on a heap of splintered wood. "Selina." He rushed to her side and dropped to his knees.

"Don't move her, Michael." Smokey's silhouette filled the doorway. "Let me check her over first," he cautioned as he headed toward Michael.

Michael nodded, even though he knew Smokey couldn't possibly see him. He reached in his pocket, pulled out the candles and matches and lit them. Candlelight flickered across his wife's pale face. He wanted to pull her into his arms and cradle her, to make everything okay.

Haydon stepped up next to them, holding a canteen. He took one of the candles from Michael. "Is—is she all right?" His words were rough and broken and mingled with fear.

Michael looked at Smokey, praying about what the next words would be.

Smokey didn't answer. Instead, he took the opened canteen from Haydon, raised Selina's head, put the canteen to her lips and tilted it. Water ran down Selina's chin and neck.

She didn't stir.

Michael struggled to remain calm, but panic was taking over. "Smokey?"

The elderly man cleared his throat. "Doesn't seem to be any broken bones or anything." His eyes slowly trailed upward at the gaping hole in the ceiling. "She's one lucky woman to be alive."

Michael drew in a long breath of relief.

After a moment of pause, Smokey tried to give Selina another drink.

She still didn't stir. His friend stood.

"Smokey?" Michael looked up at him from his squatting position. "Why isn't she responding?"

Smokey shook his head. "She has a huge knot on her head."

"I'm taking her to Doc Berg's." Michael scooped her up into his arms and stood.

"That's a good idea." Haydon's voice sounded off-pitch and strained and his eyes had a blank stare. Instantly, Michael knew why.

He wanted to comfort his brother, to ease the memories, but before he had a chance to say anything, Haydon spun on his heel and headed outside.

Smokey and Michael exchanged a knowing look. "He'll be all right, boss." Smokey's words were full of assurance, and Michael knew he was right. Haydon was a survivor. His brother would deal with his feelings and move on like he always did. Still, his heart hurt for the pain his brother had suffered. But nothing could be done about that now. Besides, Selina needed his undivided attention.

They stepped outside the old house and strode up to their horses.

"Give her to me," Haydon said.

Michael looked over at him with questioning eyes.

"I know what you're thinking, Michael, and yes, it's hard seeing her like this. But you have a chance to help Selina. I didn't with Melanie. Hand her to me until you can get on your horse. Then go. Take care of your wife."

His brother was right. He did have a chance to help Selina. With a heavy heart, Michael handed his wife over to Haydon, then swung into the saddle. His brother placed Selina's limp form into his arms and gave him the reins.

"Thanks for helping me, Haydon. I'm really sorry you had to see this." He glanced down at his wife and then back at Haydon.

"I'll be fine," Haydon assured him with sad yet sturdy eyes. "Now go on."

Michael gave a quick nod to his brother, then to Smokey. He reined his horse toward town. All the way there, he prayed, holding her close, willing her to stay alive and thanking God they had even found her.

Voices. Selina heard voices. But they sounded far away. Where was she and why couldn't she open her eyes?

"Selina? Can you hear me?"

Michael? She struggled to open her eyes. Finally, she could see through a small slit.

Michael's face blurred and pitched and swayed before her.

She concentrated on opening her eyes wider. Michael's face was no longer fuzzy or drifting.

Words tried to leave her mouth, but they never did. It was as if they were stuck in her throat.

"Here." A cool hard surface touched her lips. "Drink this?"

The liquid pooled into her mouth. She coughed, then swallowed. More liquid. "What happened?" she asked like a croaking frog.

"You fell and hit your head, love."

Love? Did he just call her love? She must have hit her head a lot harder than she thought. Now her mind was playing tricks on her. She tried to sit up, but pain shot through the back of her head. She reached toward that spot, but Michael's calloused hand clutched hers.

"Don't. You have a bump the size of an egg back there."

Another round of pain sliced through her head like the sharp blade of a hunting knife.

"How's our patient doing?"

Selina's attention wobbled over to the door. Doc Berg came walking toward her.

"Hi, Doc."

"How you feeling, Miss?"

"Like someone took a moonshine jug and smashed it against the back of my head."

Michael moved so the doctor could sit in the chair he'd been sitting in.

"You're one lucky young lady. From what Michael here tells me, you fell through the upstairs floor. You'll be sore for some time, but I didn't find any broken bones, only a few scrapes and bruises. You would have ended up with a whole lot more if you hadn't been wearing those pants."

She looked over at Michael and gave him a look that said, *see, pants ain't always a bad thing.*

He offered her a half grin.

"I'm going to keep you here overnight so I can keep an eye on you and make sure that bump doesn't get any bigger and that you don't get a fever."

"I can do that," Michael said, shocking Selina plumb down to her toes.

"I thought everyone at your place was busy harvesting the wheat."

"No, we're all done with that."

Doc Berg stood and faced Michael. "I'll be honest with you. I don't like the looks of that bump on her head, Michael. Someone needs to stay with her around the clock for at least a couple of days."

"I can."

"How can you do that and get your chores done, too, Michael?" Selina asked. "Haydon will probably stay home a couple more days with Rainee. So that leaves Jesse, Smokey and your hired hands to do the rest. I can't do that to them. So I think Doc's right. It's best iffen I just stay here."

"I'd feel a whole lot better if she stayed here, too, Michael. Me and the missus can take turns keeping an eye on her. We know what to look for, where you wouldn't."

Michael didn't say a word, but finally he nodded. "Okay. Well, I'm going to head on home, then. I'll be by sometime tomorrow to check on you." He leaned over and gave her a kiss on her cheek. "Do what Doc says and don't be giving him a hard time, okay?"

"Me? I never do stuff like that."

Michael narrowed one eye and hiked a brow before turning to the doctor. "You have to watch her, Doc. She's a feisty one who doesn't take kindly to being told what to do."

She saw a look pass between the two men along with a smile.

"Okay, y'all. I promise I'll behave and do what Doc says."

Michael flashed her a satisfied grin. "I'll see you later, love." And he was out the door.

Love. So her mind hadn't been playing tricks on her after all. She really had heard him call her *love* earlier. She liked the sound of it. Things were finally looking up between them. The two of them just might have a chance at a real marriage after all. That thought curled her lips and toes and warmed her heart.

Michael hated riding off, leaving Selina behind. Seeing her lying on the floor of that old house made him realize how important she had become to him. Who would have thought he would ever even think of her in a romantic, loving way? After all, to him she was the lady in trousers. And when he first saw her in those trousers, *lady* wasn't really the word that came to mind.

Today, the thick denim trousers had actually protected her legs from getting shredded with lacerations. He was glad she didn't listen and do everything he liked or wanted and that she stayed true to her real self. Because if she hadn't, she could have ended up... He didn't, no, couldn't, think about that.

Tack rattling, leather creaking, branches breaking and leaves rustling filled the silence, along with wolves howling in the distance. Their low mournful sounds made him lonely.

More lonely than he'd been even back when having a wife was just a nice idea. Strange how life kept bringing him around to how nice it was to have Selina as his wife.

Chapter Fourteen

Outside Doc Berg's house, Michael checked his pocket watch for the tenth time. 7:00 in the morning. The lights had been on for more than an hour, and Michael couldn't stand the wait any longer. He hurried up the porch and rang the bell.

Through the glass he could see Doc Berg walking down the hall toward the door. When Doc opened the door, he said, "I figured you'd be early. Only I figured you would have gotten here long before now." He stepped aside to let Michael in. "Are those for me?" Doc grinned, looking at the bunch of goldenrods and asters in Michael's hands.

"Sorry, Doc, but they're for Selina. And I've been here since six. I just didn't think you'd appreciate me waking you up."

"I've been up most of the night."

Concern squeezed Michael's heart. "Is Selina okay?"

Doc removed the spectacles off his nose and eyed Michael. "She had a rough night."

"Is she okay now? May I see her? I promise not to wake her."

Doc paused, then nodded. "Let me take those. I'll have the missus put them in some water."

"Thanks." Michael handed him the wildflowers then quietly opened the door to where Selina was. The shades were drawn and the lantern in the corner was turned down low. Michael sat in the chair beside her bed.

Even in the dim light, her cheeks looked pale against the white blanket. She might act tough, but seeing her like this showed him that wasn't the whole truth. Just like she had in the old house, she once again looked frail and helpless. But now she had him to take care of her. And take care of her he would.

Michael bowed his head and closed his eyes. He clasped his hands, rested his elbows on his knees and prayed silently. "Lord, I pray for a complete recovery for Selina. Help me to love her the way she deserves to be loved." That familiar fear shrouded him like a suffocating cloak.

Would he ever be free to trust in their relationship? To trust in love?

Michael shifted his gaze to her and watched her sleep. Minutes dragged by. He stood and paced the room, then watched her sleep some more. He kept the vigil for almost two hours.

Worn out from worry, he sat back down in the chair.

Still sleeping, Selina turned her face toward him and a strand of hair fell across her cheek.

Careful not to wake her, he brushed it aside, letting his finger linger on her soft skin. He longed for her to wake up, even if it meant eating crawdad tails and possum stew. He shook off that thought, knowing he must be completely losing it to even think such a thing.

But no matter how far he pushed those thoughts away, he couldn't shake the feeling of what it would be like to lose her. "Please, God, just let her be okay. Please."

"Michael." Mrs. Berg rested her hand on his shoulder.

Startled, he stood.

Doc's wife set the flowers on the stand near Selina's bed and motioned for him to follow her.

"You've been here more than two hours now. There's no reason for you to stay. She's heavily sedated and will probably be asleep for a few more hours. Why don't you go on home?"

Michael's heart yanked him back and forth, stay or go, stay or go. He hated leaving his wife. But sitting here, watching her like this was driving him nuts. "You're right. I don't want to risk waking her, especially after Doc said she had a rough night. Would you please tell her I was here and that I'll be back later?"

Mrs. Berg nodded.

Michael turned his attention toward Selina. Needing the connection to her, he wanted to lean down and kiss her cheek but he was afraid he would wake her, so he didn't.

As hard as it was to do, he headed toward the door.

Selina sat up in bed. Her head pounded and her stomach felt queasy. All night her head had ached something fierce and she'd thrown up every time the doctor fed her broth. Fresh-cut flowers on the nightstand caught her attention. She lay back down and stared at the clusters of tiny yellow and light purple flowers in a jar.

Mrs. Berg, the sweet brown-haired lady who carried

herself with poise and grace, entered the room. "You still feeling sick?"

"Yes, ma'am. I am."

"How's your head?"

"Feels like someone took a sling shot and slung a rock at it."

Mrs. Berg leaned over and peered at the back of her head. When she moved back in front of Selina, her gray eyes were comforting.

"That was so sweet of your husband to bring you those goldenrods and asters," Mrs. Berg said.

Selina glanced at them again. So that's what they were…goldenrods and asters. "Michael was here? When?"

"Early this morning. He stayed quite a while. You were sleeping so soundly he didn't want to wake you, especially after the night you had. He asked me to tell you that he was here and that he'd be back later."

Disappointed she has missed him, she wanted to pick up the flowers and smell them, but her stomach hadn't settled. "You got any ginger?"

"Ginger? No. Why?"

"'Cause nothin' works better for an upset belly than ginger."

"I'm sorry. We don't have any. Would you like me to bring you more broth?"

"No. No." She waved her hand. That was the last thing she wanted. "What I would like is to go home."

"I can't let you do that. My husband wants to make sure you're better before he lets you leave here."

"But I have to go. We're havin' an end-of-harvestin' party at the ranch, and I wanna help."

"Well, even if you could go home, you're going to have to take it easy for a few days anyway."

Selina hated sitting around, wasn't used to it. She liked to keep busy. Normally no aching head would stop her, but she'd promised Michael, and she wouldn't go back on her word.

"Do you have any mendin' that needs doin'? I've gotta have somethin' to do."

"I do. But I'm not bringing it to you, dear. You need to rest."

"Can't rest. I don't want to. I want to—"

"Are you giving Mrs. Berg a hard time?" Michael strode into the room looking more handsome than anyone had a right to. He looked at Selina with raised eyebrows then at Mrs. Berg. "Hello again, Mrs. Berg. I'm sorry. I can't leave my wife alone for a minute without her giving someone a hard time. She's one stubborn, determined woman."

Selina crossed her arms. "I ain't stubborn. Just don't like bein' stuck in bed is all."

"Well, like it or not, doctor's orders."

"Hmmpft. Don't you got chores to do or somethin'?"

"Nope. Finished them so I could come here and bother you."

"I'm sick, remember?"

"I'll leave you two alone." Mrs. Berg looked from one to the other with a smile on her face. She turned and headed toward the door. "Young lovers are so cute."

Selina felt the blush from the tip of her toes plumb up to tip of her head. Lovers? If only the woman knew. "Thank you kindly for the flowers, Michael."

"I knew you would enjoy them. You enjoy everything."

Not everything. She didn't enjoy knowing Michael didn't love her. Oh, he was trying to and all, but love didn't shine through his eyes. Not the way it did betwixt her ma and pa and her friends who had married for love.

"What are you thinking about?"

"You." Again heat fired up her cheeks.

"What about me?" He took her hand in his.

"Was mighty thoughtful of you to bring me flowers. When did you find time to do that?"

"Early this morning. On the way here, I picked them."

"I was sure sorry I didn't get to see you earlier."

"I didn't want to wake you. Doc Berg said you were up sick all night. How are you feeling now?"

"Not too good. I'd feel a whole lot better iffen I was at home in my own bed."

"Now, Selina. You know what Doc said."

"I know, I know. But I don't have to like it."

He sat on the bed and pulled her into his arms. "I hate seeing you like this."

"I hate bein' like this."

He held her and gently rocked her and she let him.

Michael held her in his arms until she fell sound asleep.

Doc Berg stepped into the room.

Michael held a finger to his lips and pointed to her.

"She sleeping?" Doc Berg whispered. "That's good. You should go and let her get some rest."

He didn't want to go. He'd just gotten here. Besides, it was lonely around the house without her. Boring even. As much as he hated to admit it, he was getting used to her antics, her high-spirited ways, even to having critters in the house and strange foods on the table. Truth was, it just felt odd being there by himself.

But he couldn't very well expect her to listen to the doctor if he didn't. Careful not to wake her, he laid her back on the bed and stood. He gazed down at the woman who was beautiful inside and out.

He felt a tug on his shirtsleeve.

Doc Berg motioned for him to step outside the room and into his office.

"Have a seat." Doc sat behind a mahogany desk covered with papers and sprinkled with medicine bottles.

Michael sat in the cushioned chair across from the desk.

Doc Berg rested his arms on the desk and leaned toward Michael. "I'm worried about Selina, Michael. That lump on her head hasn't gone down. In fact, it's gotten a little bigger. I'm concerned there may be some bleeding on the brain. Sometimes bleeding comes slow or fast. If that spot doesn't go down or get any smaller by this evening, I'm afraid I may have to operate."

Michael listened in horror as Doc explained in detail exactly what he had to do to relieve the pressure. His stomach roiled as he thought of the drilling procedure. "Sounds dangerous." He swallowed hard.

"It is. That's why I'd like your consent to do it if I need to."

How could Michael give his consent to do something that was so dangerous? "I need to talk to Selina about this first and see what she says."

"No. I don't want to worry her about this. Her getting upset could cause more problems." He stood and so did Michael. "Think about it and give me your decision. Don't wait too long. Her life may depend on it."

Hearing those words was like a stab to the heart. Michael watched Doc's back as he headed down the hallway, rounded the corner and disappeared. How could Doc ask him to make such a decision?

He needed guidance. Michael hurried down the stairs, stopping only long enough to tell Doc he would be back later.

On the way home, he prayed for wisdom. None came. In the field, he saw Jesse riding in the midst of the cows. Michael coaxed his horse to go faster, slowing only when he neared the herd.

"What's wrong?" Jesse rode out to meet him. "Is Selina all right?"

"I'm not sure." He told him what Doc said.

"Sounds to me like you have no choice."

That's what he was afraid of. Worry and fear crawled inside him, and he closed his eyes to block them out.

"You love her, don't you?" Jesse asked with gentleness.

Did he? He didn't even know anymore. "I've been trying to."

"That's part of your problem. *You're* trying to do it under your own strength. Jesus said, 'Apart from me, you can do nothing.' But God didn't leave it there, Michael. The Bible says, 'I can do all things through Christ who strengthens me.'" Jesse draped his arm over the saddle horn. "Any time we try to do things under our own strength or our own power, we are setting ourselves up for failure.

"The Lord wants His children to depend on Him, Michael. You may not be able to love Selina on your own, but God can do it through Christ as you submit to Him. Ask God to give you a deep, lasting love for your wife, Michael, and He will."

"I'm so confused, Jess. I thought I loved her when she was like Rainee. Then when she got here and wasn't, I didn't think there was any way I could love her. Now part of me can't imagine life without her and part of me thinks I'm crazy for even thinking that."

"Oh, I get it. You thought you married a fantasy woman."

"No, that's not what I did."

"Yeah you did. You thought if you married the perfect woman you dreamed of, then everything would always be perfect and you'd never get hurt. Well, I hate to tell you brother, but that's not reality. Real love ain't no fantasy—it's messy, and sometimes it's downright hard. And with real love there's no guarantee you'll never get hurt. You can't love somebody with one foot out of the door. If you love her, it's got to be all the way, no matter what happens. That's real love—not this straddling the fence thing you've got going on."

Michael put his head down as every fear he ever had attacked him. Jesse was right. That's exactly what he had wanted—the perfect woman who would never hurt him. But that woman didn't exist. Never did and never would. And now love looked even scarier than it had before.

Jesse's words applied to letting go of his fears, too. To be free to love Selina, he needed to keep on giving his fears to Christ every time they came knocking on the door of his heart and mind. "Will you pray with me, Jess?"

"Sure."

They bowed their heads and prayed not only that he would make the right decision about Selina's medical condition but also about the state of his heart. When Jesse was done, Michael had hope and a renewed vigor to continue courting his wife. But first he needed to decide what to do about the consent to operate.

He thanked his brother and headed back into town, racking his brains about what to do. "Michael, what did Jess just get through telling you not even ten minutes ago? God wants you to depend on Him—not yourself." Michael's voice echoed through the trees, bounced back at him and whipped him upside the head. "Didn't you just read the other night about if you needed wisdom to ask God?"

Over the green rolling hills, he rode. He closed his eyes. "Lord. I need wisdom. You said if I asked for it, You'd give it to me. Well, Lord, I'm asking. Show me what to do about Selina. Give me wisdom beyond my own understanding because I sure need it right now."

He opened his eyes and raised his head. "Even better, I'm asking for Your mercy and Your grace to heal Selina. I pray these things in Your Son's name. Amen." Peace unlike any he'd ever known before nested inside him.

Selina opened her eyes. The first thing she saw was Michael. "Hi." She smiled.

"Hello yourself." He leaned closer to her. "How are you feeling?"

"Better. My head doesn't smart near as bad as it did."

"Thank the Lord for answer to prayer."

"You prayed for me?"

"Sure did. Does that surprise you?"

"Everything you do lately surprises me."

"Makes life more interesting, right?"

She sat up.

Michael jumped up and propped an extra fluffy pillow behind her back.

"I sure could use somethin' to drink." She moved her tongue around inside her mouth, trying to moisten it.

"I'll get Mrs. Berg." He returned with a glass of water and a bowl of broth and sat down beside her.

Selina took the water from him. Concerned she might not be able to keep it down again, she sipped it. Her stomach was fine. She drank a little more. Still fine. Then a little more. She grinned. No more upset belly. "I'll take that broth now." Her hand reached out to Michael.

"You don't feel sick?" Hope sparked his eyes.

"No. In fact, I'm so hungry I could eat the hide off a grizzly. Ain't they got anything more than broth to eat around here?"

"Yep. You're feeling better." He smiled.

"I sure am. So you'd better watch it, mister. I just may feed you some more crawdad tails. Or better yet, some possum stew."

His blue eyes widened. "You're kidding right? Tell me you're joking."

Selina giggled. "I'm joshin' you. But, just so you know, iffen we were back home in Kentucky, we *would* be eatin' possum stew."

"I'm glad we don't live there." The serious, relieved look on his face tickled Selina. And yet at the same time, she realized once again just how wide the gap was in their worlds. They sure did live differently.

Truth was…in the short time she'd been here, she

was getting used to his ways and even liked some of them better. Some she didn't. Like wearing dresses. She wasn't sure she'd ever get used to that. Trousers were a whole heap better and more comfortable, too. Only thing was, trousers didn't put a light in Michael's eyes like dresses did.

His eyes held hers gently. "What you thinking about?"

"Trousers."

Michael laughed. "Trousers? What about them?"

"Oh, I was thinkin' how I'm still tryin' to get used to not wearin' them all the time." She tapped his chest with her finger. "You'd better appreciate it, mister. I ain't ever changed for anybody before. And to be honest with you, I'm not right sure how I feel about that or iffen I can ever learn to talk like y'all do. I'm sure you noticed I ain't doin' too good with that so far."

"I hadn't noticed." His lips held a smirk.

"You'd better be nice to me, or I'll fix you not only possum stew but gopher stew, too."

"It's nice to see you're doing better. Even if I have to put up with your threats." He grinned.

She smiled.

"I see someone is feeling better." Doc Berg entered the room, smiling.

"I sure am. Can I go home now?"

He walked around the other side of the bed and gently pressed the back of her head. His eyebrows rose.

"What's wrong?" Michael asked.

"Nothing's wrong. I'm just surprised."

"About what?"

"The lump is almost gone. This morning it was…and now it's…" He shook his head. "I don't understand."

"I do. It's called the power of prayer, Doc."

"Does this mean I can go home?" Selina asked.

"It sure does," Doc said. "But you need to rest and take it easy for a few days. And gradually introduce solid food as you can tolerate it."

"Will do, Doc." She tossed the covers aside and set her feet on the floor. "Where's my clothes?"

Doc laughed. "They're in here." He walked over to a large cabinet, opened the door and lifted her clothes off a hook. "The wife washed them for you."

"That was mighty nice of her. Please be sure to tell her thank you for me."

"I'll do that. I'll leave and let you get dressed. Don't forget—nothing strenuous for a few days, young lady."

"I'll try."

"I'll see to it." Michael sent her his take-charge look. She sent one of her own back at him. Nothing would stop her from helping with the after-harvesting party. Nothing.

After what seemed like forever, Michael pulled the buggy to a stop in front of the house. "Stay," he ordered.

She rolled her eyes, but wanting to please him, she obeyed.

He came around, swooped her into his arms and carried her onto the porch. "Close your eyes. I have a surprise for you."

Her eyes closed, he carried her inside and put her down. "You can open your eyes now."

"Oh, my." Her hands went to her face. "Oh, Michael." She walked over to the kitchen table and picked up the drawing she had done of her home back in Kentucky.

He stepped up behind her. "Do you like it?"

She turned and clutched her picture in the beautifully handmade frame to her chest. Tears leaked from her eyes but she didn't even care. "Like it? Oh, Michael, I love it. Thank you." She threw her arms around him and pressed her head into his chest.

"I thought we would hang it above the fireplace mantel, if that's okay with you. Then when you get lonesome for home, you could look at it."

"That's the sweetest, most thoughtful thing anyone's ever done for me." She stood on her tiptoes and pulled his head down to hers and kissed him. Every ounce of love she had for him she poured into that kiss. When he responded and didn't push her away, her heart smiled with even more hope.

Chapter Fifteen

~

"Selina! What are you doing?" Michael wrinkled his nose at the smell of wet pig. "You're not supposed to be doing anything strenuous, remember?"

"I ain't. I'm just givin' Kitty a bath. Besides, it's been four days since Doc told me to take it easy."

"What do I have to do, tie you to the bed?"

"You'd have to catch me first." She kept her eye on Michael while she continued scrubbing the sow.

"That can be arranged." He cocked his head, wiggled his eyebrows and took a step toward her.

Selina tossed the bucket of cold water on him, drenching the whole front side of him.

He sucked in a sharp breath. "Oh, you're going to pay for that one."

Selina tossed the bucket aside and darted off through the trees.

Michael followed her and so did Kitty, oinking all the way.

Last time he had chased Selina, she'd gotten away. This time he was ready. He glanced upward, behind him and off to the sides, making sure she didn't take him by surprise again.

Branches rustled nearby.

From the corner of his eye, he spotted her ducked behind a bush. He stopped and let out a dramatic, disappointed sigh. "Well, Kitty. It looks like we lost her. We'll just go back to the house and wait for her." Turning on his heel, he walked past Selina, pretending not to see her.

Kitty waddled behind him.

Suddenly, he whirled and latched on to Selina. "Got ya." He started tickling her neck and shoulders with one hand while the other held her tight.

In between giggles, she said, "Remember. I'm not supposed to do anythin' strenuous."

"If you can wash that pig, you're well enough to get tickled." His fingers found the spot on her waist that made her squirm the most.

"Stop, stop," she begged through her laughter.

"Not until you promise you'll rest."

"Kitty, help me!"

Kitty stuck her snout in the air and shifted her head back and forth between them.

"She can't help you. Now promise me, or I'll keep it up."

Without warning, her lips latched on to his.

Shock rippled through him so ferociously that he froze. Then as if his fingers had a mind of their own, they snaked their way through her hair at the back of her head. Michael pulled her closer.

She wrapped her arms around his neck and smiled at him.

"Uh-hmm. Am I interrupting anything?"

They yanked apart. Jake. Michael groaned. The man's timing was terrible.

"Jake, what are you doing here?"

"I heard about Selina's accident and thought I'd stop by to see if she was okay."

Selina fussed with her hair, putting even more distance between them.

"She's better now. Thank you." Michael only glanced at her.

"Glad to hear it. I was sure worried about you."

"Won't you come to the house and sit a spell, Jake? I'll fetch us somethin' to drink."

"I'd like that."

He might, but Michael wouldn't.

Selina and Jake walked side by side toward the house, leaving Michael to walk with Kitty. He wanted to say something, but he didn't want to sound like a jealous, insecure husband.

Jake stopped and turned around. "Michael, did you know that Mr. Drakes is selling out? I was just telling Selina about it."

"No. I hadn't heard that. Why?" He picked up his pace and without being too obvious he stepped between Jake and Selina.

"The missus is tired of the long winters. She wants to go back east and live in the city. Told him if he didn't, she was going without him."

Michael's gut twisted.

Jake looked past Michael to Selina. "Can't picture you ever living in the city."

"Ain't never lived in a city before. Don't plan on it, neither."

His stomach relaxed.

She scurried ahead of them, sprinted up the steps and disappeared inside the house.

Jake turned his attention back to Michael. "I hope you know how lucky you are to have found someone like her."

"I do."

Loneliness covered Jake's eyes.

"Hey, why don't you place an ad? Maybe you can get lucky, too."

"I've been thinking about it. I used to think people who did that were desperate. No offense, buddy."

"None taken."

"But there aren't many women around here who can handle the harsh winters. Even though the town's grown and the train comes through here now, the women still don't seem to stick around. Especially them city women. Good thing you got yourself a good country woman and not some highfalutin city lady."

Michael had never thought about that. What if the woman in the letters had turned out to be one of those who couldn't handle the harsh winters? Without a doubt, his fears really would have come true then.

They stepped inside the house. Selina had coffee and oatmeal cookies ready for them. An hour later, Jake stood. "Well, I'd better get on home. Got chores to do." He faced Selina. "Thanks for the coffee and cookies." Jake turned to Michael. "Thanks for the visit."

"Any time." As soon as he said it, he wanted to snatch back his words. Every time Jake came, Selina and Jake talked while he remained quiet, having nothing at all to add. Those two would have made a great pair. The thought of them together felt like someone had slung a stone into his heart. They might make a good pair, but she was his wife, not Jake's.

Standing outside on the porch, Selina said to Jake, "Are you comin' to the after-harvest party tomorrow afternoon?"

"Nothing could stop me from coming. I'm looking forward to it. I'll see you there. You too, Michael."

"Yeah. See you tomorrow." Just what he wanted to do, watch Jake occupy all of his wife's time.

"He sure is nice. I enjoy talkin' to him."

"You two sure seem to have a lot to talk about."

"We sure do." She smiled. "Do you know he keeps a goat in his house?"

"Yes. I was sitting there when he said that. Remember?"

"Oh, yeah. That's right. I plumb forgot."

That hurt.

"Well, I'd better get supper on."

"No."

"What do you mean, no?" Puzzlement darkened her brown eyes.

"Come on." He clasped her hand in his.

Her steps were like a one-legged turtle. "Where we going?"

"You'll see." He led her upstairs into the east bedroom and stopped just outside the closed door. "Okay, now close your eyes."

She eyed him suspiciously. "Why?"

"Come on, Selina. Just do it."

Her chest heaved and she nodded.

Once her eyes were closed, he waved his hand in front to make sure she wasn't peeking. Then he opened the door and led her inside. "Okay. You can open your eyes now."

Her mouth dropped open and her eyes blinked. "Oh, Michael. Are those for me?"

"Who else would they be for? Of course they're for you."

Selina walked to the bed. She glanced at the silk slippers before picking up the blue silk dress and holding it under her chin. "I ain't, I mean I have never had anythin' this purt...pretty before." She gazed up at him, then frowned. "But where would I ever wear anythin' this fancy?"

"At dinner."

"Dinner?" She looked down at her yellow muslin dress. "What's wrong with what I got on?"

"Nothing. But you'll want to wear that—" he pointed to the dress in her hands "—because I'm taking you to the finest dinner theater in town."

Selina's heart sank. She knew *finest* meant a place where she would never fit in.

"Do you like them? Mother made them."

Selina numbly ran her hand over the soft material and itchy lace. "She sure did a fine job."

He took the dress from her and laid it on the bed, then handed her a blue velvet box.

She had a feeling she knew what was in that box. When she raised the lid, her fears came to life with a punch to her gut. The dress, the shoes, the expensive jewelry, all of it represented the type of woman Michael wanted. Deserved even. And it wasn't her.

"I can't do this, Michael." She handed the box back to him.

"I don't understand. What's wrong?"

"Michael, I can't change my roots, who I am. You deserve a whole heap more than I could ever be." She bolted past him and flew down the stairs and out the door.

The trees swiped her face as she ran through the forest to the hilltop. Tears streamed down her cheeks. She hated treating Michael like that, especially after he went through all that trouble to have a dress made for her.

Tired from running, she sat down against the trunk of a large tree, wrapped her arms around her knees and rested her head on them.

"God," she said, sniffling. "I know I said my vows before You and all, and I promised to stay with Michael until death parted us. But I have to break that promise. I'm right sorry, but I shoulda seen it afore now. We're just too opposite. Michael deserves someone much better than me.

"So, I'm askin' You ahead of time to forgive me for breakin' that promise. I won't get married again and sin against You that way, but I have to set Michael free." At that thought, a thousand knives cut through her heart, shredding it slowly, torturing her soul until breath became hard to catch. Tears flooded her cheeks like a gulley wash.

She leaned her head back against the tree and closed her eyes, letting her heart have a good cry.

Suddenly, the hair on the back of her neck and arms stood.

Her eyes darted open.

She had a feeling she was being watched. By who

or what, she didn't know. But she'd hunted enough to know when she was in danger. And right now, she was in a heap of danger.

Two hours had passed since Selina left. It was dark now, and Michael was starting to get worried. He wished he'd gone after her when she first ran out. He was still nursing his wounds over the rejection of his gifts. He tried to do something nice for her by having his mother make her a beautiful gown and shoes. He'd even had the sapphire and diamond necklace and earrings shipped in from back east to go with them. But she wanted nothing to do with his gifts. It was time to put his hurt feelings aside and go looking for her.

Michael lit a lantern, grabbed his rifle and headed into the woods. "Lord, please show me where she went. And show me what to do to make things right. I'm so confused by everything right now. Please help me."

He climbed the hill, following the path, hoping to see her somewhere along it. Holding the lantern high, he checked the trees. Checked everywhere.

A loud scream pierced the air.

Michael set the lantern down and raced toward the sound.

Moonlight shed its silvery light in the darkened forest.

Dry foliage crunched under his feet.

Another scream.

He ran faster, harder, ignoring the branches slapping against his face.

"Help! Somebody help me!"

That was Selina.

His heart pounded against his ribs.

"Help!" Her voice got louder.

And then he saw her—and it.

A bear standing on its hind legs just yards away from her.

Selina held a stick almost as long as she was tall in front of her like a weapon. But that stick was no match for a hungry bear.

Instinct kicked in and Michael raised his rifle, aimed at the bear and pulled the trigger.

He missed.

The bear turned toward him, dropped on all fours and ran straight toward Michael.

Michael reloaded, aimed again and pulled the trigger.

About seven yards away, the bear dropped to the edge of the path with a crash.

Everything was silent.

Forcing his hands to stop shaking, Michael reloaded and waited, making sure the bear didn't get up. He inched his way to the animal and poked the bear with the barrel of his rifle. It didn't move. Relief poured through him, and his gaze shifted to Selina.

She stood still as a statue, staring in his direction.

He rushed to her and pulled her into his arms.

"Is it—is it dead?" Her voice trembled along with her body.

He glanced back at it, then at her. "It's dead."

Selina sunk against his chest. Her shoulders shook.

"Hey, it's okay." He rubbed her back in what he hoped was a soothing gesture. "Everything's okay."

"No, it isn't. And it ain't never gonna be, neither."

"What do you mean?"

"I'm leavin', Michael. I'm goin' back home."

He yanked his head back and stared down at her. "What? What do you mean?"

"Just what I said." She pulled out of his arms and swiped at her eyes. "I can't stay here anymore."

He wanted to snatch her back, but her look sent him a warning not to.

"You can't go. I don't want you to go. You're my wife."

"I'm sorry, Michael. But my mind is made up." With a shudder and a sigh, she turned to walk away from him.

Michael caught her by her arm and turned her around to face him. "Look, I know this isn't the ideal marriage for either one of us. But we need to work at it."

"I can't never be like Rainee. Or Aimee."

"I'm not asking you to."

"But that's the kind of woman you want. That dress and them slippers told me that. Can you look me in the eye and tell me that I'm wrong—that you don't want a woman who can wear those things and act all proper?"

Michael looked away. As much as he wanted to, he couldn't.

"Just as I thought." She yanked her arm away from him and headed down the mountain.

His head hung low in shame as he followed her. Ever since Rainee had arrived, he'd dreamed of a woman like her. One who could fit into his ranch-style life *and* the elite social life if need be. Knowing he had hurt Selina over his discarded dreams made him feel lower than low.

Selina headed upstairs to pack her meager belongings. She wouldn't be able to leave until morning, but when morning came, she'd be ready. She would ask Rainee to loan her the money for a train ticket and when she got back to Kentucky, she'd take in sewing to pay her back.

She opened the closet door and reached for a dress but stopped. Those weren't hers. She closed the door and sat on the bed.

The stairs creaked. Michael was coming.

Selina sprang up to close the door, but Michael stuck his foot inside and blocked it before she had the chance. "Please move your foot, Michael."

"Not until you let me in."

"We have nothin' more to say to each other."

"Well, maybe you have nothing more to say, but I've got plenty to say." He pushed on the door, and she was no match for his strength. His body filled the doorway.

She stepped back, crossing her arms over her chest.

"Look, Selina," he said, his voice going ragged. "It doesn't matter what I want or don't want. God chose to put you and me together and we need to stay together. We need to try and work this out. I care about you, Selina. I really do." His eyes searched hers.

She blinked. "I can't live like this, Michael. I tried wearin' dresses to please you, to be the type of woman you wanted. But when I saw that fancy ballgown, it reminded me that that was the type of woman you really want. That even with all the changes I made, I still ain't good enough for you. And never will be."

"I'm so sorry you took it that way." He took a step toward her.

She held up her hands. "Please don't come any closer."

"Why, Selina?" He took another step toward her.

"You know how I feel about you, and you comin' closer ain't helpin' things none. I ain't made of stone, you know. I got feelin's."

"So do I." He took another step.

"But they ain't for someone like me." She stepped back.

"How do you know that?" He took another step.

"I just do." She took another back.

"Are you sure?" He stepped closer.

She moved back farther until her back touched her bedroom wall. Against her will, his eyes held hers prisoner, and she was unable to pull her attention from him.

He pulled her to him.

She stiffened, but he tugged harder until she found she couldn't resist him.

His arms went about her, and he pressed her head into his chest, settling his chin atop her head. "Please stay. We need more time."

Being in his arms, breathing in the spicy forest scent that was all Michael, her heart skipped like a stone across the pond, and she found she couldn't say no.

Chapter Sixteen

Clean and refreshed from his dip in the creek, Michael headed to the house and stepped inside. In front of the fireplace, with her back to him, Selina stood wearing a blue dress and matching ribbon in her hair that flowed freely past her waist. He was glad she hadn't left, but things were far from settled between them and he knew he had a lot of ground to make up with her.

"You look beautiful, Selina." He wanted to step toward her but his feet wouldn't move, and that was a good thing because he didn't know what he would do.

"You look mighty fine yourself."

"Shall we go?"

"I'm ready whenever you are."

"What all needs to go?"

"That picnic basket." She pointed to the large basket on the table.

"What's in here?" He picked it up and opened the lid to find cloth-covered platters nestled inside. One peek and he saw his favorite cookies, Swedish oatmeal cookies, Brunscrackers, and his favorite one of all—Swedish tea cookies. The thought of the buttery sandwich cookies with the buttercream frosting in the middle made his mouth water. When he reached to grab one, she slapped him on the hand.

"Those are for the party."

"What if they all get eaten before I have a chance to get any? Can't I have just one of each?"

"I know they're your favorites, so I made plenty of extras for you. They're in the cookie jar." Was there no end to her sweetness? Making his favorite cookies. She really was a thoughtful little thing. He shoved his arm through the picnic basket handles and scooped it up, then offered her his other arm.

She looped her arm through his, and out the door and down the steps they went. "You brung, I mean, you *brought* the buggy?" Surprise fluttered through her eyes, eyes that endeared her to him.

"Can't have my wife walking and getting all dusty, now can I?"

The scent of roses surrounded her.

He set the basket on the floor of the carriage and offered her a hand up. She settled her skirt, and he climbed in next to her. Their shoulders brushed, then melded together.

Michael looked at her and smiled.

Innocent eyes gazed up at him, blinking, and her lips parted.

Like a moth drawn to flames, those sweet lips lured him to her until he found himself leaning into her and capturing her mouth in a brief but pulsating kiss.

Their lips separated and they smiled at each other before he picked up the reins. Maybe things would work after all. "Giddyup." Michael turned his horse toward the ranch yard. A quick glance at his wife and his shoulders straightened. This time he would not be embarrassed to ride in with her. Not because the lady who'd worn trousers when he'd first introduced her to everyone was now wearing a dress and looked prettier than a field of buttercups. No, it was because she was beautiful on the inside and he was proud to call her his wife.

Joining the reins in one hand, he reached over and clasped hers.

Her gaze slid to their adjoined hands, then turned up at him, questioning him with a look only. He answered with one of his own—admiration and pride.

Buggies and wagons nestled against the base of the trees in the ranch yard. Tepid air drifted down the mountain, but the sun balanced it, making it a warm, but not too scorching, day.

"There's Rainee. I can't wait to see Haydon Junior again."

He parked the buggy and helped her down. His eyes scanned the crowd of neighbors. Unlike the last time they'd gathered together, surprised looks were quickly replaced with admiration.

He grabbed the picnic basket with one arm and offered her the other, leading her into the crowd.

Women gathered around Selina, gushing about how beautiful she looked and crowding him away from her. "I'll go put this on the table," he said over the flock of ladies' heads.

She nodded and turned her attention back to the women.

On his way to add their basket, Rainee, carrying Haydon Junior, came walking toward him.

"Hello, Michael," Rainee said passing him by.

"Whoa, just a minute there. Where are you going in such a hurry that you can't even stop and let Uncle Michael see his nephew?"

"I wanted to see Selina."

"Seems like you and everyone else." He glanced over to where she stood.

"She sure looks lovely."

"She sure does."

"Her reading has improved greatly, too."

Shock slammed into him. "Her reading?"

"Yes, she—" Rainee stopped. Her eyes widened in horror. "Oh, Michael. I was not supposed to say anything. She would be quite displeased if she knew I had. Oh, my. Please, do not tell her I told you. It slipped out."

He rested his hand on her arm. "Relax, Rainee. I won't say anything." Michael darted a glance over toward Selina, then turned his attention back onto Rainee. "How long she been learning to read?"

"Ever since she arrived."

Michael didn't know why, but the thought of her trying to improve herself blessed him.

"Please, do not tell her I let it slip. Promise me you will not."

"I won't, Rainee. I promise. Now let me see that baby."

She handed Haydon Junior over to him. Michael tucked him to his chest, and the hunger to be a father returned. His attention once again slid over to Selina. Maybe there was a chance for them to be a family after all.

"Okay. Give me my son back. I want to go see Selina."

Michael did as he was told and watched Rainee walk

away and inch her way into the crowd surrounding his wife. He continued to watch as Selina took his nephew from Rainee. She looked so natural holding a baby in her arms. He visualized her holding their child, and he smiled at the image.

The dinner bell rang. The ladies separated from Selina in search of their spouses. Michael strolled over to Selina and offered her his arm. They gathered around the table with the rest of their neighbors, family and ranch hands.

Haydon's voice boomed as he spoke, "Let's bow our heads." When he finished praying, women bustled about uncovering dishes. Families lined up at the tables, filling their plates with a menagerie of foods.

Once he and Selina had their plates filled, they found seats.

Within seconds, Jake strode up. "Mind if I join you?"

Yes, he minded. What was with Jake coming around so much lately? Michael thought he meant no harm, but now he was beginning to wonder.

Selina nudged him in the side.

"No, no, don't mind at all."

Jake smiled at Selina as he lowered his bulky frame down. "You're looking prettier every time I see you. Is that a new dress?"

"Yes." Selina's cheeks tinted to a light shade of pink. Was she blushing because of Jake's compliment, or was she embarrassed by the attention he had just lavished on her? Michael wasn't sure why Jake's attention to Selina bothered him so much.

This time, however, Michael wasn't going to be left out of the conversation. "Selina."

She pulled her attention away from Jake and onto him.

"Back home, did your neighbors get together after harvest season?"

"Sure did, but we gathered together when the weather changed, any time someone had a baby or when the first frost gathered on the ground. Why, any excuse we could find, us neighbors used it to get together."

"You had parties that often?"

A strand of her molasses-colored hair slipped over her shoulder. He wanted to reach over and slip it back, but not in front of Jake. Touching her always did funny things to him and he was afraid it would show.

"We sure did."

"What were they like?" Michael asked before Jake had a chance to.

"Well…" She set her fork down. "Ain't much different than this one. Except we always set up a wooden floor in the middle of a clearin' or the meadow and had us a dance. Folks brought their fiddles, guitars, banjos. Some folks even made music blowin' into empty moonshine jugs. Others would play spoons. Anythin' that made music, they used it. Always had a heap of contests, too."

"What kind of contests?" Michael found he really wanted to know.

"Contests to see who could toss an ax closest to the center of a circle. Horseshoe toss. Log sawin'. Iron skillet toss. Just about every kind of contest you could think of. Everything from gunnysack races, to berry pickin', to corn shuckin'. Womenfolk entered their pies in the pie tastin' and eatin' contests. Well, one man did, too. Piney Baker. He'd enter his blackberry pie over and over again. And every time he lost on the count of his pie crust had the texture of uncooked grits."

"What's grits?" Jake piped in.

"Y'all ain't never had grits?" Shock sang through her slow melodious voice. A voice he now enjoyed listening to. "You don't know what y'all are missin'."

"What is grits? What does it taste like?" Michael shot up his hand. "Not that I want you to make me any," he added quickly, afraid she'd make him another crazy food he wouldn't like. "I'm just curious what it is and what it's like."

"Well, it's kinda bland. But it's mighty tasty iffen you add lots of butter or cheese or sugar or syrup to it. Some folks mix it in with their eggs. Some pour redeye gravy on top. I never did that. Don't care much for the taste of that stuff."

"What stuff?" Jake asked, and Michael frowned.

"Redeye gravy."

"Never heard of it. What is it?" Jake tore off a huge chunk of buttered bread slathered with jam and shoved it into his mouth, but his focus never left Selina's face.

"It's made from ham drippings."

"Sounds like you grew up with some unusual foods," Jake said.

Frustrated that once again Jake was occupying Selina's attention, Michael tore off a chunk of Selina's Southern fried chicken. There was nothing unusual about it. She made the best chicken he'd ever eaten.

"Wasn't unusual to us." She looked at Michael, her eyes and lips twinkling. "There was one contest you could've never done, Michael."

"Oh, yeah. What's that?" Michael suddenly felt challenged.

"The crawdad eatin' contest."

She was right. He would have never been able to enter that one. The others sounded fun, though.

"Crawdad tails?" Jake looked shocked. "You eat fish bait?"

"That's what I asked her. She made me some for dinner one night. I hate to admit it, but they weren't too bad. Even though they tasted all right, I still couldn't eat them once I knew what they were. But at least they weren't frog legs. I'm glad for that."

Jake's eyebrows rose toward the sky. "You eat frog legs, too?" He looked horrified.

Michael understood Jake's reaction firsthand. He chuckled.

Selina shot him a scowl. "We sure do," she said proudly. "Y'all don't know you're missin'." Defensiveness stole her voice.

He hadn't meant to hurt her feelings by laughing.

"They're right tasty."

"Did you ever enter your fried chicken?" Michael asked. "If so, I imagine it won."

Her cheeks brightened to a light shade of red. Her gaze fell to her lap. "Sure did. Won first place every time."

"I can believe it." Jake tore off a chunk. His cheeks bulged like a chipmunk.

Conversation continued to flow as they ate. As Michael finished the last bite of his chicken, Jesse headed toward him. "Michael, can you help me a minute?"

"Sure." He stood and looked down at Selina. "Be right back."

She nodded.

Several yards away, he glanced over his shoulder and

noticed Jake had moved around to the other side of the bench and was now sitting next to Selina. He hurried and helped Jesse chase Kitty down and put her back into her pen, then strode back over to her. "Excuse me, Jake. But I believe you have my seat." He forced his lips to curl into a smile.

"Oh. Um. Sorry about that, buddy." Jake picked up his plate and hurried back to the other side of the table.

Michael sat next to Selina and faced her. "What would we need to set up a few of those contests you were talking about?"

Her eyes brightened. "You mean it?"

"Yes. I think everyone here would really enjoy them."

She threw her arms around him. "Thank you, Michael." Her breath sent shivers skittering through him. "Okay." She yanked out of his arms and leaped up from the bench. "First we'll need—"

"You need to finish eating first. And no crawdad eating contest. No mention of it, even."

"Oh, you big old teasin' polecat. Ain't time to catch any today and you know it."

"Can I help with the contest?" Jake asked.

"I don't see why not. Let's get to eatin' so we can have some fun."

Michael refused to let his jealousy come between his wife's happiness in sharing a part of her culture here in the Idaho Territory. He would work with Jake and be grateful for his help, too.

They finished eating and cleaned up.

"Okay, let's see." Selina glanced up at Michael standing near the barn. "We need to fetch a couple of cast iron skillets, an ax or two, four horseshoes, somethin' to use as a spike. Need two of them. And as many empty grain sacks and gunnysacks as you can find. I need a few dozen eggs and some clean soup spoons."

"What do you need the spoon and eggs for?"

"Well, you have teams of three. You place an egg in the spoon and carry it to the next person on your team without dropping it. Iffen you drop it, you have to go back to the startin' line. If you don't drop it, you hand off the egg and spoon to the next person. The first one to reach the finish line with a whole unbroken egg wins."

"What do they win?"

Selina pressed her finger to her lip. Just what would they win? Back home there were homemade quilts for the women who won and axes for the men. No time to do that now. Or was there? "Just a minute. I'll be right back." Selina scurried over to Katherine.

"Excuse me, Mrs. Hansen, but I need to ask Mother a question."

"I'll leave."

"No, no. Don't leave." She ducked toward Katherine.

"Mother, you know that quilt we finished?" She still couldn't get used to calling her new ma Mother. Maybe one day she would.

Katherine smiled. "Yes."

"Well, I know I made it for Michael for Christmas, but I was wonderin' iffen I could have it now."

Katherine paused, a confused look on her face.

"Is that all right?"

"Oh, sure, sure. You just took me by surprise is all."

"What do you need the quilt for?" a neighbor standing nearby asked.

"You'll see. It's a surprise."

"Oh, I love surprises," Katherine chirped. "I'll go get it."

"No. Not yet. Iffen it's all the same to you, I'll get it when I'm ready."

"That's fine, Selina."

"Thank you kindly." She gave her a quick hug and raced back to the barn.

Horse flesh, hay and saddle oil swirled up her nose. And so did dust. Oh oh. She felt a sneeze coming on. Achoo! It echoed through the barn.

"Selina's here," she heard Michael say from inside the tack room.

"How do you know it's her?" Jake asked.

"I know her sneeze."

"You two are strange. You know that?"

"Yep. Makes life interesting." Michael stepped out of the tack room with Jake on his heels.

"What you got there?" she asked Michael.

"Prizes."

"Jumpin' crickets! You're giving them away?" Her attention stuck on the brand-new halters in Michael's hand.

"Yep."

"Those sure are mighty nice prizes. Ain't ever gave anythin' that nice before back home."

"What did you give for prizes?"

"Oh, jars of preserves and pies and sometimes a pocket knife iffen it was a good crop year."

"Those sound like nice prizes," Michael said.

"I agree." Jake licked his lips and rubbed his belly.

When they finished gathering and setting everything

up, the three of them climbed onto Katherine's porch and Michael rang the bell.

Everyone stopped talking and the kids stopped playing. All attention was on her husband.

"This year, I want to do something different," Michael announced. "Something fun." He pulled Selina to him and tucked her under his arm. "Back in Kentucky, where my wife is from, when the harvesting is over, they have a get-together something like this. Only they hold contests. They even give away prizes."

Selina saw the surprised look on everyone's faces, especially her brothers- and sisters-in-law.

"So that's what we're going to do. First, we're going to start with an ax-throwing contest. Anyone who wants to participate can follow me when I'm finished talking. The other contests will be…" She listened as Michael explained the rest. When he finished talking, there was silence.

Selina's heart sank.

Michael's smile vanished.

Jake looked shocked and angry.

Suddenly, whoops and hollers filled the air.

Selina found herself being picked up and swung around. "Put me down, you ole polecat. We got contests to run." She giggled.

Three hours later, the last contest was the sack race.

"Come on." Michael grabbed Selina's hand and took her over to the table where the empty gunnysacks were lying. He picked one up and tugged on her hand, pulling her to the starting line.

"I can't do that with you, Michael. I'm too short and you're too tall."

"If it gets complicated, I'll carry you."

She hesitated. "I don't know."

"Chicken."

"Polecat. You got yourself a partner."

"Sure do." He winked at her and her heart winked in return. Only he couldn't see her heart, so she flashed him a wink of her own, and he chuckled.

Excitement and anticipation bubbled over her like water over river rocks.

At the starting line, they each put a leg into the gunnysack. A feeling of being protected washed over her. She'd always had to be the protector, and now she had a sense she could give that job to Michael. After all, wasn't that what God intended all along?

"Ready?"

"Sure am."

"Then put your arm around my waist." He smiled down at her. That one dimple peeked at her.

"Oh" was all she could manage. Her arm slipped around him. Being this close to him always turned her mind to mush.

She glanced to the left. Six other teams had joined them. Two couples, whose names she couldn't remember. And Tom and Sadie, which surprised Selina since it hadn't been all that long ago that Sadie had had her baby. But one thing she knew about Sadie, she came from tough stock. Sadie leaned past her husband and smiled at Selina.

Selina smiled back and gave a quick wave.

Abby and her friend Betsy stood next to Sadie. Next to them were Jesse and Hannah. Jake and Leah were teamed up, too. Those two made a mighty fine-looking couple, too. She wondered why the two of them didn't get hitched.

"Ready?" Haydon hollered from the end of the finish line. "On the count of three." Pistol raised, he counted. "One. Two. Three."

Bang!

Selina struggled to keep up with Michael, but she did. As they got closer to the finish line, only three couples were left. Tom and Sadie, Jake and Leah and Selina and Michael.

Yards away from the finish line, they were lagging behind, so Michael picked her up. Her legs dangled as he rushed toward the rope stretched between Haydon and Smokey.

Tom and Sadie were ahead of Jake and Leah and she and Michael by inches.

From the corner of her eye she watched Leah and Jake tumble to the ground.

Only feet left to go.

Strain and determination wrinkled Tom and Sadie's red faces as they struggled forward, stretching their necks out as far as they could just as she and Michael tumbled to the ground.

"The winners. Tom and Sadie!"

Cheers filled the yard.

Michael stood and reached his hand toward Selina, helping her up. "That was so much fun. Thank you, love." He kissed her cheek, then led her over to where the crowd stood.

"Time to give out the prizes," Michael shouted.

"Be right back." Selina rushed inside Katherine's house, snatched the quilt from the trunk and ran back to Michael's side, puffing.

Michael called out each winner's name. Men who didn't win moaned, saying they wished they'd a won a nice halter, too. "Now for the winners of the gunny-sack race… Tom and Sadie." Selina handed Michael the quilt she'd made. Her very first one.

"Oh, Tom. Look. A quilt." Sadie beamed. "We sure needed one," Sadie gushed.

Selina's heart grew to bursting.

It was getting late, so everyone pitched in and cleaned up the yard, putting tables away, loading their wagons and thanking Selina and Michael for providing such a wonderful fun-filled day with the games. Finally, the last wagon pulled out of the yard.

"I don't know about you, love, but I'm ready to head home."

"Could we do somethin' first?"

"What's that?"

"Can we take the buggy up the hill and watch the sun set?"

"Sounds nice." He gazed down at her, smiling.

They said their good-nights to the family, and Michael offered her his hand to help her into the buggy.

Up the trail they headed until they reached the top. Michael reined Bobcat to a stop.

For a few moments, neither said a word.

Michael slipped his arm around her shoulders and pulled her closer to him. Selina rested her head on his shoulder.

They sat back to watch God's masterpiece at work.

Above the shadowed rolling hills an orange sky with yellow clouds outlined the fading sun.

A perfect setting to a perfect day.

"I know why you tripped me."

"What do you mean?" Selina whispered.

"You know what I mean." His soft voice melted her

into him further. "You knew Sadie and Tom needed blankets for the winter so you tripped me so they would win."

"Are ya mad?" she whispered again.

"Mad?" He tilted her head. Their eyes connected and held. "How could I be mad at one of the sweetest gestures I've ever seen? Where'd the quilt come from, anyway?"

"From me. It was the first one I ever made."

"You're kidding?"

"I'm not."

"You really are something. You know that?"

"You keep tellin' me that. Still not sure if being somethin' is a good thing or a bad thing."

"Trust me. It's good." With those words, his lips found hers and held them for a long time.

Now, that was an even more perfect ending. The only thing that would make it better was if Michael would whisper those three little words against her lips.

Chapter Seventeen

"**Y**esterday was great," Michael told Selina over breakfast. "I don't know when I've had a better time."

"Me, too." She refilled his coffee cup.

"What are your plans for today?"

"Well, I need to go to town and pick up some supplies."

"Me, too. You want to go together?"

"Sure. I'd love to."

"Can you be ready in about," he glanced at the clock, "ten minutes?"

"I'm ready now."

Michael looked over her new black trousers. Before he'd gotten to know Selina, it would have bothered him to be seen with her wearing men's trousers, but not anymore. Now that was just Selina.

She followed his gaze. "Oh. I plumb forgot I was wearin' pants. I got up early and fed the chickens and horses."

"What time did you get up?" Michael sipped his coffee. His eyes never strayed from her.

She looked down at her lap. "I never went to bed."

Michael frowned. What did she mean she'd never gone to bed? He'd seen her climb the stairs.

"I tried to sleep but couldn't. So, I got up and read—" Her wide eyes darted to his.

"You can read?" He already knew the answer to that question, but he promised Rainee he wouldn't say anything and he intended to keep his promise.

"Some. I'm still learnin'. Gettin' easier everyday, though. I can write some, too. Now iffen I could just talk better. But—" she sighed heavily "—I talked this way my whole life and the words fall out before I have a chance to correct them."

Michael set his coffee down and pulled Selina's hands into his. "Selina, I think it's great that you're learning to read and write…for your sake. But…I don't want you to change the way you talk. I like it."

"You—you do?"

"Yes."

"But I heard you tell Jess I talked funny."

She heard that? What else had she overheard? "I must admit, it did bother me at first, but now I like it." He kissed her hand. "It's you."

Her face lit up like a candle in a dark room. She smiled. "I'll be right back." She whirled and ran upstairs.

Minutes later, the rustle of skirts drifted over to him. He glanced toward the stairs. His breath hitched and his heart bucked like a wild horse in response to seeing her in a soft pink cotton dress that showed off her feminine curves. He couldn't wait to show *her* off in town.

Twenty minutes later, Michael stopped in front of Marcel Mercantile. The first person he saw was Ethel. He groaned, knowing how cruel the woman could be and knowing that she had spread rumors about how he had feelings for her daughter.

He helped Selina down from the wagon and draped his arm around her shoulder. "Morning, Ethel."

"Morning, Michael." Ethel turned to Selina. "You sure look nice, Selina. I heard how you helped save Rainee and her son's life. And Sadie, well, she can't say enough good things about you." The woman babbled on and on about all of Selina's attributes. "Next time you're in town, drop in. I live in the green house at the end of this street."

If Michael hadn't heard it for himself, he would have never believed it. Ethel being kind? Inviting Selina to her home? Ethel never invited anyone to her home.

They finished gathering their supplies and headed back to the ranch.

At the house, Michael had just finished unloading the wagon, when Doc Berg came to the door.

"Is Selina home?"

"Yes, she's inside. Why?"

"The Barrison twins' wagon rolled over and I'm headed to their house now. Your place was on the way, and after I saw the great job she did sewing Jake's head, I thought I would see if Selina would be willing to come and help me. That is, if you don't mind."

"I don't mind. But it's up to her. How are Bo and Sam?" Michael asked as they headed into the house.

"Won't know until I get there."

They stepped into the kitchen. Selina was standing at the sink. "Selina, Doc's here. He needs your help."

Selina wiped her hands off on her apron. "What can I do for you, Doc?" She removed her apron and hung it on a peg near the sink.

He explained the situation.

"You don't mind iffen I go, do you, Michael?"

"Before you decide," Doc interjected, "you need to know she won't be home until way after dark. It takes almost an hour alone to get there."

"No, I don't mind. I have a lot of work to get caught up on this afternoon anyway."

"Thank you, Michael." She kissed his cheek and headed out the door with Doctor Berg.

Hours later, after branding and fixing fences, Michael made his way home. A light was on inside his house. He knew it wasn't Selina—she hadn't gotten back yet and wouldn't be home until later that evening.

Lately, a few shady prospectors looking for gold had started making themselves at home in other people's houses when they were not at home.

Michael pulled his derringer out of his boot and crept up the steps, careful to not make a sound. At the window, he stayed back far enough to not be seen and peeked inside.

What in the…?

Who was that?

He took a minute to study the woman sitting on his sofa.

Starting at her feet, his eyes made their way up.

Pink silk slippers peeked out from under a pink ruffled dress. Her head rested on the back wing of the sofa. Her face was covered by a row of long ringlet curls.

Was the woman hurt or asleep? Only one way to find out.

Because the front door squeaked when it opened, Michael went around back and slipped inside through the back door, then made his way into the living room.

"Uh-hmm." He cleared his throat.

The woman's head wobbled upward and turned his direction.

Michael's breath hitched in his throat.

Misty gray eyes stared up at him through a haze of sleep. She sat up and pushed the curls off her face. "You. You must be Michael," she said.

Before him was a very beautiful woman.

Who was she?

And what was she doing here?

"Michael?" She rose from the sofa. When she tilted her head a curl fell across her porcelain cheek.

"Yes. I'm Michael. And you are…?"

"Aimee. Aimee Lynn Covington." Her words came out slow and precise and she curtsied just like Rainee had when she first came here.

His eyes widened. "You're Aimee?"

"Yes, sir. I am." She looked behind him. "I hope you don't mind but when your sister, Leah, and I got here no one was home. I asked her if it would be all right if I waited here. I wanted to surprise Selina."

She'll be surprised all right. He knew *he* was.

"Where is she?"

"Who?"

She frowned. "Selina? Your wife. My best friend." Her delicate brows rose.

The woman had done her friend a huge disservice. Aimee was no friend. "What are you doing here?" His teeth ached from biting them so hard. This woman had nerve showing up here like this.

Aimee frowned, and the gray in her eyes darkened like thunder clouds. "I told Selina I was coming for a visit. Didn't she get my post?"

"Your letter said you would be coming sometime to visit us, but it didn't say when." He knew he should have written back to tell her she wasn't welcome here and never would be.

"Well, I just missed Selina so much, I had to come and see her. Where is she?" She looked around again.

So many emotions were running around in Michael's head that he had a hard time catching up to any of them. He stared at the beautiful, genteel Southern lady in front of him. All those years when he had pictured a wife for himself, he had envisioned someone just like Aimee. But now the only vision to fill his mind and his heart was Selina.

In that instant it dawned on him. He loved Selina. Not only loved her, but he was *in* love with her. Happiness flowed through his veins like warm, liquid sunshine.

"Michael, are you okay?"

"What?" He placed his attention onto Aimee. "I'm fine." He couldn't keep the joy out of his voice or from his face. "I'm better than I've been in a long time."

"You haven't answered my question. Where is Selina? Is she okay?"

"Oh, yes. She's more than okay. She's great." He knew he sounded stupid but he couldn't help that, either. "She's helping Doc Berg."

The woman's rigid shoulders relaxed. "I'm so glad she's okay. I don't know what I would do if something happened to her. She's the most amazing person I know."

"She sure is."

"I'm so glad you feel that way." She looked down

at the floor. "Michael, by now you know that I didn't write everything Selina told me to."

That snagged his attention. "Why didn't you?"

"Because if I did, you wouldn't have sent for her."

Anger coiled inside of him. How dare she talk about his wife like that. "Why not?"

"Because most people listen to her talk or they look at her outward appearance and judge her unworthy. They don't get to know the real her. I just knew if someone did, they would love her, like I do. They would see that underneath her rugged exterior is a heart of pure gold. A lovely person who deserves the best. Who deserves the love of a good man." Her gaze came up to his. "I could tell from your letters that you were an honest, decent man. I'm sorry I deceived you, Michael. Are you sorry I did?"

He could see how important his answer was to her. She really did love her friend. He heard it in her words and saw it in her eyes.

"No. At first I was. I'm ashamed to say I did just what you said everyone else does. I judged her by her outward appearance and her speech. But then I got to know her. To know her heart, and you're right. She is a wonderful person." He paused, and all the anger he held toward Aimee and himself relinquished its hold on him. Selina had told him he deserved someone better. She was wrong. "I don't deserve her. But I love her so much I'll do whatever it takes to deserve her."

"Oh, Michael, I'm so happy for you and Selina." Aimee threw her arms around him and hugged him. He hugged her back, happier than he had ever been.

* * *

Selina slid from the buggy, bone tired. All she wanted to do was to head straight to bed.

Lights were on in the house. Michael must still be up.

Anxious to see him in spite of how tired she was, instead of climbing the steps she hopped onto the porch. On her way to the front door, she passed the living room window and glanced inside.

Jumpin' crickets!

She backed away from full view of the window and peeked inside.

Michael and Aimee had their arms around each other. When they separated, Selina right away noticed the joy on her husband's face, and her heart shattered into hundreds of tiny pieces.

She closed her eyes and refused to let the tears stinging the back of her eyes fall. Her fears had come to life. She knew something like this would happen if Michael ever laid eyes on Aimee. Everything he said he wanted in a wife, Aimee was it, and Selina wasn't.

Well, he could have her. They could have each other.

She quietly made her way back across the porch and hopped down. Where she would go this late, she had no idea, but she wouldn't go back into that house ever again. She couldn't. It hurt too much seeing them hugging and seeing the happiness on Michael's face.

Michael paced between the living room and kitchen, peering out the windows occasionally. With Selina gone, he hadn't felt right about having Aimee in the house, so he had taken her to his mother's to see if she could stay the night there.

For the twentieth time, he looked at the grandfather clock. Doc said it would be late, but Michael thought he meant eight or nine, not midnight.

Every time he prayed, deep in his gut he felt something wasn't right. He'd waited as long as he was going to. He grabbed his jacket and rifle and one other thing from his dresser and headed down to the barn.

When he stepped inside, he heard the muffled sound of crying. He strained to listen where it was coming from. Quietly he made his way to the ladder leading up to the loft.

The crying grew louder.

He climbed the ladder only as high as his head so he could peek around to see who it was. Laying on one of the blankets they kept in the barn was Selina, curled in a ball. Michael scurried up the ladder, rushed to her and dropped to his knees beside her. "Selina?"

She curled up tighter, keeping her back to him. "Go away, Michael." She sniffed.

"What's wrong, love?" He laid his hand on her arm. She shoved it away with one swipe.

Fear clutched his insides. "Selina, what's wrong?"

"You know good and well what's wrong. Now go away."

"No, I don't know. And you're scaring me. What's wrong?" He dropped into a sitting position and pulled Selina onto his lap, cradling her stiff body against his.

She twisted, trying to get away, but he held her securely without hurting her. His wife refused to look at him. "Let go of me," she whimpered before going limp in his arms.

Now he really was scared. Selina's spunk usually rose to the occasion. So whatever had her upset must be huge for her to give up so easily. Whatever it was, he was going to find out. "I'm not letting go until you tell me what's wrong."

She yanked her tearful gaze up to his. Even in the dark shadows of the barn the moisture in and under her eyes sparkled. Seeing her pain, his heart rent into pieces. He laid his thumb under her eye to wipe away the tears, but she brushed it off with a yank, too.

Without warning, fire flashed through her eyes. She stiffened in his arms and tried to sit up, but he held her so she couldn't move. "I'll tell you what's wrong, you no-good polecat."

"No-good polecat? What did I do?"

"Don't think I don't know what's goin' on. I may not be the most learned person in this world, but I ain't stupid, neither."

"I never said you were. What's this all about, Selina?"

"I saw you and Aimee huggin'."

That was what was bothering her? Relief replaced his fear and he laughed with the release of knowing that was it.

"You think that's funny? Well, I don't." Selina jerked upward, but he captured her around the waist and pulled her back onto his lap. She fought him, but he gently restrained her.

"Selina, listen to me. Yes, you saw me and Aimee hugging. Do you want to know why?"

"I already know why." She squirmed some more. "'Cause she's more what you're wantin' in a wife than me, and you couldn't help yourself when you laid eyes on her."

"Oh, my love." Out of pure joy, Michael laughed

again. "You've got it all wrong. It's you I want. When you saw us hugging, I had just told her that I realized I love you. That I'm *in* love with you."

She stopped squirming and looked up at him. "What?"

"I said…" He gazed down at her tenderly, willing his eyes to show the depth of love in his heart for her. "I love you, Selina."

"You—you do?"

"That's what I said." He tossed her own words back at her with a hint of humor and a small smile.

"Oh, Michael, you mean it? You ain't in love with Aimee?" Her eyes searched his.

"Now, how could I be in love with her when I'm so madly and completely in love with my wife?" He held on to her securely with one arm and pulled out a little cloth sack from his vest pocket with the other. He reached for her left hand and slipped the gold band with blue sapphires and diamonds onto her finger.

She gazed down at it. "A wedding ring? For me? It's so beautiful."

"So are you." He cupped her chin and with a voice husky with love, he said, "And now, my love, I'm going to prove to you just how much I really do love you." His lips touched hers. She surrendered her lips to his in the sweetest, most passionate kiss he'd ever received.

Nine months later, Michael paced the floor of their house. From their bedroom a loud cry pierced the air. He rushed inside.

"Here, Michael. Take your son." Doc wrapped a blanket around him and handed the baby to him. "I have to deliver another one."

"Another one?" Michael swallowed hard. Twins? Selina was giving birth to twins? Shocked to the essence of his being, all he could do was stare into the face of his son until he heard another cry. His attention flew to Doc. "Another boy?" he asked.

"No. This one's a girl."

Michael gazed over at Selina. Their eyes joined as their hearts and bodies had so many months before. Contentment wrapped around him like the blankets around his children. Children.

He was a father.

And a husband.

Michael thanked God that He hadn't answered his prayers the way Michael thought He should. That the Lord knew what was best for him and had blessed Michael far beyond any desire he'd ever had the day God sent him a very unlikely wife in trousers.

* * * * *

Dear Reader,

Difference isn't always easy, is it? Yet those differences make life interesting. How boring life would be if we all looked, acted, dressed and talked alike. If every bird, tree, flower and scent resembled one another. I'm so glad God made His entire creation unique. Those diversities make for such a fun, interesting life, don't you think? Yet how many times do we reject those differences based on appearance only? Look at what Michael would have lost out on if he had rejected Selina based solely on her outward appearance. He almost did. I'm so glad he was a Godly man who honored his vows even though Selina wasn't what he'd desired in a wife. Or so he thought. But God knew differently. He knew what Michael really needed. Michael learned that outward appearance does not represent the heart and soul of a person, that God cares enough about people to send His best, and that God's ways and God's plans are unfailing.

Thank you for reading my story *The Unlikely Wife*.

Debra Ullrick

Questions for Discussion

1. Is there someone you have judged by their outward appearance as Michael had Selina? Please explain.

2. Like Selina had done with rich folks, have you ever clumped a certain type of people together and deemed them all alike based on your personal experiences?

3. How would you deal with finding out the person you thought you loved was really a stranger? Do you feel Michael handled the situation with Selina well?

4. How would you have handled Selina's different ways?

5. What do you think it would be like not to be able to read or write?

6. What talents do you have that others would never guess you have, like Selina and her doctoring skills and artistic ability?

7. What are current stereotypical male and female social rules or standards?

8. If you were stuck with someone you couldn't get along with, what would you do differently than Michael did?

9. What would you do if you loved someone who didn't love you back?

10. Would you change who you are to please another? If so, where do you draw the line at changing who you are to please someone?

11. What options do you think were solutions to Selina and Michael's ill-conceived marriage? Divorce? Annulment? Something else?

12. Michael had a fantasy woman who he thought would make him happy. In what ~~way~~ is the experience of love often different in real life than in movies and books?

13. Michael was scared to fall in love because of what he'd witnessed in Haydon's first marriage as a young boy. Is there anything you experienced in your childhood or youth that now affects the decisions you make? The way you live?

14. When Selina fell through the roof, Michael had to assess his true feelings for Selina. What crisis have you experienced in your life that changed your view of a situation?

15. What was the funniest thing Selina did, and why?

INSPIRATIONAL

Wholesome romances that touch the heart and soul.

Love Inspired.

celebrating 15 YEARS

HISTORICAL

COMING NEXT MONTH
AVAILABLE FEBRUARY 14, 2012

THE COWBOY FATHER
Three Brides for Three Cowboys
Linda Ford

HOMETOWN CINDERELLA
Ruth Axtell Morren

THE ROGUE'S REFORM
The Everard Legacy
Regina Scott

CAPTAIN OF HER HEART
Lily George

REQUEST YOUR FREE BOOKS!

2 FREE INSPIRATIONAL NOVELS
PLUS 2
FREE
MYSTERY GIFTS

Love Inspired
HISTORICAL
INSPIRATIONAL HISTORICAL ROMANCE

LIH11B